WILDCAT

USA TODAY BESTSELLING AUTHOR
REBECCA JENSHAK

CHAPTER ONE

LEO

THAT ONE IS A WILDCAT

I plug one ear with a finger and press my phone into the other as I walk away from my table toward a quieter corner in the bar.

"Yo, College, where you at?" My buddy, Ash, asks on the other end of the line.

"A bar near campus. I had a meeting with my advisor this afternoon, and a couple of buddies from my summer classes invited me out."

"I'm bored. What time will you be back?"

"Probably not until late. It's trivia night."

"Trivia night?" Ash snorts with laughter. "You don't get enough of that in school?"

I roll my eyes, letting him get his jabs in. I'm used to the guys poking fun at me for taking classes while playing in the NHL. It's all in good fun. Mostly.

"Wait." His voice goes serious, and I can almost picture him sitting up straight and preparing to move from his favorite spot in the middle of the couch in his living room. "What's the girl situation? Are hot girls still into trivia?"

"Doesn't matter. They're all totally out of your league," I say as I glance around the busy bar that's popular with Whittaker students. My gaze lands, not for the first time, on the gorgeous bartender working tonight. She's new, or at least I've never seen her before.

This place is packed. A month into the new semester and it looks like all those good intentions to stay in and study during the weeknights have been tossed out the window. Man, some days I really miss college. Nights like this are few and far between for me during the season.

For the next eight months, I will live and breathe hockey. With any free time, I'll hang at Ash's house, or he'll be at mine. We're neighbors and teammates. He has the better TV setup, complete with every gaming system you can imagine, but I have the better patio and pool.

"Maybe I should drive down," he says. I can hear him punching buttons on the controller and the video game in the background. "I've got you covered in Philosophy and History. I bet some other guys would be up for it, too."

"By the time you get here, trivia will be done."

"Then we can still have a beer and get you tucked in by midnight, Cinderella. If I didn't know better, I'd think you were trying to keep me away. Afraid I'll steal all the hot girls for myself?"

"Yeah, that's it," I say dryly. "I'll see you in the morning." I hang up before he can goad me anymore or talk himself into coming for real. It isn't that I don't want to hang with him, but if the entire Minnesota Wildcats team shows up here, it's going to be a shitshow.

I can usually go undetected in a crowded bar, save the occasional hardcore fan. On the ice, I might want the attention, but not here. At the reminder, I pull my hat down a little lower over my eyes and keep my head down as I walk.

Before I've made my way back to the table, Ash has sent me a series of texts with the middle finger emoji.

Brad and Micah stop their conversation when I slide onto my chair.

"What'd I miss?" I ask.

Micah leans forward, elbows on the table and beer bottle dangling from one hand. "Settle a bet for us. Did you or did you not hook up with that reporter after you eye-fucked her boobs during this interview?"

I groan, and their cackles fill my ears.

Brad slides his phone onto the table, the infamous video playing. Last week, guys from teams all over the league attended a pre-season strength and training camp. It was a great week. Lots of media stopped by. It was interview after interview on how strong we were feeling going into the new season, our expectations for our teams, blah blah blah. Interviews are not my thing. Guys like Jack, our team captain, and even Ash are much better at handling the mundane and repetitive questions.

I press pause on the video and slide it back to him. "I wasn't staring at her boobs."

Or I hadn't meant to be anyway. I was tired and hungry and concentrating on coming up with something more to say than *"I'm feeling good" and "The team looks good,"* which I'd already said a half-dozen times that day alone.

"You are hardcore staring at her cleavage, Lohan." Brad holds up his phone, the screen paused on a frame where my eyes are downcast, and indeed it very much looks like they're focusing on her boobs. And they're great boobs, so I get why people would think that, but I was so exhausted after a long ass day of workouts, she could have been topless, and I still might not have checked her out.

The other problem? She's very obviously checking me out. Her gaze dips several times in the video over my sweaty chest and abs, even dropping to my crotch at one point. Yeah, not my best interview.

"We didn't hook up."

"Dammit. Really?" Brad's shoulders slump, and he finishes off his beer.

"Sorry to disappoint." I'm not breaking his heart and telling him I'd never hook up with someone in the media. I have a hard enough time with interviews. I don't need to piss off any of the reporters.

Micah sets his empty bottle on the table with a clang. A victorious smile pulls at his lips. "Make sure they grab one from the back of the cooler. I like it ice cold."

Brad starts to get to his feet to grab the drinks.

"I've got this round," I say, standing and placing a hand on his shoulder. "Shots? Pitcher?"

Their eyes light up. I remember all too well what it was like to be a poor college kid. I won't get to hang much since the season is about to kick off. All summer long, we drank here after our Wednesday night finance class. It was nice.

Until next summer, I'm only taking one class a semester online. I wish I could do more, but I'll finish my degree eventually.

The bar in this place spans one long wall. It's a narrow space with tables scattered in front of it. There's no dart board or pool table and only one TV. It's a total dive, but the proximity to campus keeps the cramped space in business. It has a friendly, fun vibe and is obviously the place to be tonight. It's busier than I've ever seen.

I choose the less crowded end of the bar closest to the new hottie bartender. I've come to know some of them. Mike, the owner, is the only one I recognize tonight. I don't think Mike knows who I am, but he doesn't seem like the kind of guy that would make a big deal out of it even if he did.

They're really slammed, so I settle in to wait.

Hottie bartender moves slowly as she pours a line of tequila shots. She's concentrating so hard like it might be her first night. She's holding up the line, but she's damn fine to look at, so no one is complaining much.

Her long brown hair is the color of aged whiskey. It's pulled back in a ponytail that sways around slender shoulders. People are calling out to get her attention, but she continues taking her sweet-ass time like she isn't bothered by the chaos around her.

The guy buying the shots says something to her with a cocky tilt to his mouth before he hands over his credit card. He holds on when she tries to take it and leans in closer. She recoils, and I don't have to be a genius to know he hit on her, or more likely, propositioned her. She snatches the card away and turns to run it. As if he didn't get a clue by her avoidance, he bends over the bar and smacks her ass.

Damn. Ballsy. I stand tall ready for… fuck, I don't know. Mike catches the dirtbag in action, scowls, and comes over, presumably to defend his employee and kick the guy out, but before he can, she stomps back with a wild look in her eye, picks up one of the shots, and tosses it at him.

I laugh. Mike, not so much. Most of the other patrons have a good chuckle and then slide down to the only remaining bartender. Not me. I'm enthralled.

"I'm sorry, Mike," she says, hands balled up in fists, looking about as sorry as I feel that she doused that guy in alcohol.

"That guy had it coming," Mike grumbles. The two of them move my way to talk more privately. "But you can't go around tossing top-shelf liquor in every douchebag's face, Scarlett."

Scarlett. I try her name out in my head as I get a better look at her. Her tank top and denim shorts are the standard attire of half the girls here, but it shows off her lean body and slight curves. Her eyes are dark, but the way she smiles, a little mischievously and a whole lot sexy, makes them light up under the glow of the bar.

"We need to start trivia. Why don't you help Jade?"

She pulls a bottle opener from her back pocket and hands it to him. "Sure."

"Good. I think that'll be a better fit for you."

"Why? Because they'll be too busy to grope me?" Her voice is raspy, annoyed, and sexy as hell.

He smirks. "No, because the drinks on that side of the bar are already paid for. Toss away."

She brushes past me, and Mike meets my gaze and moves in position to help. "Wildcat."

"What'd you say?" In all the times I was here this summer, he never mentioned the team or let on that he knew I was an NHL player.

"That one is a wildcat," he says with a head tilt in the direction Scarlett went. "What can I get you, man?"

I breathe a sigh of relief that I haven't been outed. I can go most places with a minimal invasion of privacy, but here hanging with guys from class, I don't want to be Leo Lohan, NHL player. I just want to hang with some friends and relax.

And maybe get Scarlett's number.

CHAPTER TWO

SCARLETT

DELAYED JET LAG

The tray of shots in my hands tips to the side and clatters to the floor between customers. I squeeze my eyes shut. *Fuckity fuck.* It's safe to say that bartending is not my calling.

Mike's heavy sigh breaks through the noise of the bar as he comes around to help me.

"I'm sorry," I say for at least the tenth time tonight as I squat down to clean up another mess.

"It's okay." He picks up the tray, and together we retrieve the tiny plastic cups (thank goodness they weren't glass) and mop up the sticky liquid. "I got it. Why don't you go ahead and close out? I think we can handle it from here."

The look on his face right now—the downturned, tight-lipped smile and apologetic eyes— I've seen it before. Just last week, my boss at the coffee shop gave me the same one when I confused the vanilla and hazelnut syrups for an entire shift. Oops. I was politely "let go" from that job, but I wasn't too sad about it. I am not a morning person, and mixing me with other fellow caffeine addicts before the sun rises is a recipe for disaster.

"I guess I'm not any better on the other side of the bar," I joke.

"You'll get the hang of it," he reassures me. "And, hey, thanks for your help getting the word out. I haven't seen this place so busy in years."

"Welcome." I untie the little black apron and set it on the tray with the empty cups. "You'll let me know if you have any nights you need covered next week?"

I like the energy of this place, so I'm hoping that despite my less than stellar bartending skills, he might call me to work again.

"I might have some liquor promotions this week. They're…" He bobs his head side to side. "More casual. I think you might do well with that. I'll be in touch once I check the schedule." Mike reaches over the tray to give my shoulder a squeeze and then gets back behind his bar. As bosses go, he seems like a good one.

My best friend appears by my side. "What's going on? Did he cut you for the night? Please say no. We're still packed in here. Where are the shots for table Smart and Handsome?"

I snort a laugh at her nickname for the table of trivia winners. "I dropped the tray."

She winces and gives me one of those *maybe this isn't your thing* smiles that have become routine in my hot mess of a life.

"Sorry," I say. "I appreciate your putting in a good word for me, but I don't think Mike will be calling me up to cover another night shift."

"Don't even worry about it." Jade sets her tray on the bar and expertly pours three shots. She's been working here for two years and makes it look so easy. She blows out a breath that sends her bright red bangs out of her eyes. "This is really a problem of your own making.

Your photos on the bar's social media page brought all of these people here."

"It was nothing," I say. Last week I came to the bar to hang out while Jade was working. I had my camera on me and took a few photos of her working trivia night. Mostly, I was just messing around, but Mike loved them, and when they posted all the images, I guess other people did too. It's a cool bar, so I'm glad people are coming in. A total dive, but cool.

"Whatever. It's a crazy night to have your first shift. Besides, you were fine out on the floor."

"Yeah, as long as I didn't have to carry anything but empties." The number of beers and mixed drinks I spilled tonight or messed up somehow and had to re-pour is too many to count.

"Are you staying and hanging out at least? I should be off in thirty. Usually, at midnight, it clears out a little."

"That depends." I glance up at the TV at the exact moment my ex-boyfriend's face pops on the screen. Ugh. As if it weren't stressful enough starting a new job, I've had to work all night with excited chatter on the TV for this weekend's Russian Grand Prix and all the highlights from the qualifying sessions. Rhyse is the favorite, which is nothing new. He's almost always the favorite. "Can we change the channel in here?"

"Sorry. Mike has an ESPN-only rule. Sit at the far end and do not look at him." Her gaze flicks to the screen. "He does not deserve it. *Prick*."

"I'm not sure I should even be in the same vicinity as anything glass or spillable. Every mistake is making me more jittery and klutzy. I might be sending off bad juju just by hanging around."

"You are stunning and majestic and not klutzy. Well, not usually.

Maybe it's delayed jet lag?"

"More like a crushing blow to my self-esteem," I mutter, and because I'm obviously a glutton for punishment, I steal another glance at the TV where Rhyse is smiling through an interview in his red racing suit.

"Forget him." Jade tries to hand me the tray.

"Uh-uh." I try to back up, but I'm already against the bar.

"Yes," she insists and edges it forward until the rounded edge hits my chest. "I'm not letting you leave here without going out on a high note. Take these shots to the trivia winners and end the night with your chin up. Rhyse is an idiot. There are a lot of great guys out there. His loss. He's going to have a 'come to Scarlett' moment and run back to you. And when he does, you're going to have moved on, realized you deserve so much more, and be living your best life."

"That is a lot of growth." I laugh lightly, but I cling to her words with hope.

"Yep, and it starts tonight. Take these to the table and then grab a seat at the bar and wait for me."

"Come to Scarlett moment?"

"Like come to Jesus, but with memories of how freaking awesome you are."

God, I love her. "Okay, fine, but if I drop it—"

"You won't." She nudges me forward. "And maybe while you're over there, get hottie trivia guy's number or better yet ask him to take you out back and talk nerdy to you while he fucks you back on your feet."

"Oh my god," I mouth at her ridiculousness as she winks and hurries off.

I take baby steps across the bar, holding my breath any time someone walks in front of me or gets too close, which is often, considering how packed this place is. I'm staring down at the tray, which Jade tells me actually makes it more likely I'll spill than if I don't, but I can't seem to stop. *I am stunning and majestic.*

I make it to the table and am mentally giving myself a high-five when one of the guys calls out, "Victory shots," and reaches for the tray. I panic and move it closer, which throws off his aim.

I brace myself for a collision that doesn't happen. The guy closest to me stands and steadies me and the tray with reflexes and a grip that temporarily stun me. I don't make any move to untangle myself from him or stand firm on my feet. Nah, I'm perfectly content to lean into him and inhale his masculine and woodsy scent.

"Are you okay?" His voice is quiet confidence wrapped in a deep baritone.

He meets my gaze from under the bill of an old, worn hat. I was able to sneak some glances at him earlier. He's hard to miss. My heart might be a little broken, but I'm not so distraught that I don't notice hot guys. And he is hot. Really hot. Straight nose, square jaw, hazel eyes, full lips, and also super smart. He carried his buddies to victory on the trivia front. He knew so much obscure sports trivia; my dad would be over here shaking his hand.

I realize I'm still staring and haven't answered him. "Perfect."

One of us sets the tray down. I'm pretty sure it's him. The other two take their shots, including his, and place them on the table. I'm still in some sort of weird stare-off. I can't seem to look away, and he's still standing next to me.

"Can we get another round of beers?" One of the other guys drops a twenty-dollar bill on my tray.

"Oh, uh, you'll have to get it from the bar because this is my last table."

"For the night?" That deep voice beside me asks.

"Forever, probably. I think I just got fired." *Omg, shut up, Scarlett.* How mortifying. I turn on my heel and scamper to the safety of the bar, where I grab my wallet and phone. Okay, so not stunning and majestic. I'm a work-in-progress.

I say goodbye to Mike and am rounding the bar when I come up short. Mr. Smart and Handsome Trivia Nerd stands waiting for me with the shot I just dropped off at his table still clutched in his fingertips.

"Is something wrong with the shot? Because I didn't pour it. You're safe."

His eyes twinkle with humor, and his lips turn up into a smirk. "Thought you might need it more than me."

"Oh."

He holds it out, and I reach forward, fingers brushing his as he hands it to me.

"You didn't spit in it or anything, right?"

"Would I tell you if I had?" Laughter makes his lips pull into a smirk that somehow makes him even hotter. "Nah. Spit-free."

"Thank you." I hesitate, but eventually toss it back, ignoring the burn coating my throat. "What is that?"

"Shouldn't you know?"

"Did you miss the part where I was fired for failing spectacularly on my first night as a bartender?"

His laughter warms my insides. "It's Fireball."

"Thanks. I needed that." I set the empty on the bar.

"I'm Leo." He reaches a big hand out to me.

I place my palm in his, and my breath hitches. "Scarlett."

Neither of us lets go right away, and I am very much enjoying the feel of his rough hand against mine and the warmth spreading through my insides.

"Can I buy you a drink?" he asks, still holding my hand hostage in his.

"Are you taking pity on me because I got fired?"

"Pity?" He withdraws his hand and shakes his head. "I saw you toss a drink in a guy's face earlier. I don't think you need my pity."

"You saw that, huh?" I cringe, even though that guy totally had it coming. I motion to the table he left. "What about your friends?"

"They're heading out soon anyway."

He drags a stool out for me at the bar and then takes the one next to it.

"Oh," I say as I perch myself on the other side of the bar I worked tonight. "I see. I'm the last resort so that you don't have to drink alone."

As soon as I say the words, I realize how silly they are. I bet he could get any girl in here to have a drink with him. He laughs it off, and when Mike comes over to take his order and places a couple of coasters in front of us, I lift a hand in an awkward wave.

"I think I like you better when you're on the paying end of things." He winks and tries to play it off like he's kidding, but I don't doubt the sincerity of that statement. "What can I get you?"

"Can I get a vodka soda?"

Mike nods, and we both look to Leo for his order.

"Just water. Thanks." He places a twenty on the bar.

"You're not having a drink?" I angle my body toward his, which is also, thankfully, away from the TV, as Mike places the glass in front of me.

"Wish I could. I've got to be up early in the morning for—" He stops himself, and then a half-smile tugs at one side of his mouth. "I have to be up early."

"You signed up for an eight o'clock class, didn't you? What kind of monster are you?"

He chuckles and takes a drink of his water. "What about you? Do you go to college here?"

"No. Well, it depends on who you ask." I shake my head. How many embarrassing things can spill out of my mouth in front of this guy? "It's a long story."

One dark brow lifts. "Well, now I'm intrigued."

He leans a big bicep against the bar and gives me his undivided attention, so I give him the basic rundown of my messy life. At this point, he's either a glutton for punishment or enjoying my disaster of a night/life.

Footnotes: I did a study abroad program in London for a year, then met a boy and decided to stay an extra year, and now I'm back in Minnesota and supposed to be starting my sophomore year of college, but instead dropped all my classes after the first week.

My parents don't know that last part yet, and yes, I know I need to tell them, but they are traditional and sometimes a little overprotective. I wanted to have a steady job lined up before I told them, so it would look like I have some inkling on what I'm doing with my life.

"Sorry you bought me that drink about now, aren't you?" I cringe at the honesty with which I just dumped my messy life on his lap. It felt good to tell someone besides Jade, even if it's just a stranger.

"Not at all. College isn't the right track for everyone, and no one says you have to do it in the four years right after high school. If you decide later you want to get a degree, you still can. I think it's cool. You'll be far better equipped for the real world and probably happier, too."

"Wow. Can I get you to come over and repeat that when I tell my parents that instead of going to classes all day, I'm hanging out on my friend's couch watching Friends reruns?"

He flashes me another big smile. He has a small dimple on the left side of his cheek. His hat comes down so low, I wish he'd take it off so I could get a better look at his hair. The ends poking out on the side are a light brown.

Jade slumps in front of me, forearms resting on the bar. "One more table, and then we can go." Her gaze slides to Leo, and a slow smile splits her lips. "Or not."

"Jade, this is Leo," I interject before she says something to embarrass me.

"The trivia nerd," she says.

He tips his head. "Nice to meet you."

"You know an incredible amount of boy band facts and sports history. Weird mix."

"What can I say?" He grins. "It's a gift."

"Impressive. Truly." She looks at me with wide eyes. "Are we still on for the karaoke bar?"

"Yeah, of course."

"You should come with us," she says to Leo. "I bet they even have some Backstreet Boys songs for you." Jade stands tall and smooths a hand over her braid. "Back in five."

"You could come if you wanted," I say. "Jade is a lot of fun. Her boyfriend works for the karaoke company, so we get to sing as many songs as we want."

He checks the time on a flashy watch adorning his left wrist. "I really wish I could."

"Damn those early classes." Seriously, damn those classes. I'd forgotten what it feels like to sit and talk with someone new. I haven't dated since I've been back. It's only been a couple of months, so it isn't like I've been hiding away. Not much, anyway. Still, this is nice.

"What's your major?" I ask. "Wait, let me guess."

He sips on his water and leans an elbow on the bar. He's confident and smart, personable. I wrack my brain for possibilities.

"Pre-law?"

He shakes his head and grins, that dimple twinkling.

Before I come up with another guess, his buddies step up next to us.

Leo stands. "Are you guys heading out?"

"Yeah," the taller of the two guys steps forward, and they do the bro hand slap hug thing. "We have international finance in the morning, and without you to cheat off, we have to actually pay attention."

The other guy offers a fist bump. "Thanks for coming out. Good luck next week."

"Thanks." Leo flicks his gaze at me uncomfortably, and I stare down at my glass to give him the illusion of privacy.

They say their goodbyes, and Leo drops back to his seat. "Sorry about that."

"No worries." I finish my drink. "So, a finance major?"

"Business with a finance emphasis."

"I'm impressed. Math and numbers always intimidated me."

"It's simple, really. It's all rules and order."

I swear I get a little involuntary body shiver the way he says rules and order. This guy looks the opposite of both those things, and somehow the combination makes him sexier. Or maybe I just needed a reminder that hot, smart guys still exist in the world. Jade's right.

Forget Rhyse. There are good guys out there, and I think Leo might be one of them.

When my best friend is done, the three of us head out. Leo insists on walking us the two blocks to the other bar. Jade rushes in to see her boyfriend Sam, and I hang back to say goodbye to Leo.

"Are you sure I can't convince you to come in for a little while?"

"Another time."

We exchange numbers, and I have that giddy feeling of hope and excitement that he might call. Neither of us is drunk, so I don't think I'm imagining the chemistry between us. He takes my hand and smooths his thumb over the top of my knuckles. The light touch sends a shiver up my arm.

"Night, Scarlett." He keeps holding my hand until his backward steps pull our fingertips apart. Then he jolts forward and recaptures my hand. "Fuck it. I'll nap tomorrow afternoon."

CHAPTER THREE

SCARLETT

THAT POST-VACATION GLOW

Two hours pass like a video montage. Jade and I sing our hearts out to 90s and early 2000s songs. I even do a little Backstreet Boys for Leo. We talk, we laugh, we get handsy, and now, now I'm back at his place. I can't believe I'm doing this. Thank Jade and her insistence that I need hot Leo to fuck some confidence back in me.

Though, I'd be lying if I said I was here only because my best friend wants me to move on. I want to, too. No, I need to. I'm tired of driving the hot mess express.

And Hot Leo… yeah, he's the kind of guy you rebound with. He's like vacation sex personified, and I'm hoping to leave here tonight with a fabulous post-vacation glow and renewed belief in men and relationships.

"You live here?" I ask as he opens the passenger side door for me. The house is in a big, gated residential neighborhood.

He nods and takes my hand to help me out of the sporty car. I know cars, thanks to Rhyse, and this is a nice one.

"I was expecting a cramped apartment you share with like ten other guys or maybe a grungy dorm room."

"Sorry to disappoint," he says with a grin. "Though my buddy Ash lives across the street."

"You drive to campus every day from here?" We're at least twenty-five minutes away. And yeah, this neighborhood is amazing, but getting to campus for classes every morning is a pain. I know because I'm supposed to be doing it. My parents only live about five minutes away, and as far as they know, I am making the drive to campus every day instead of sleeping in and then going to Jade's or downtown to practice my photography.

"Uhh…" For the first time tonight, he lifts the hat from his head and runs his fingers through the light brown strands. It's thick and a little unruly. He rests the tattered hat back on top of his head. "About that."

Oh no. I stop walking and check my pocket to make sure I have my phone for the Uber ride I'm five seconds away from calling.

"I do go to Whittaker, but I am not a full-time student. I'm mostly online."

"You don't have an eight o'clock class tomorrow?" I ask dumbly.

"No, but I do need to be up in…" He tilts his wrist to check the time on his watch. "Three hours for work."

"Is your name really Leo?"

"Yeah." He steps to me and places each of his big hands on my hips. "Wanna see my driver's license?" He twists his face up into a horrified expression. "Scratch that. I have the worst photo of all time."

"Well, now I absolutely have to see it." I rest my hands on his chest. "I don't care if you aren't a full-time student. Or that you live with your parents." I look behind us to the beautiful house. His parents have money, that's for sure. The car, the house—it's all way too nice for someone his age. His interest in finance makes sense now, too.

It feels a little weird that he brought me back here, but maybe his parents are gone on vacation or something. It doesn't look like there are any lights on inside. Maybe they're just asleep like my parents most definitely are.

"I don't—" he starts, head cocked to the side like he's considering how to phrase the next sentence.

I stop him by pressing a finger to his full lips. "I live with my parents too. Temporarily, if I can ever get and keep a job. We'll move out someday, right?" I laugh softly to myself. "Who am I kidding? On my current track, I'll be lucky to have a good job by the time I'm thirty." I give my head a shake. I need to stop opening my mouth and giving this guy more reasons to call this off. "All I mean to say is, I get it. This time of our life is about figuring it all out."

He kisses me then. Soft lips slant over mine, and for a few moments, it's tender and gentle, and holy shit, I wonder if he can feel it. Never mind, there's no way he doesn't feel the ground shift beneath us like I do. His head tilts, his mouth opens wider, and I copy the movement. His tongue sweeps into my mouth, and then it isn't tender anymore.

We fumble toward the front door and inside, breaking the kiss only when absolutely necessary. Down a long hallway and toward the back of the house, he leads me while his hands roam over my body. The back wall of the house has large windows that look out into a back yard with a pool that sparkles in the moonlight.

"Is anyone else home?" I ask when his hands slide under my tank top.

He shakes his head to the side slowly. "It's just us."

Well, that's a relief.

"Can we get in the pool? Is it heated?"

Nodding, he leads me out the back doors. "Anything you want."

Woah.

"Leo, this is amazing." I kick off my shoes and walk into the water. It's one of those zero-entry pools and takes up most of the yard. There's also a hot tub and patio area with a TV and a big outdoor sectional.

He watches me wade in, smiling as I turn in a circle, taking it all in. When he still doesn't come in, I slowly walk back to him. "If I had a place like this, I'd never leave."

He brushes a hand along my face and tucks my hair behind an ear.

"Want to swim?" I ask.

"Do you want to swim?"

I nod and pull my tank top over my head. The early fall air is crisp, and goosebumps dot my arms. He stares at me for a beat before following suit and removing his shirt over his hat and then his jeans. We strip down, him in his black boxer briefs and me in my bra and panties.

I hesitate now that we're mostly naked in front of one another. His body is incredible. Broad, muscular, oh so sexy.

He scoops me up and runs into the water. I squeal as he takes us under, holding on to his neck. When we emerge in the deep end, I do what I've wanted to do all night. I lift his hat from his head and toss it on the patio. "Some guys look better in a hat. But you? You're just doing a disservice to the world by hiding behind that thing."

"You're something, Scarlett." His arms go around my waist under the water. I don't have to ask if that's a compliment. I can see it on his face. I didn't even know how much I needed someone to look at me like that until now.

Weeks of worrying about dropping out of college and disappointing my parents, of thinking I made a mistake leaving London and not giving Rhyse another chance, and more than anything, feeling like I'm royally screwing up my life, but the way Leo stares at me, every decision feels exactly right. At least for tonight.

His mouth dips to my collarbone while his hands skim over my ribs, thumbs brushing against my breasts. "Beautiful."

While his mouth explores me, I glide my hands over his chest and stomach.

"Personal trainer?"

"Hmm?" His mouth skims over the top of my bra.

"Your job. It was a guess based on your incredible body."

Long fingers slide under the straps and pull them down off my shoulders. Then he pulls my bra down until my boobs spill out.

"Model?" I ask through a groan as he covers my nipple with his lips.

He laughs. "I am not photogenic, so no."

"Oh right, the driver's license. It can't be that bad."

He moves to the other nipple then looks up at me with water droplets hanging on his eyelashes. "It's that bad."

I wrap my legs around his hips. "It isn't possible. Your cheekbones and jawline are a photographer's dream."

Yeah, I'm not buying it. If I had my camera, I'd prove it to him. Also, not going to lie, I'd love to capture the way his hair spikes up all over, water dripping off his amazing muscles and the glint in his eye that's playful and hot. And this back yard, and this pool.

"Male stripper?" I unclasp my bra and toss it on the patio.

"If you'd seen me dance, you'd already know the answer to that one." He captures my mouth again, and there's more urgency this time. Leo holds me against his chest. His dick is hard underneath me, and the breeze is cool on my wet skin, causing me to shiver.

I'm lost in his kisses and the feel of his hard body pressing into mine, only partially aware he's walking us out of the pool and toward the hot tub.

"Better?" he asks as we sink into the warm water.

Nodding, I tangle myself around him. My back hits the edge as he pins me against it, hands framing my face as he kisses me hard and deep.

I could kiss this guy for days. His hands span my waist and lift me onto the edge. My panties basically melt off as he hooks his thumbs under the wet material. They're tossed to the side, and he slides those big palms down my legs, stopping at my knees and pushing them open.

The way he stares at my pussy makes me shiver for an entirely different reason.

"Tell me if you get too cold, okay, gorgeous?"

And then he puts that beautiful mouth on me, and I fall back onto the patio. The way his tongue and lips work me over keeps the chill at bay. His shoulders push my legs farther apart, and he hooks an arm around one, lifting me slightly.

"Porn star?" I ask through a gasp.

A rough chuckle vibrates against my clit. I reach out and grip his forearm as the orgasm builds. He dives back in, kissing and licking, inserting a finger, and then a second. Nothing has ever felt this good. I come hard and go limp underneath him.

Water drops onto my chest and face as he leans over me. I open my eyes. "Porn star, right? I can pay in badly made drinks and horrible life advice."

He silences my rambling with a kiss and pulls me back into the warm water. My body reacts like I didn't just have the best orgasm of my life. I need more of him. More of this. I kiss him and grind over his hard length. When we're both panting, we get out of the hot tub and move to the outdoor couch. The night air nips at my skin, but I'm burning on the inside.

Wow, he's hot. This is hot, and so not at all how I pictured my night going. Zero complaints here.

He pushes his boxer briefs down, and his long dick points up. I need another word for wow because it's the only thought floating around in my head and it does not adequately capture this feeling.

His body covers mine, and we go back to making out. Leo doesn't seem to be in any hurry, even as I arch into him, eliminating every centimeter of space between us.

The dark sky is starting to lighten with the threat of sunrise when he finally runs inside to get condoms. I've had hours to reconsider, but I am so all in. I'm going to let hot Leo fuck me back on my feet. That's a thing, right? Jade didn't just make it up? I sure hope so.

"You're stunning." He twirls a strand of my damp hair around his finger. He's been so quick to hand out compliments and attention, and I am living for all of it.

I pull him down on top of me and kiss him as he pushes inside. His moan fills my mouth. Several seconds pass where he doesn't move.

"Everything okay?"

"You're squeezing me so tight."

I twist my fingers through the hair at the nape of his neck. "Maybe you're just too big."

He lifts his head from where it rests on my chest, and a cocky smirk graces his lips. That look makes the walls of my pussy squeeze tighter as I clench around him. My head falls back as my body tingles.

His hips move at a slow pace, each thrust going deeper and deeper until he's buried inside of me. Tears prick behind my eyes. I was only partly kidding about him being too big. The way he fills me so completely is like nothing I've ever felt before.

I cry out. I might even chant his name as my second orgasm takes hold of my sanity and shakes it.

"I could watch you come all day long," he says as he takes me into his arms and sits with me on his lap. He guides me back onto his cock. The words, I don't think I can get off again, were on the tip of my tongue, but this new angle has me second-guessing that.

I lean forward and kiss him as he drives into me, hands caressing my back and then squeezing my ass as the third orgasm rips through me. He follows, and I can't be sure I don't get off twice more because it goes on so long I feel like I'm having an out-of-body experience. I rest my forehead against his while we catch our breath.

His eyes lock on mine, and we stare at one another like neither of us can be sure the other is real.

Best vacation sex ever.

CHAPTER FOUR

LEO

SHE THINKS I LIVE WITH MY PARENTS

The Uber driver sighs loudly. As if that's going to hurry me along. I've got Scarlett pinned against the back passenger door of his car, kissing her like that isn't what we've been doing for the past three hours. I don't remember when I've had such a good time with a girl. Or with anyone, for that matter. I barely know this chick, but last night was like none other.

The driver lays on the horn, making Scarlett jump in my arms. I take a step back and glare at him through the window.

"I should go before he leaves me," she says, staring up at me with those big brown eyes. Her hair is wavy and still a little damp on the ends. She's wearing one of my old Boston University sweatshirts over her tank, and it comes down past her shorts. I hook my finger in the neck of it and pull her back to me.

"Oh right." She makes a move like she's going to take it off.

"Nah, keep it. Looks better on you."

She opens the car door, and I hold it as she slides into the back seat.

"Thanks for last night, hot Leo," she says as I shut her inside. The car pulls out of my driveway, and I look up to see Ash standing in his driveway across the street with a smile so big I might be tempted to regret getting caught walking a girl out, if it hadn't meant I got a few more minutes with Scarlett.

He crosses the street, pulling a long-sleeved T-shirt over his head. "Looks like you had a much better night than I did. Are we running this morning before we hit the road?" He does a scan of my bare chest and jeans.

"Give me five minutes."

For the first three miles, Ash interrogates me while simultaneously giving me shit. I offer few details, which just makes it worse. Ash is my best friend, he knows me better than anyone, so it isn't that I don't want to tell him. I'm just not sure I can put it into words. I had my share of one-night stands back in the day, but they've never been like that. And I'm not just referring to the sex that was off the charts amazing. It was like I'd known her forever.

"I knew I should have gone out with you last night," he says. "God, I passed out on the couch with my hand down my pants. When are you going to see her again?"

"It hasn't even been an hour. I think I'll wait until, I don't know, at least lunchtime to hit her up."

He cocks a skeptical brow. "I know you. You wouldn't have brought her home unless you really like her."

I don't bother denying it. I'm not big on random hookups anymore. Been there. Done that. Have the cringe-worthy photos splashed on social media and tabloids to prove it. I made plenty of bad decisions my first year in the league. Since then, I've dated infrequently and no one more than a few months at a time. Dating is always hard, but it's almost impossible at the beginning of a season.

The point is, I could have just as easily gotten Scarlett's number and waited to take her out another night when I didn't have to be up so damn early. I'm going to be tired as shit later, but I can't find it in me to regret it. Last night, this morning, whenever it was, was awesome. And the thing is, I didn't want to wait. I haven't been that excited about spending time with a girl ever.

"The timing is awful," I say. "We'll be gone all weekend, and when we get back, we start camp, then right into practice, media events, then pre-season games..." I trail off as I realize just how true it is. Even if her schedule was wide open, I have no idea when I'll have a free night to see her again.

"It'll always be tricky. Invite her to a game. Oooh, invite her to one of the events Daria's been trying to get you to attend." He snaps his fingers like he's given me a genius idea.

Daria is my agent, and she would love that idea. She's always pushing for me to attend more A-list events, where I'm seen schmoozing with other local celebrities. I use that term loosely since it's mostly athletes and influencers. "I can't do that."

"Why not? That's a pretty baller date setup if you ask me. Formal attire guarantees she'll be in a dress and all done up. The dinner and drinks are free, and I'll even come along to make sure you don't screw it up."

"Yeah, I've seen you in action. I know exactly what type of wingman you are. You end up in deep conversation with chicks, talking about great loves and the one that got away."

He grins and doesn't even try to refute it. He's totally that guy. Ash is likable and easy to talk to, and unexpectedly deep. He has this way about him that people want to open up and tell him their life story. It also means he attracts the emotionally damaged chicks sometimes because they latch on and feel seen or some shit. If I were a psych major instead of a business one, I'm sure I could have a field day dissecting him.

"She thought I was just some college student," I say as we get back to our neighborhood.

"You are."

"You know what I mean."

"Are you sure she didn't recognize you?"

"Positive." She guessed just about every occupation except professional athlete. And truth be told, I enjoyed connecting with a chick and my job not being at the forefront.

"And she still hung out with you?"

I shove him, sending him jogging off on the shoulder of the road.

"That's not the worst part."

"Don't hold out on me," he says with a grin. He's enjoying this way too much.

"She thinks I live with my parents."

"What?" He busts up laughing and comes to a halt in my driveway.

"She assumed, and then I felt weird about correcting her."

"Wow, this just gets better and better. Okay, well, what's the move then? Invite her to lunch at McDonald's? Splurge on a large nugget meal with a couple of apple pies? Damn, actually, that sounds real good about now."

I don't answer. I'm not sure what the move is. I know it's not that. And after the amazing night we had, where she had no idea that I was a professional hockey player, I don't want to invite her to some team thing like I'm trying to show off.

"Okay, not lunch. That's a weak follow-up to an all-night fuck fest. Besides, you might need the glow of the moon and stars to re-engage her bad decision-making. This girl sounds too good to be true. Hence the need for nightfall. She's probably already regretting hooking up with you and blocking your number."

I flip him off. Even with him busting my balls, my good mood can't be beat. She liked me. I felt it. And I liked her too. Last night was a damn dream.

"I'll figure it out when we get back. I don't want to bring her to some team event where I can't give her my full attention."

"Yeah, I get it. This is why Talia is perfect. She's only interested in the hockey stuff, and she's cool with a last-minute invite. One bird, two stones."

"Talia is sleeping with half the league."

He shrugs. "When she's in town, we're exclusive. It works."

"When she's in town?" I counter. "You say that like she's an international businesswoman instead of a part-time model who goes from city to city to hit up her many boy toys."

Ash laughs lightly like he doesn't care. Maybe he doesn't. His relationship with Talia, if we're even calling it that, makes no sense to me.

"Scarlett was different."

"I can see that, Romeo. You haven't stopped grinning. Well, if you're serious about this chick, then yeah, your timing is awful."

"Gee, thanks. In the future, I'll try to randomly bump into the hottest girl I've ever laid eyes on at a more convenient time."

"Hottest girl you've ever laid eyes on, huh?" He makes a face to show his surprise.

"Definitely. She was a dream. Too good to be true."

"Damn. I knew I should have met up with you last night."

By the time we get on the road for our guys trip, staying up all night is starting to catch up with me, but I've got big afternoon plans that include napping the entire ride up to Ash's lake house and then chilling on the boat with a beer in my hand.

Jack, Declan, Ash, and I go every year just before camp, and this year, we invited two rookies: Tyler and Maverick. It's a chill weekend away from the arena where we have a chance to hang out and let loose before the season starts.

We take two vehicles and, unfortunately, I picked the wrong one to ride up in. Ash is at the wheel, and I'm riding shotgun. Johnny Maverick, a rookie straight out of college, is yapping a mile a minute from the middle seat in the back of Ash's truck. Maverick is a cool dude—funny, high-energy, and as a teammate, he's going to be a blast to play with, but right now, when all I want is the lull of the tires rolling down the road, I'm wishing he'd gone with the other guys.

Two hours later, we pull into the driveway of Ash's place behind Jack, Dec, and Ty. The house sits just off the lake, has a great back yard for playing washers, grilling, and drinking, and the inside is big enough for all of us guys to have our own room. Not that we'll spend a lot of time in them this weekend.

I've barely dropped my things in one of the rooms when Jack appears in the doorway with a basket. He holds it out toward me, and I can see the other phones he has already collected.

"Seriously?"

He smirks but doesn't say a word. He doesn't need to. Jack is huge on disconnecting. I think it's the only way he stays sane.

"Can I just send a text first?" I ask, thinking of Scarlett. I bring up her contact on my phone. Fuck, what do I even say? It isn't like I can see her this weekend or next week. We get back Sunday night, and camp starts early Monday and goes all day, all week long.

The beginning of the season is brutal, but I enjoy the onslaught of hockey each year. Unfortunately, it also means that I'm looking at an entire week before I can see Scarlett again.

Last night was fun. Work is crazy right now. Call you soon.

It isn't the greatest text ever composed, but it'll do for now. I toss my phone in the basket. I'll follow up next week after camp is over when I have more than two hours I can devote solely to her.

CHAPTER FIVE

LEO

ALTERNATE CAPTAIN

'm in the locker room, pulling on my shoes, every muscle in my body screaming, when Jack stops in front of my stall. It's the last day of camp, and contented exhaustion flows through me. What a fucking week.

"Coach and Blythe want to see us before we head out," my captain says.

I groan but get to my feet and follow him. Blythe, the head of marketing for the Wildcats, is the first one I see. She's holding onto a game jersey, and dread washes over me at the thought of another press conference. It feels like the worse I do in interviews, the more they shove at me like they're trying to fix it. I think this might be one of those instances where we should let sleeping dogs lie.

"Lohan." Coach smiles, stepping next to Blythe. He's a nice guy—tough but fair. It's only his second season as head coach, but he's earned our respect. He's smart, and he works hard, and he isn't afraid to switch things up, which is nice. We're a young team, the youngest in the NHL in fact, so we have a lot of eager and energetic guys ready to jump around and do whatever's needed.

"Hey, Coach." I nod to Blythe. "Not sick of me yet, huh?"

"Never." Her smile is genuine. She must really love her job because I have not made it easy.

Jack runs a towel over his face, watching me like he's in on whatever's about to happen.

I glance between the three of them. *Oh shit.* What have they signed me up for? What do you get when you cross the coach, the captain, and the VP of marketing? Something that I can't get out of.

"What's going on?" I ask tentatively.

Coach speaks first. "I'm appointing you to alternate captain along with Declan."

Blythe holds out the jersey—mine—to show the "A" now proudly displayed on the upper left of the green material. I'm speechless.

Jack claps me on the shoulder. "Congratulations."

"Woah." I take the jersey and continue staring at it. My hands shake with nerves and excitement. It's my fourth year in the league, which in NHL years feels like a lifetime. It hasn't always been an easy road, but the hard work I've put in feels like it's starting to pay off.

I did not expect this, especially after my latest interview blunder. I swear, I wasn't looking at her boobs. Really. "Thank you. I'm honored."

Coach smiles and places one hand on his hip. It's his calm but serious speech stance, usually reserved for those moments just before a big game. "You really stepped up for us last season. We have a lot of new guys looking for leadership, and I think you're going to be a great addition to that."

"Thank you, sir."

Blythe continues her wide smile as she starts talking rapidly, "We'll be putting out a statement, and I'd love to get a few signed jerseys that we can give away on our social media pages. We'll want to do a couple of interviews as well."

Another groan slips out before I can stop it. Jack laughs.

"I'm sorry," I say, "I am thrilled to help lead the team, but the strong, silent type might be a better role for me."

"Your last interview was… unfortunate," Blythe says, her smile not faltering. "But these will be controlled, and I will prep you in advance."

It doesn't look like I have a choice, so I slap on a professional smile. "I appreciate it, Blythe."

She takes a step back. "I'll be in touch next week. Enjoy your weekend."

"Congratulations," Coach says when she's gone. His posture relaxes. "I'll see you boys tomorrow at my house."

"Looking forward to it," I say.

Jack follows me back into the locker room. "Are you ready to celebrate tonight?"

"Do I have a choice?" I sit on the bench in front of my stall, still holding the jersey. Jack is hosting a team party, and the way the invite was worded didn't make it seem like it was optional. I'd go either way, but after being gone last weekend, then a long week of camp, I'd prefer a chill night at home where I speak to no one.

"No, but since you're the man of the hour, you do get to pick up the booze. I'll send you a list of everyone's favorites. It shouldn't get too crazy tonight, and I keep most of it stocked, but it's always good to have a surplus. Especially with the rookies."

I shake my head. My first official duty as an alternate captain is to pick up the booze for the party? Yeah, that sounds about right.

Ash goes with me to the liquor store. I read from the long list of all the guys' favorites.

"Where do you think they keep MD 20/20?" I ask as we wander down the aisle, tossing various liquors and beers in the cart.

Ash doesn't respond, and I stop and look back to find him staring down at his phone.

"Talia?"

"Yeah, she just got back in town," he answers while still smiling at his phone.

"What's her favorite drink?" I ask with a sigh. Might as well add another item to this long ass list.

He finally looks up. "I don't think we'll be doing any drinking tonight."

"Jack will kick your ass if you duck out at his party."

"I'll come for an hour or two." His thumbs fly over the screen in his hands. "She needs a couple of hours to unpack and all that."

"It doesn't bother you that she was just with someone else?" I ask. Ash is a lot of things, a pushover isn't one of them. I can't understand why he's settling for someone that is clearly not invested in him. He's a great guy. If he was hooking up with other people too, it'd make more sense to me, but he isn't.

"What about you?" He tucks his phone in his pocket, walks in front of me, and holds up a bottle of MD 20/20. "When's your next bonefest with Scarlett?"

I nod for him to put the bottle in the cart. He does and grabs three more, too.

"I don't know. I haven't talked to her." She sent a single text in response to mine: *I had a good time, too.*

His brows raise. "Seriously? I thought you were into this chick? I believe your words were, 'She was a dream.'"

"I stand by that." Although as the days have passed, I'm starting to wonder if I didn't actually dream the whole thing. It feels like a month ago instead of seven days. "I've been a little busy. When do you think I possibly could have seen her this week?"

"You slept at home every night this week, didn't you?"

"I'm not inviting her over to fuck. I want to get to know her." I smirk. "Then fuck again."

Ash huffs a laugh as he sets a case of craft beer in the cart. "Well, don't wait much longer. If she's half as awesome as you made her out to be, she's not sitting around waiting to hear from some college dude who lives with his parents. No matter how sexy you are."

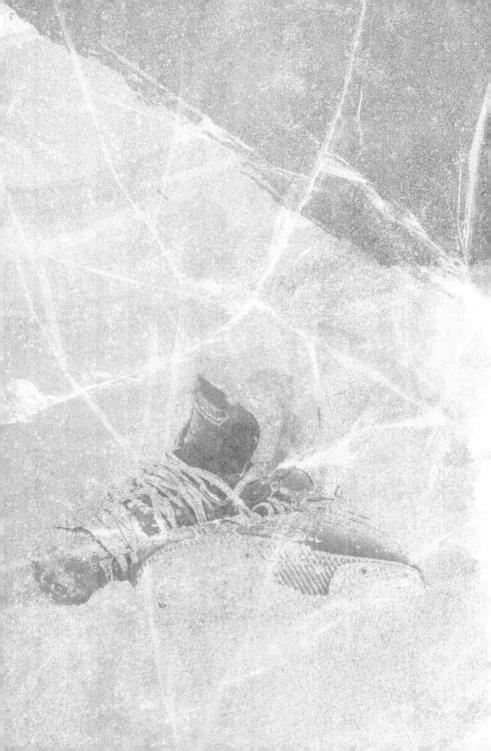

CHAPTER SIX

SCARLETT

I WAS SO WRONG ABOUT HIM

Jade lies on my bed, flipping through a magazine while I get ready for dinner with my parents. A meal with Mom and Dad wouldn't usually require such dedication to my appearance, but tonight I have to tell them that I dropped out of college. Again.

I don't have the type of parents that will yell and scream or disown me, and I'm thankful for that, honest, but the disappointment and worry etched into their features over the past couple of years is starting to wear on me. First, it was when I dropped out of my study abroad program to travel with Rhyse and then again when I came home a blubbering mess after we broke up.

I get it. I gave up everything for him. I was all in. So all in. And it didn't work out. I was shattered, and they were rightly concerned. But this decision isn't a reaction to the breakup. If I took nothing else away from my time following Rhyse around the world, I discovered just how much I love taking pictures. Something that had always been a hobby before became a passion.

I'm in a dress my mom bought me and wearing my hair in two

long braids—a hairstyle my dad likes (He's never actually said that, but he always tugs the ends and smiles when I do.).

I do not want to be this daughter, the one still living at home at twenty-one, figuring out life and disappointing her family. Even if they've never voiced it, I know my parents expect me to be like my older sister, Cadence. She is the perfect daughter and sister. She went to college, got a great job, found a nice guy, and got married. I'd hate her if I didn't admire her so much. Which is why I invited her tonight. She knows about my plans and is supportive.

Also, she has the bigger news. She's pregnant! Mom and Dad can't be upset when they're getting their first grandkid, right? *Right?*

"Still nothing from hottie Leo?" Jade asks. "I'm surprised. Tell me again how you left things."

Laughing, I indulge her for the third or fourth time this week but give her the short version. "He said he had a great time, and then we kissed some more until the Uber driver was about to leave my ass."

"And the text?"

"Said that he was busy, but would call." Which he hasn't.

"Then he'll call. He will. I know it."

"Doubtful. It's been a week since he sent that text, and I haven't heard from him," I say with an air of indifference. I'm faking. I went to sleep the morning after, or morning of, technically, since we stayed up all night, convinced he would text, but so far nothing.

"I was so wrong about him. The way he looked at you all night." She fakes a shiver.

"It's fine. It was good to get back out there." I am trying desperately to play off my night with hot Leo like it meant nothing more than a hookup to get over my ex. I can't handle another blow right now, so total delusion is my best option.

Besides, it isn't the greatest time to get involved with someone. I need to focus on myself for a little while and figure out my crap. The breakup is still fresh, and my life is a mess. Hear those weak excuses? Yeah, I know. They're true, but I have plenty of room in my schedule for mind-blowing sex with Leo. I will make room in my schedule for that.

"Can I change the subject?" she asks.

"Please."

"I applied for a job with a bridal magazine," Jade says, pulling my attention from the three shades of lipstick I'm deciding between.

"That's great." I turn from the chair in front of my vanity to look at her and smile.

"It's a long shot. I have less experience than they're looking for, but one of my classmates from college is an editor there, and she said she'd put in a good word." She sits up, and I hold out the tubes of pink lipstick to get her opinion. She points to the one in my right hand, and I swivel back around to the mirror.

Jade is two years older, and unlike me, she went straight to college after high school, worked hard, and got a bachelor's degree in journalism. She even used it for a short time, working with a local fishing magazine. Not long after, she quit and went back to the bartending job at Mike's that she'd held through college because she said she makes more money and doesn't have to write about nature. She is a girly girl through and through. The closest she wants to get to nature is a fancy-ass boat on a lake—her words.

"You really want to go back to a desk job? I thought you liked the hours at the bar."

"I do, but I miss writing and researching, seeing my name on glossy pages. Though if I get this one, it'll be mostly digital."

I catch her in the mirror staring down at the old Cosmopolitan magazine and running a hand along the paper.

"You'll get it. I can feel it. Good things are coming our way." I kiss the air. "Now, how do I look?"

She gives me a once-over, and the corners of her mouth pull up into a smirk. "Like you're heading off to eighth-grade graduation."

"I wouldn't have been caught dead in a dress with this much fabric in eighth grade," I say as I smooth a hand down the skirt of my long dress. The cotton material falls to my ankles and has cute little tie straps at my shoulders. My mother has good taste. This dress is just a little more sophisticated and girly than I'd pick out for myself.

"Are you sure you can't stay?" I plead. "My parents love you. You'll be a good distraction."

"Sorry, I have to get to the bar. I will check in later though." She stands and places her hands on my shoulders. "You've got this. You're a great photographer, and you're following your dreams."

I nod, soaking in some of that confidence. *I have this.*

I walk Jade upstairs and outside. Dad is in the garage working on his golf swing. He has a whole setup with a course simulation screen Mom got him for Christmas last year. The driver makes a loud *thwack*, and Dad curses under his breath as the ball goes left.

He looks up as we approach, and his scowl turns into a smile. "Hey, baby girl. Hi, Jade."

"Hey, Coach Miller." Jade has always called him this, even though he's never been her coach, but I think my dad loves it. Both of my parents adore Jade. She's polite, respectful, and responsible. She's also impulsive and fun, but never at the detriment to her career or reputation. I don't know how she does it.

"How's the team looking?" Jade asks him.

"Good. We have a lot of young, talented guys."

"Maybe I'll actually watch a game or two this year," she says with a sly smile. Neither of us is into sports, much to Dad's disappointment. Cadence was the sporty daughter.

Dad grins back at her with an amused expression as Jade heads to her car.

I sit on a stool at his workbench on the side of the garage. "Lots of new talent, huh?"

"Mhmm." He walks over with the golf club and takes a drink of water, then gives the end of one braid a little tug. "You look nice."

"Thanks. Mom picked this out for me."

His dark brows raise. "Uh oh. Trying to please your mother. Is everything okay?"

"Everything is great." I roll my eyes and pull away. "Cadence is coming."

"I heard." He rests the club on the ground and leans into it. "How are classes going?"

I struggle to form a response but am saved by Cadence's car pulling into the driveway. "She's here."

I hop down and jog to greet her. She hurries out of the vehicle, and we meet in the middle, hugging fiercely.

"Scar," she says. "Oh, I missed you."

"I missed you too." I squeeze her harder and then remember the baby. "Sorry."

"I'm fine." She looks me over. "You look so grown up."

"Don't worry," I say quietly. "I'm still as much of a hot mess as ever."

She links her arm through mine and keeps staring at me. We haven't seen each other since I've been back. She lives three hours away and is a lawyer, which is, apparently, code for never gets weekends off.

Dad waits for us just outside of the garage.

"How's the quest of becoming the next Tiger Woods coming along?" She steps forward and hugs him.

"I'm just out here because your mother threatened to withhold dinner if I didn't stop working. Simon at work?" Dad asks, referring to my sister's husband and my awesome brother-in-law. Simon is the best, but he's even more of a workaholic than my sister.

"Always," she answers. "If we didn't work together, we might not ever see one another."

The three of us laugh as we head inside. Dad is a total workaholic, just like Cadence, and Mom is always on the two of them to take more time for themselves. She was my biggest supporter when I wanted to study in London. She's all about experiences and traveling. You'd think that would make her team *drop out and follow your dreams*, but she's also a teacher, so education is sort of her whole life's purpose.

"Ready for pre-season games?" my sister asks as she walks beside my dad.

"We'll see. We still have a lot of work to do next week to prepare, but yeah, I'm ready to get back into it."

"I heard you made Lohan an alternate captain. It's about time. He's one of the most underrated players in the league," Cadence adds.

I fall in step behind them as we walk through the house to the kitchen. I couldn't smell it earlier, but the aroma of homemade bread and spaghetti sauce assaults us as we step through the door and makes my mouth water. Mom made all of Cadence's favorites tonight because family dinners are my mother's love language.

"No hockey talk at the dinner table." My mother comes around the big island in the kitchen to hug Cadence.

Cadence gives her a small gift bag (like I said, perfect daughter). "Don't open it now. It's for after dinner."

Mom takes it but stands in front of my sister with a scrutinizing glare. I'm familiar with that glare, but I don't think I've seen it used on Cadence since high school when she missed curfew.

"Honey, you're glowing. Are you…"

Cadence nods, and then Mom bursts into tears.

"What's going on?" Dad asks, watching the scene unfold before him with cautious eyes.

"I'm pregnant," Cadence says, then mouths *Sorry* to me.

NEEDLESS TO SAY, dinner does not go as planned. Mom sports an ear-to-ear grin as she peppers Cadence with questions about her pregnancy. Dad and I listen in, mostly, adding our excitement when we're able to get a word in. I'm so happy for Cadence, but now that she's dropped this amazing news, I do not want to be the one to ruin it. Which is why when the conversation turns to me, and I finally get an opening to tell my parents that I dropped out of college, I lie through my teeth and tell them classes are going great.

As soon as I'm finished eating, I take my plate from the table into the kitchen to rinse it off.

Cadence follows. "I should have known Mom would take one look at me and just know. I swear that woman is psychic. I'm so sorry."

"It's fine." I open the dishwasher. "Maybe I should have come upstairs in my pajamas, unshowered, looking like the hot mess I am, and she would have figured me out without me saying anything."

"You are not a hot mess."

I cut her a look. "I'm a twenty-one-year-old, unemployed, college dropout who lives with her parents."

"You are an up and coming artist temporarily staying with Mom and Dad." She bumps her hip against mine. "You could always come live with me. I'm going to need all the help I can get. Simon and I are like the blind leading the blind. I'm going to be a mom." She pauses with a faraway look in her eyes. It's the closest to unsure as I've ever seen her.

"You are going to be the best mom."

She smiles a little sadly. "Are you doing okay, really?"

"Yeah." I let out a breath. "I'm getting there."

"I'm sorry about how things ended with Rhyse, but I'm really glad you're back and that you'll be here to be Auntie Scar."

"Me too."

My phone pings in my bra, and I fish it out, earning a laugh from Cadence. "What else are you hiding in there?"

I stick out my tongue at her as I unlock the screen. For days I've jumped every time I've gotten a new text, hoping it was Leo. I felt something with him that I hadn't felt in a really long time. Maybe ever. Then again, maybe I was so desperate for someone to give me attention, I imagined the connection. But it's not Leo this time, just like it hasn't been him any of the other times a new text has come in the past few days. Jade's name displays on my screen. *I got the job! They called right after I left your house. Can you come out for drinks tonight? Invite Hottie Leo!*

"Oh, I know that smile." Cadence tries to peek over my shoulder, and I sidestep so she can't see the screen. "Who's the new guy?"

"What did I say about not dating until your thirty?" Dad winks as he comes into the kitchen carrying his and Mom's plates.

"It's Jade. She got a job with a local magazine, and that rule went out the window when this one got married at twenty-three and knocked up at… How old are you these days? Twenty-nine?"

"I'm *twenty-six*, and you know it."

Cadence is not thrilled about creeping closer to the thirty mark, and I like to tease her about it any chance I get.

"You met a boy?" Mom asks. We're now all crowded into the very space I came to escape.

"Boys are idiots," Dad says. "Thirty. That's about the time they start acting like men." He's still pissed at Rhyse. My parents only met him once, but he made a great impression. He always does. He puts on his media face—charming grin, saying all the right things, personable, likable. And it isn't even fake. He loves his job and meeting people, being in front of a crowd. He was meant for a life in front of the camera.

Cadence laughs softly. "I need to get going. I'm so tired these days, and I have to be in court first thing in the morning. The gift bag has an adorable *I heart my grandparents* picture frame in it with a photo from my first ultrasound."

"Oh!" Mom rushes for the bag and her first glimpse of the little bean.

There's a lot of oohing and ahhing over Cadence before she can get out the door, and then it's just the parents and me again. Dad goes to his office with a promise that he won't be long (We all know that's a lie.), and I help mom clean up.

"Don't forget we have the party for the team tomorrow," she says as I start to leave the room.

"Do I need to be here?"

"I think it would be nice," she says. Translation: yes. Most girls would be dying to attend a party with a bunch of pro hockey players, but I have had my fill of professional athletes. Besides, it's too weird now that my dad is the coach of the Wildcats.

"Okay. I'll be here, but I'm inviting Jade, so I have someone to talk to."

I text Jade to wish her congrats on the job, decline her invite to go out tonight because I need to edit some photos I took for Mike to keep up his new visibility and promo online, but beg her to come to the team party at our house tomorrow.

The edits for Mike don't take long. In fact, it takes me longer to select a few images from the hundreds I took than to do the actual editing. Either way, I'm happy to be doing something to work on my skills. I'm not sure Mike even cares about the photos that much. I think he just felt bad for not giving me more hours behind the bar. Since my first shift, I've worked two more afternoons, and they went about as well as the first.

After I send off the edited images, I fall into bed with my phone and scroll for jobs. There are a few places looking for photographers, but I don't feel ready for that yet. I check my messages, you know, just in case one came in from Leo, and I didn't notice (groan), and then since I'm already feeling sorry for myself, I go to Rhyse's social media page.

Someone on his team posted a video from the race last weekend. He stands on the podium as handsome as I remember. It really doesn't seem fair that he can go on living his life, winning, looking great, seemingly unaffected by our breakup, while I'm floundering with just about every aspect of my life.

I scroll through his old posts. It's weird to see his life like this, knowing I was there but not being in any of it. Half of the photos are ones I took, but I'm not in them. Rhyse's team thought it was best to keep the focus on him. When we first got together, he snapped a selfie of us at some event and posted it, tagging me as his girlfriend, and the backlash from his fans was immediate and awful.

He'd built an image—the hotshot Formula 1 racer and notorious playboy. He'd partied hard his first couple of years, dating women all across the globe. That's who people wanted him to be. They didn't want him to settle down and grow up.

They came for me in droves. I had to change my social media profiles to private. He might have been ready for a serious relationship, but after seeing the reaction, his publicist thought it was best if we kept it quiet for a while. At first, it was only going to be six months until the end of the season. I didn't love being his girlfriend in private only, then in public watching him keep up his single, fun image, but it was better than being attacked.

And I was head over heels. I really thought it was temporary. Six months came and went, and I could see that he still wasn't ready to risk his popularity taking a nosedive to really be with me. I held out hope for another six months, but on our one-year anniversary, I gave him an ultimatum.

And here I am.

I traveled all over the world with him, but there isn't a single scrap of evidence I ever existed on any of his social media pages. If it weren't for the ache in my chest, I could almost pretend it never happened.

CHAPTER SEVEN

LEO

SCARLETT MILLER IS YOUR DREAM GIRL?

Sunday, we get a day off from practice and workouts, and Coach Miller invites the team over to his house. We did it last year, right before the pre-season kicked off, to get to know the new head coach, and I guess now it's going to be tradition.

We're outside in his back yard, where a bar is set up and there's enough food inside to feed us twice (which is saying something). Everyone is on their best behavior tonight. Not that Coach doesn't know we like to get rowdy and have fun when we're on our own time, but this could be a big year for us. We've all been feeling it since that very first day we were on the ice together.

Sure, we're young, but teams that count us out because of that are going to end up icing their old man aches and pains while watching us in the playoffs come spring.

"Hey, man." Maverick corners me next to the bar where I'm standing with Ash and Jack. "Do you have any extra tickets for the home opener?"

Ash speaks before I can. "I already asked. He's saving them for his dream girl."

"Dream girl?" Maverick asks. "Is she real or fantasy? Because mine is very much real, and she's thinking of flying up for the game with some friends."

"I'm going to call her tonight. Can I let you know then?"

"Sure. Thanks, man." He walks off with a salute.

"Dream girl?" Jack angles his body, closing the small circle between the three of us. "Why am I just now hearing about this?"

"He's being stingy with details," Ash answers for me. "Met her at a college bar. She doesn't know he's a hockey player."

"What am I a toddler? I can answer for myself."

Ash smirks.

"I met her at a college bar. She doesn't know I'm a hockey player," I repeat his words.

Both of them laugh.

"She was gorgeous and unexpected and…"

The guys are hanging on my words and grinning like a bunch of idiots. Fuck them. I don't even care.

"Whatever. I'm going to call her tonight and invite her to the first home game and then out to Wild's after." I shouldn't have put it off this long. It's been more than a week since she left my house at sunrise, smelling like chlorine and sex, but I've been trying (and failing) to come up with a better follow-up date to our fuck-a-thon. Don't get me wrong, I'm hoping that's how the end of this one turns out too, but I'd like to spend some more time getting to know her.

She was funny and enchanting, and I felt good hanging out with her. She liked being with me, not Leo Lohan. I forgot what that was like. But, I think my only option is to invite her to a home game and hope she wants to hang out after.

"Why wait?" Jack asks. "That's another almost two weeks. Give me your phone. Let's text her now."

"No."

Jack thrusts his hand out toward me. "Come on. We both know I'm better at talking to chicks."

He isn't wrong, but I need to do this myself. I push my hand in my pocket and grip my phone. "I've got this."

"All right, but if she's forgotten you or doesn't answer or agrees to come to the game and then ghosts your ass, don't say that I didn't—"

My arm slices through the air, and I place my hand on his chest, silencing him, as my gaze snags on the other side of the yard near the back door where more people are arriving. I have to convince myself my brain isn't playing tricks on me as Scarlett steps off the porch, wearing a yellow dress. Maybe I've conjured her up by thinking about her nonstop.

"That's her. That's Scarlett." I blink a bunch of times, but she's still there.

"Which one?" Ash asks.

"Yellow dress. Do you see her?" I'm still not totally convinced that I'm not imagining her.

The smile on my face falls as Coach Miller embraces her. A sick feeling washes over me, settling like a rock in the bottom of my stomach.

"No fucking way." Jack cackles. He fucking cackles. "Scarlett Miller is your dream girl? Get in line, buddy. Coach will trade your ass faster than you can say, *Stay away from my daughter.*"

His daughter.

"I didn't know." I look at Ash.

He shrugs. "Never seen her before. Are you sure?"

Jack gives a definitive nod. "She was studying abroad the past couple of years. Paris or Australia or…"

"London," I say.

I'm gonna be sick.

As if she can feel me staring at her, she looks in our direction, eyes quickly flitting over and dismissing us, then snapping back to me. Her gaze widens, and she stops in her tracks.

"Looks like she remembers you." Jack slaps my back. "Congrats."

"Sorry, man." Ash's words are a consolation I don't want.

Fuck me. Did I get played? Was all of that guessing my occupation a joke because she knew exactly who I was?

I move toward her, hoping I figure out what to say before I reach her. She's just as gorgeous as I remember. Brown eyes framed with thick lashes and a mouth that looks like it was made to be kissed. I should know because despite being confused and irritated, I still have the overwhelming urge to drop my mouth to hers.

I'm grappling for words when I reach her side, but I don't get a chance to say anything. Coach's voice booms with pride next to her as he introduces her to a couple of our assistant coaches. "This is my daughter, Scarlett. Just back from London and attending Whittaker."

She says hello and shakes each of their hands, then introduces Jade standing beside her. Jade. Fuck.

"Hi," I say from just behind Coach when her gaze snags on me again.

"Leo." Coach opens his stance to include me and gives my shoulder a squeeze. "Honey, this is Leo Lohan, our newest captain. Leo, this is my youngest daughter, Scarlett and her friend, Jade."

The back of my shirt sticks to me as I start to sweat. How the hell did I get myself in this situation? His daughter!? Fuck me.

Scarlett offers me her hand. "Nice to meet you, *Leo*."

The slight taunt in her tone when she says my name is the only indication that she knows me. Well, that and the snicker from Jade as she watches us pretend to meet for the first time.

Coach falls into conversation with someone else, and I take Scarlett's hand and practically drag her around the side of the house and out of view.

"Slow down," she whispers in a haughty voice that goes straight to my crotch. "These shoes were not made for running in grass."

"Did you know?" I ask, reaching for calm. Here she is. The girl I've thought of nonstop since she left my house. My fucking coach's daughter.

"I thought you were a college student still living with his parents, so no. Did you know? Is that why you were so cagey about telling me what you do for a living?"

"I wasn't cagey."

She crosses her arms over her chest. "Yeah, okay."

"I had no idea." I run a hand through my hair. "I can't believe this."

"It's fine. I'm about as eager for my dad to find out I had a one-night stand with one of his players as you are. So neither of us says anything. Are we cool?"

Are we cool?

I'm silent for too long, and she adds, "We don't have to make a big thing out of it. It was one night."

"Are you serious?"

"Umm... yeah. I have enough chaos in my life without worrying about a hot hockey player who doesn't know how to work a phone." The ice in her tone solidifies my fuck-up.

Ah, shit. "I was going to call. Just now, I was talking to my buddies about it."

She laughs and lets her arms fall to her sides. "Let's make a pact. I won't tell my father, and you won't pretend to care when I walk away and act like I don't know you."

She starts to leave, and I reach for her, wrapping my fingers around her wrist. The contact sends tingles all the way up my spine. "I was going to call. I swear. My schedule is nuts right now, but I wanted to invite you to the first home game."

"You wanted to invite *me* to a game? A girl you didn't even tell you played hockey."

"I'm sorry," I say. Damn, am I sorry.

She shakes her head, making her brown hair move around her shoulders. "It doesn't matter. There's no reason we need to run into each other again."

"Come to the game," I beg.

"I'll be there… for my dad."

"How about after?"

"You don't need to do this. I'm a big girl, and I knew exactly what I was getting myself into the other night." Her eyes drop, and she does a sweep of me from head to toe. "Just not who I was getting into it with." She inhales sharply. "All the things I told you. Oh god. Please don't say anything about me dropping out of school. I will tell him. I just haven't found the right time."

This is what she's worried about? That her dad will find out she quit school, not that she spent last weekend riding my dick? Well, that feels… honestly, I'm not sure.

"Your secrets are safe with me."

She tenses. "Ditto."

I imagined this moment—seeing her again—a whole lot

differently. For starters, I thought the expression on her face would read more excitement than repulsion.

"I don't have any secrets. Don't get me wrong, your dad may very well send me across the country if he learns what I did with his baby girl in my hot tub, but I'll tell him myself right now if it means I can do it again." I bring my hand to the curve of her neck. "You're all I've thought about for the past week."

Her lashes flutter, and her pulse races under my touch.

"Scarlett." Jade appears around the corner, a warning in her gaze as she waves Scarlett over. "Your mom is looking for you."

She nods, walking away from me, and toward her friend. I have so many more things I want to say, but this isn't the place, so I don't follow. Before she disappears, she glances over her shoulder to find me still staring after her. "See you around."

She can count on it.

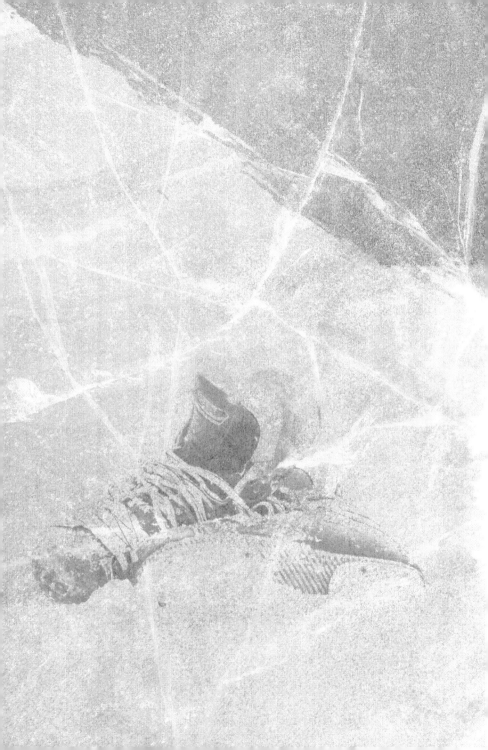

CHAPTER EIGHT

SCARLETT

THE INTERNET SUCKS

J ade brings the bottle of wine from the kitchen and refills my wine glass while peering down at the screen of my phone. "Stop torturing yourself."

"It doesn't even look like him. Seriously. Would you have known this guy was Leo?" I hold up the Wildcats roster photo of him. His hair is shorter, and his eyes are wide, like someone startled him seconds before they took the photo. I've never seen a more perfect "deer in headlights" impression.

My best friend drops into a chair across from me in the living room. I'm hiding out inside, trying to convince myself that I don't care, Leo, *my* hot Leo, is actually Leo Lohan, Wildcats star forward, and currently in the back yard of my family home.

"You know I don't follow sports, but he does look better in person."

I groan, drop my phone, and bury my head in my hands.

Her voice is the calm to the chaos raging inside of me. "Do you think he really would have called and asked you out again?"

"I don't know. It doesn't matter. We'll never know now. I blocked him."

"You *blocked* him? Why?"

I slump back into the couch. I haven't blocked him yet, but I'm seriously considering it. "He plays hockey for my dad. He's a professional athlete. He lied. Pick a reason."

"Lied is a bit of a stretch."

I glare, and she snorts a laugh.

"Sure, now that he knows who I am, he can't stop thinking about me and wants to see me again. Where was all of this a week ago when I was still hoping he might call?" No one is so busy they can't find a second to text. I replay his words earlier and try to make them line up with the facts. He was full of sweet words, but was it all just to save his ass?

"So, are you mad because he plays hockey for your dad and seeing him again would be complicated or because he didn't text when he said he would?"

The back patio door opens, and I lower my voice to keep our conversation private. "I don't know. Both. Why?"

Her gaze lifts, and she looks behind me over my head. "Because he just walked in."

I hold my breath as his footsteps approach. He stands in the space beside me. I don't look directly at him, but I know it's him. I hate that after only one night together, my body is so tuned to his. Goosebumps race up my left side where he stands closest.

"I'm going to go… anywhere else." Jade gets to her feet.

Neither of us speaks in the time it takes Jade to cross the room and exit the same way he came in. I'm too agitated to sit, so I stand and move to the kitchen with my wine. He follows.

"What are you doing in here?" I ask. I finally look at him and then wish I hadn't. He skipped the hat today, and his light brown hair sticks up like he might have been running his fingers through it recently. He's dressed casually in jeans and a T-shirt, but even so, he looks every bit as good as I remember. His roster photo really doesn't do him justice.

"We need to finish talking."

"I don't have anything else to say to you, Leo Lohan."

"Maybe I have something to say to you, *Scarlett Miller*." His lips turn up, and that dimple in his left cheek appears.

The look on his face reminds me of the night we spent together. How fun and easy it all felt. But nothing about this is easy. I'm not going to fall at the feet of another athlete who knows how to turn on the charm to get his way.

"Save it. I'm not interested."

"Why not?" His brows pull together. "I thought we had fun the other night."

I glare.

"Your dad being the coach isn't ideal," he admits, like that's the only reason I'm not falling over myself with excitement to see him again.

"Do you even go to college, or do you just hang at the campus bars trolling for girls?"

"I went pro after my sophomore year, but I've been working on finishing my degree. I took a couple of classes this summer, and I'm enrolled in one this fall. The guys I was with the other night are buddies from my summer class."

"Do they know you're… you?" I flick a hand in his direction.

One side of his mouth quirks with a hint of a smile. "Yeah."

I drop my wine glass to the counter and cross my arms over my chest. "Why didn't you tell me? If you really had no idea who I was, then why not tell me? If not at the bar, then at least when I was at your house. It is *your* house, right?"

He drops his head and pushes his hands down the front pockets of his jeans. "I guess I liked spending time with someone who wasn't interested in what I do more than who I am. And when we got to my place, and you went off on how you didn't care that I lived with my parents because you did…"

I groan as I remember my heartfelt speech. I meant every word, and it turns out I spewed all my baggage, thinking we had something in common. "You still should have told me. I feel like an idiot."

In two long strides, he closes the distance between us. His voice is deep and low as he says, "You're not an idiot. You're smart and funny, and I've been thinking about how gorgeous you look when you come for a solid week."

I breathe in his words like helium. My throat tightens, and my chest expands. My skin tingles as I remember how it felt to be kissed by him, touched by him.

"We have a busy week, and we're traveling next weekend, but we have a home game the following week."

I give him my best "duh, I know" glare.

"Right. You probably know the schedule." His mouth pulls into a tight smile. "After home games, we usually go to a bar called Wild's. It's a couple of blocks from the arena. Meet me there and let me make it up to you for not calling sooner."

It would be so easy to give in. It would feel good. I know it. My body freaking knows it, too. Every nerve ending crackles with desire.

Easy and good, but also dumb.

Ignoring the heavy thrum of my heart, I step back. "I'm not interested, Leo Lohan."

THE NEXT MORNING I'm in the kitchen eating a bowl of cereal while I replay yesterday like a horror movie. Leo *freaking* Lohan. Of all the guys to go home with, I would pick the one that's totally off limits to me. I'm a freaking mess.

Mom's voice cuts through my thoughts. "Can you run this to your dad at the arena on your way to class? The man was going to wear a suit from the nineteen nineties in his team photo." She groans and lays the garment bag over the chair beside me.

The seemingly simple request sends panic pulsing up my spine and I sit straight. "I can't."

Mom fills her travel mug with coffee and grabs her lunch bag from the fridge before she responds. A wrinkle forms between her brows. "Why not?"

I don't come up with an answer quickly enough because I don't have a good excuse.

She cocks her head to the side. "Please? I cannot bear the thought of your father being the worst-dressed NHL coach two years running. I'll never live down the shame."

"Worst-dressed coach?" I ask. "That's a thing?"

"I believe the exact words of the online article were, *That suit belongs in the dumpster along with the Wildcats post-season performance.*"

"Man, the internet sucks." Except for odd animal friendship videos and military members reuniting with family. Those can stay.

"Well, they aren't wrong, at least about the suit." She has her hands full but comes around to lean in and place a kiss on my forehead.

"I don't even know where his office is." It's true. I haven't been to visit Dad at work since I've been back. It wasn't intentional. At least not until twenty-four hours ago.

"You're a smart girl, Scarlett Marie. I'm confident that you'll figure it out. See you tonight."

I take my time finishing my cereal, then shower and get ready. The extra effort I put into my hair, makeup, and outfit is entirely unrelated to the possibility of running into the hockey player I'm hell-bent on avoiding. *Completely* unrelated.

At the arena, I walk through the front doors, and a security guard ushers me to a sign-in desk.

"Name and purpose of your visit?" A woman asks without looking up from her computer.

"Scarlett Miller. I'm here to make sure Coach Miller doesn't commit a crime of fashion." I lift my arm to show off the garment bag as her eyes slowly glance up from her screen to me.

I can't tell if she believes me or not—she has the piercing, take no shit gaze of a woman who takes her job seriously—but I'm eventually guided to an elevator and down to a lower level by a security guard who whistles lightly the whole way.

"Let's check his office first," the guard says. "If he's not there, then he'll be on the ice."

I nod like I know. But I don't. Not anymore. It's one of those things that I knew had changed since I'd left for London two years ago, but until now, I didn't realize that meant I didn't know how he spent his day in the same way I used to.

Dad was still coaching at the junior hockey level then. I'd

occasionally pop in to have lunch or just to see him. It was nothing like this. Everything about this place is bigger and nicer.

The guard in front of me stops in a doorway while I'm still admiring the massive hallway with its green paint that smells like it was recently done, the framed photos of players and coaches, and the light music playing over speakers in the hall—Taylor Swift, which for some reason makes me smile.

"Your daughter is here to see you, Coach."

"My daughter?" Dad's voice snaps me back to my purpose for being here, and I walk through his office door.

"What are you doing here?" He smiles behind a messy desk stacked with papers, so many papers, along with stick tape, hockey pucks, a brown banana, and those are just the things visible. Who knows what's buried underneath?

"Mom sent me." I hang the bag on an open filing cabinet and unzip it.

"Thanks, Mick." He waves to the guard and then loosens the brown and white tie he's wearing, walking toward the mom-approved outfit without a word of complaint. That is true love. Or twenty-seven years of experience telling him that changing his shirt and jacket are easier than listening to Mom gripe.

I take a seat behind his desk in a big, worn leather chair that I know for sure he had at the last place. It creaks as I lean back.

"They couldn't spring for a new chair?" I spin around in it. "Or a maid." I lift the banana and toss it into the wastebasket, which is empty, so maybe they do clean in here.

"I've had that chair for fifteen years. It's lucky." He winks and goes about switching his shirt and tie.

I move a few items on his desk and uncover a sandwich that

definitely shouldn't be eaten and another ugly brown tie that Mom would probably pay me to make disappear for good.

"How do you work in here?"

"It isn't usually this bad." He takes out the jacket and pulls it on, grimacing as he rolls his shoulders and shifts to get comfortable. "Anna needed to take some time off to visit her family in Michigan."

"Who's Anna?" I stand and straighten his tie.

"My assistant."

"I don't remember you being this disorganized at the last place."

"It's been busy with camp and practices. I'll get to it eventually."

A phone rings from somewhere on his desk. I stifle a laugh as he rummages around until he pulls the receiver free and answers.

"I'll be right there." He fidgets some more with his tie after he hangs up. "Look okay?"

"Yep, and now I have fulfilled my daughterly obligations."

"You don't want to come check it out? Media day is pretty impressive. Lots of fancy cameras and photography equipment."

My eyes light up, and he grins like he knew the mention of cameras would have me following him down a hallway and into a tunnel that eventually leads to the ice. A quick look, and then I'm out of here.

On the ice, a big green backdrop is setup, and in front of it, another man in a suit sits on a stool, smiling as a woman snaps pictures of him. She moves from left to right, to center, capturing every angle. They have music going and lots more people with cameras and video equipment mill around the ice.

Eventually she has him stand and takes more photos that way, then has him don a Wildcat hat and takes a few more.

Dad sneaks a glance over his shoulder to check my expression.

The buzz of excitement that's worked its way into the very core of my being must be radiating from me because he smiles and says, "This is just for the coaches. Once the players get here, the real fun starts."

"Coach Miller."

At his name, Dad and I both look up to see the man on the stool has vacated his seat, and the photographer is walking toward us with a friendly smile.

"Lindsey, this is my daughter Scarlett," Dad says, adjusting the cuffs on one sleeve.

"Hey. Nice to meet you," she says. She removes the camera from around her neck and hands it to someone else. "Are you ready for us, Coach?"

"Yeah. Let's get this over with." He messes with his tie. If they manage to capture a photo with the thing not crooked, I will be amazed.

"Great. Give me two minutes." She starts off the ice with a bounce to her step that makes her short blonde hair sway around her head, then stops. "Oh, hey. Do you have the schedule for the rest of today and through the week? Anna mentioned there were a few changes. She was going to email it over, but…"

"Right." Dad frowns. "It's probably on her iPad, but I think she printed me a copy."

Green catches my eye on the other side of the bench, and I glance over in time to see the first players arriving. Three of them huddle together in their full uniforms. I don't see Leo's head, but I pull my gaze away so quickly, I can't be sure he isn't among them.

"I'll grab the paper," I say, a little too eager.

Dad's forehead crinkles as his brows lift, but he nods. "It's on the desk. If you can't find it, bring the iPad. It'll be on there somewhere."

"I've got this," I say with far more confidence than I feel the second I step back into the tunnel. I'm not even sure I can find his office again, let alone a single sheet of paper on his disaster of a desk.

When I get to the end of the tunnel, I pause and look left and right, then left again. More green jerseys are headed this way from my right, so I gamble and go left.

Dad's office isn't that hard to find, thank goodness, and I start sifting through the piles of paper. I don't know exactly what I'm looking for, but Lindsey said it was a schedule, so I look for dates and times.

As I work, I stack the piles neatly and throw away more spoiled food. Gross, Dad, seriously.

I finally find what I'm looking for. Two pages stapled together with the word 'schedule' and this week's date on it. I hold it up and kiss it, then remember it was on a desk with old food.

I start toward the door, but a mass of green fills the escape route. A very handsome mass.

"Coach—" Leo stops with his hand up like he was about to knock on the open door. Two very long seconds pass before he speaks my name. "Scarlett."

He starts to smile, but my horrified expression must scare it off his handsome face.

I hold up the paper to indicate why I'm in here, but don't speak. I'm incapable of forming words as I take him in, all six feet and two inches of him covered in padding and wearing skates that make his already big frame mammoth.

He takes a step closer at the same time I do, then we both stop.

"What are you doing here?" His deep voice snaps me out of the trance.

"Finding a schedule. Coach is on the ice." I try to brush past him, but he steps in front of me.

"I'm glad I ran into you. I wanted to clear the air."

"I already told you I won't tell my dad." Talk about an awkward conversation with dear old dad. He can't really think I'd be eager to share the details of my one-night stand.

"Thank you, but that isn't it. You and I are bound to run into one another, and there's no reason it should be weird between us."

"You mean except for the fact we've seen each other naked?" I ask in a hushed tone.

His mouth curves up. "Except that."

I fight the flush climbing up my neck from standing this close to him. "Like I told you yesterday, I'm not interested in a repeat. It was just one night. Zero weirdness coming from me."

He studies my face without speaking. The office is quiet. Way too quiet. Noise in the hallway gets louder, and Leo finally steps back, and I can breathe again. "Perfect. Zero weirdness."

CHAPTER NINE

SCARLETT

HOCKEY PLAYERS ARE AWESOME

Oh, it's weird all right. My legs carry me down the hall away from him, but my heart pitter-patters in my chest. Holy crap. Leo in a bar as a regular guy, hot. Leo in his hockey uniform, ugh, I hate myself a little for admitting this, but so, *sooo* hot. What is it about a guy in a uniform?

I glance back as I turn into the tunnel. He hasn't moved from the outside of my dad's office, and his eyes are pinned on me. He lifts a hand, cocky smirk on his face. Damn him.

No hockey players. No jocks. No men. No dating.

I say each phrase under my breath like a pledge as I march back to the ice. Dad is in the hot seat now. He smiles stiffly as Lindsey moves in front of him. *Good call on the jacket, Mom.* He looks sharp against the green backdrop.

My gaze moves past him to the hockey players hanging out, waiting their turn. More have arrived, and they're a swarm of green muscle. I find Leo in the back of the group talking to another player. While he's preoccupied, I take the opportunity to appreciate how good he looks.

He's had a haircut since our night together, but the light brown strands still have a mind of their own. He holds his stick in front of him, both hands resting on it casually.

He tips his head back and smiles at something his buddy says, and when he does, he catches me staring. I know I should look away, but I drink him in for a few good seconds first. It feels much safer with my dad acting as a barrier between us. A reminder that this can't happen.

Why did he have to be a Wildcat?

"All right," Dad's voice startles me as he appears in front of me. I glance back at Leo to find an amused smile on his face at my being caught off guard.

"Mom did good," I say.

He mumbles his agreement, even as he continues to mess with the knot of his tie.

I lift the schedule. "Is this what you were looking for?"

"Ah, yes. Thank you. I knew you'd find it."

"Your desk is disgusting. I hope Anna is coming back soon."

"Yeah. Me too." He looks over it before calling to Lindsey.

The players begin taking the ice, and someone lines them up. I see all of this out of my peripheral, but I keep my focus on Dad as he and Lindsey chat about today's schedule. It's time to get out of here.

"Dad, I'm going to go," I say and jab my thumb behind me.

He looks up. "Already?"

"Umm… yeah?"

The watch on his wrist catches the light as checks the time. "Oh, crap. I have a meeting in five."

I laugh. Dad isn't usually this disorganized, or maybe he's just always had an Anna working her magic in the background.

"Is this everything you need?" he asks Lindsey.

"Yeah. We're all set unless you can figure out how to get my two assistants back." She rolls her neck. "Whose idea was it to do photos and social media on the same day?"

"Sorry." He finally undoes his tie completely. That didn't last long.

"We'll figure it out. We always do. Thanks, Coach." Lindsey moves into action, bossing people around for the team photo.

Dad pulls off the tie and undoes the top button of his shirt. "I have a meeting, but if you want to hang out and wait for me, I'll buy lunch."

My stomach growls. It's in direct opposition with my need to get the heck out of here and away from Leo Lohan.

"How long?"

"Thirty minutes. Forty-five tops." He smiles and starts off like it's a done deal. "Stay and watch. They haven't even gotten to the really impressive stuff yet."

On cue, it goes dark in the arena, and neon green lights come to life on the backdrop.

My mouth makes an O, but I'm not sure any sound comes out.

Dad chuckles. "Enjoy."

By the time I find my voice, he's long gone. I move to a seat in the first row and watch Lindsey work. After they've taken a bunch with the team together, they move to individual photos.

Jack Wyld is up first, and she moves around him as he stands naturally in front of the backdrop. Then she switches cameras, and another guy steps in with a camcorder. Jack skates to the side and grabs a stick and puck and then moves around the ice.

I can tell he's done this before. Lindsey too. Their movements are choreographed like a dance, slow and controlled, and Jack seems to know exactly when to look up, flashing a practiced smile that I'm sure the fans love.

I'm enthralled watching when Leo takes the seat beside me. His shoulder brushes mine and I suck in a breath.

"You're still here."

"I'm having lunch with my dad." I move my arm away from his and point to where Jack shoots the puck into the net and then skates toward the camera, coming up short and spraying ice. "They do this with every player?"

"Yeah. It takes damn near all day to get through everyone. When we're done here, they send us through another room where they have someone from the social media team ask us questions- like ice breakers that they use as footage during games."

Now I understand what Lindsey meant about doubling up with social media. I get why they'd want to do it all in one day while the guys are dressed and available, but she has a long day in front of her. They all do.

"Still working at the bar?" Leo asks like we're just old friends catching up.

"What are you doing over here? Shouldn't you be in makeup or something?"

He grins. "You think I need makeup?"

I look him over as if I'm considering it. He has nice skin. It isn't shiny and is blemish-free. He has a straight nose and a sharp jaw. His hazel eyes are bright and framed with thick, dark lashes. No, he definitely doesn't need makeup.

I mumble as much under my breath. Apparently louder than I mean to because he chuckles softly.

"I'm up next." He bumps my shoulder. "Maybe I'll see you around."

"Not likely."

He shakes his head. "I'm going to win you over, Scarlett."

Not in this lifetime.

I take a deep breath when he's gone. He sets my every nerve ending on edge. Blocking him out, I walk down to the ice. Lindsey rolls her neck again as she sets the camera down and takes a long drink of water. She smiles as I approach.

"This is incredible. Did you put all of this together?"

She nods. "More or less. I come up with a few different ideas, and someone above my pay grade decides which one they like best."

"I'm a photographer. Or, I'm interested in it. I don't do it professionally or anything. I dabbled a little in sports photography for my ex. He is a race car driver."

"No shit? If I'd known that, I would have already strapped a camera to your hand. Do you prefer a Canon or Nikon?"

"I'm very much a newbie. I don't think I'm ready to shoot anything like this, but I could help with lighting or setup or... whatever you need."

"Really?"

"I can't seem to force myself away from the action and I'm waiting on my dad for lunch, so..." I shrug.

"Okay, yeah. If you take over for Joe, that'll free him up to swap off with me. I'll take any and all the help I can get."

She introduces me to Joe, who's running the schedule, making sure the next player is ready to go and that everything is set.

"Got it?" he asks me as Lindsey hands him a camera.

"I think so."

"Good enough for me." He smiles. "Send the next guy out."

Leo's already close enough that he walks onto the ice without my calling him.

"Where do you want me, boss?"

"You're enjoying this too much," I tell him.

"Hell yeah, I am. Did you really block my number?"

"It isn't like you were going to use it." I roll my eyes.

"I would have," he says. "Honest."

I don't believe him and the scowl I give him must tell him as much.

"I should have done it sooner, I know. We were busy with camp, that's true, but I had plenty of opportunities to shoot you a text."

"Exactly."

"The thing is, I knew as soon as I contacted you, I'd want to see you, and I couldn't. I was waiting until I had more time where we could really hang out, get to know one another."

My pulse races as he speaks and I swallow thickly. "They are ready for you." I take a step away from him, but he closes it.

"How do you follow-up a night like that with a text, you know?" he mutters more to himself than me. "Anyway, I'm sorry."

He skates into position and the lights drop. Breathing is easier when he's a good distance away and not saying all the right things. He looks good against the neon green, too. He looks good. Period.

I check the schedule to see who's next. "Ash Kelly?"

"Here," someone calls.

Ash Kelly moves to the front of the pack. He's about the same height and build as Leo but with longer hair that's slicked back and touches his ears.

"You're next after Leo."

"Thanks." He continues to stand next to me as Leo stares seriously at the camera.

"Would it kill him to smile?"

Ash huffs a laugh. "Yeah. After the shit we gave him for last year's photo, he isn't taking any chances."

Well, I can't blame him there. He's nearly unrecognizable in last year's roster photo.

"I'm Scarlett," I say.

"Oh, I know who you are."

My face heats and a memory from my and Leo's night together flashes in my head. "Right. The neighbor."

"That's right." His smile is pleased. "He wouldn't shut up about you last week at camp."

Kill me now. I don't respond. Seriously, what do I say to that? He could brag to his buddies, but not pick up the phone?

"If I hadn't seen you with my own eyes, I would have thought he dreamt the whole thing up. Never seen him so spun up about a chick."

"I don't date athletes."

"Why not?" Ash gives me a horrified look. "Hockey players are awesome. Or at least we are. Especially Leo. Best guy I know."

His face reads sincere and I don't doubt he means it. I divert my attention back to Leo. He's skating around, shooting pucks now. He catches my eye and butterflies swarm in my stomach. Wait, no, I'm pretty sure that's just hunger pains. It has to be. Yep, that's my story and I'm sticking to it. No hockey players. Definitely no Wildcats.

I'm still helping out when Dad comes back down to grab me for lunch.

"Go," Lindsey says. "We're going to break for lunch soon, too. Thanks for your help. Next time, maybe you'll pick up a camera."

Dad takes me to the cafeteria on-site. We get our food and sit at a small table off to the side.

"How was it?" he asks.

"It was really cool. Lindsey's great. How long has she been here?"

"Not sure. She was here when I got here. How can you tell she's good without even seeing the final images?"

"She has a way with the players. She knew exactly how to get each one to relax. They were having fun."

He nods and smiles. "She does do that. I hadn't really put it into words like that, but you're right."

He asks me about my photography as we eat. I can ramble all day long about it, so I do most of the talking. He smiles and nods along as I tell him about all the things I've shot recently.

When we're done, I walk with him back to his office. The cyclone that's still his desk makes me laugh. "When does Anna come back?"

"I don't know." He runs a hand over his hair. "Her mom is sick."

"Can you get a temp or someone to cover until she returns?"

"I could, but Anna knows how I like things. By the time I train someone new, she'll be back. You know how crazy the beginning of the season is. I don't really have the bandwidth."

"What if I helped?" I stop. "Wait, assistants don't have to interact with the players, right?"

"Not often." He smiles. "I'd love to have you here every day with me, but are you sure? What about your classes?"

"About that…" Big gulp. "When I was in London, I spent a lot of time thinking about what I want to do and what makes me happy. I don't think that is getting a college degree. At least not right now." Before that furrowed brow of his can formulate a question or disappointed remark, I add, "So I dropped all my classes and I'm going to try to make a go of it with my photography. I know it isn't what you or Mom wanted for me, but it feels right."

He makes a noise deep in his throat.

I charge on. "I'm already so far behind from taking a year off and I don't need the degree. There are lots of workshops and classes I can take, and I've been working on finding something with more hours than the bar so working here with you is sort of perfect."

One of the things I love about Dad is that he can just be. He doesn't need to fill the quiet. That might have something to do with being married to my mother who talks incessantly. Opposites attract, I guess. But right now, as he nods slowly, seconds feel like an eternity. That thing I said I love about my dad being comfortable in silence becomes his worst trait. Mom would have already said something. I don't know what, but something. I'd know what's going through her head immediately instead of being in my current hell.

"Okay."

Wait, what? "Okay? Really?"

"You don't need to convince me that photography is the right path for you."

"I don't?" A small, nervous laugh escapes.

"No, sweetheart. You're an adult and your decisions are your own. I don't know how it happened. I blinked and you grew up."

All the air and nerves I've been carrying since I returned leave my body on a giant exhale.

"Thank you."

"Your mother, on the other hand," he says as he sits behind his desk.

"Any chance we can just keep her in the dark?"

He doesn't respond, so I guess that's a no.

One parent down. Dad took it so well, but I am not expecting that from my mother.

"You really want to work here around a bunch of rowdy athletes?" he asks. The look he gives me, full of pity and understanding, makes me positive I need to, if only to prove that I can. Maybe I need to prove it to myself, too. I can work here, around athletes and Leo, and be fine. Rhyse broke my heart, but he didn't break me.

"I think it would be good for me. Less time to sit around and sulk. And maybe I can pick Lindsey's brain a little when I'm not busy." I want to know everything about how she got to where she is.

"Okay. If you're sure." Another coach steps in the doorway, and Dad greets him. "This is my daughter, Scarlett. She's going to be helping out while Anna is gone."

He steps forward and extends a hand. "Nice to meet you, Scarlett."

"You too."

He looks to Dad. "Are you ready to do the film analysis?"

"Yeah, let me get Scarlett settled and I'll come down to your office in two."

He taps the jamb of the door and nods. "Great. Welcome, Scarlett."

Dad glances around the office and works his jaw side to side. "I'm not sure where to have you start. Anna's office is next door, but I've moved everything I need in here."

"How about with that?" I point to his desk.

"Good idea. There's a filing system, but I don't really understand it. If you're not sure, leave it and we'll go through it when I get back. Need anything?"

"Rubber gloves?" I push up my sleeves.

He laughs and starts toward the door, stopping before he reaches it. "This is going to be nice having you here."

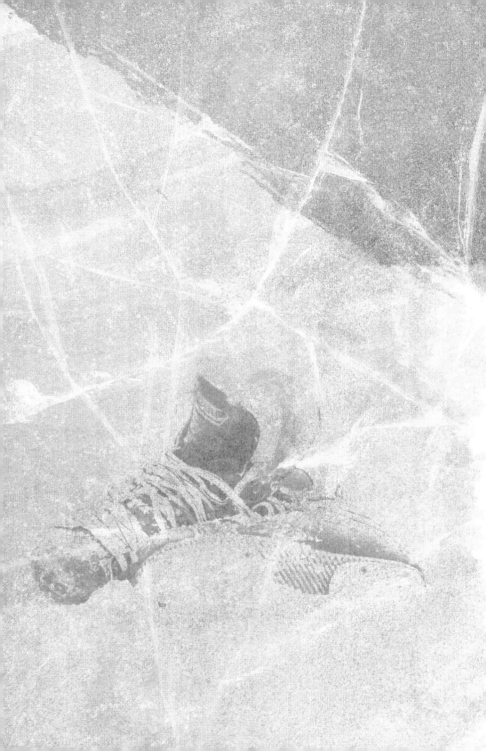

CHAPTER TEN

LEO

I LIKE MORNINGS JUST FINE—ALONE AND WITH COFFEE

Tuesday morning, I get to the arena early for a meeting with Blythe. When I was a kid dreaming of being a pro hockey player, I never imagined that would include media training.

As I'm walking into the building, I spot a dark head in front of me. She walks to the next door, peers in, then continues down the hall. Smiling, I quicken my steps.

She does it three more times before I reach her.

"Lost?"

Scarlett jumps and then stands tall with a hand to her chest.

"Good morning," I chirp.

"'Morning," she grumbles.

"You're here again." *Hello, Captain Obvious.*

"I'm helping my dad until his assistant is back."

"No way." My smile grows bigger and something warm spreads in my chest. "Congrats."

She moves along and I follow, passing the stairway to Blythe's office. Scarlett goes to the next open door, looks in, and then does this cute little growl.

"Who are you looking for?"

"Not who. *What*. I need coffee." She looks at me and lets her gaze slide over me. "I needed coffee five minutes ago before you appeared."

"Not a morning person, huh?"

"I like mornings just fine—alone and with coffee."

"Oh, I don't know. You seemed pretty peppy and happy the other morning without caffeine."

Her eyes narrow. "If I'm going to work here, I'm going to need you to forget that ever happened."

"Not a chance."

She cocks her head to the side.

"I'm sorry. Couldn't even if I tried." Every detail of that night is burned into my brain.

"Can you at least not speak about it?"

I make a motion like I'm zipping my lips and stop outside the break room. "Coffee is in here."

She walks in and lifts the empty carafe.

"Oh. I think Anna usually made the coffee. She was always the first one in."

Scarlett groans and tips her head back. After a few seconds of looking like she wants to throw herself to the floor, she moves to the cabinets and opens two, looking inside.

Without saying anything, I move forward and pull a filter and coffee packet from another cabinet while Scarlett watches my every move. Once I've dumped the water and flipped the coffee maker on, I lean against the counter. "It'll be ready in a few minutes. Do you think you can survive that long?"

"I knew I should have made my dad stop at Starbucks. He was all,

"Five dollars for a cup of burnt coffee is ridiculous."

Her impression of her dad loosens a laugh from my lips. "There's a coffee shop next door, for future reference."

Coffee starts pouring into the carafe. She leans in and inhales.

"Looks like you're going to make it." I push off and start toward the door.

"You don't want to wait for coffee?"

"Nah. I don't drink coffee."

She looks appalled. "What kind of monster are you?"

Her innocent words make me think all sorts of dirty things. She must read it on my face because her eyes widen.

"See you around."

AFTER MY MEETING with Blythe, we have practice and then conditioning. It's lunch time when I file into the media room with the rest of the team. Lunch is catered and we fill our plates and take a seat.

Coach comes in with Scarlett. The way she holds herself so stiffly, eyes trained on her dad, I know she feels me watching her. She's dying to look and find me amongst the other players.

"What's dream girl doing here?" Ash asks with a nod in Scarlett's direction.

He and Jack, on his other side, look to me for an answer.

"She's the new Anna."

His head moves slowly up and down. "That explains why the coffee in the break room was burnt this morning."

Oh shit. I forgot to tell her to turn off the burner.

Coach introduces her and tells us she'll be coming around to get our sizes for the new warmups and other gear, as well as updating our travel preferences.

She heads to the opposite side of the room and Coach starts the film.

"What's your move, Romeo?" Ash leans closer and whispers.

"I don't know. Looks like she'll be around though."

"Might want to clear your intentions with Coach and Blythe, get ahead of any drama."

He's mostly joking, but it wouldn't be the first time a player hooked up with someone that worked here and caused a shitstorm. It isn't strictly against the rules; relationships just need to be disclosed.

"What am I going to say? Hey, Coach, I'd really like to take out your daughter, but she's still pissed that I didn't call her after the last time we hooked up."

Ash's chest shakes with laughter. "Needs just a little tweaking."

"No shit."

He angles his body toward mine and leans on one elbow. "Are you sure about this?"

"About what?"

I meet her gaze from across the room and she looks away. She stands beside Morris as he denotes his choices on the forms she's shuttling around for us to fill out. Scarlett brings her thumb to her lips staring anywhere but at me. If she's trying to appear cool and collected, she's failing.

A chuckle escapes. I can't help it. Damn. I've never met anyone like her. It's cliché to say, I know, but it's just a fact.

It isn't like girls are throwing themselves in front of me at every turn, but I've never had one try so hard to avoid me either.

I look back to Ash and take in his lifted brows and concerned gaze.

"Dude, she's Coach's daughter."

"I know." Fuck, he's right. "I know."

"Be careful. All I'm saying."

When she makes her way to me and Ash, I pass him the form first and focus on Scarlett. "How's your day going?"

"Good. Thanks."

Ash chuckles next to me. "Oh boy. This is going to be a disaster."

I elbow him and lean forward to block him out of the conversation. "Did you get some food?" I tip my head to the spread up front.

"That's for the players."

"Do you want me to grab you a plate? The chicken wraps are delicious."

"I'm good. Once I get done here, I'm going to lunch."

She refuses to look at me, but it's fine. I'm too happy that she's working here to be annoyed about how she keeps insisting our night together "was nothing" and treating me like the worst one-night stand in the history of casual sex. Maybe it should sting, her ability to so easily dismiss me, but it doesn't for one simple fact: I know she's bluffing. If she truly felt nothing, she wouldn't need to put up a front.

Maybe it's because of her dad or because she's working here, maybe it's because of the prick in London that broke her heart, maybe she really is pissed I didn't call sooner—but if it's the latter, then that just sort of proves my point.

Ash nudges me with the clipboard. I scan the questions on the form, then tip my head up to look at her. "This is all you need from me?"

"Yeah. I think Anna got everything else before she left. Dad promised I wouldn't need to interact with the players much. Thank goodness." She looks at Ash. "No offense."

"Lots taken. We're awesome."

I tap the pen on the clipboard. "So after this, you won't have any reason to speak to me?"

"That is the hope," she says, voice climbing to a playful sing-song.

I skim over the form again. It's basic information we provide every year. I hand it back without filling it out. "I need to check a few things first."

She balks. I bite back a smile at the look on her face—the one that says she knows exactly what I'm doing."

"I'll come back to you," she says in a sugary-sweet tone that hardens when she adds, "Figure it out."

"If you're trying to make her like you, you might try making her life easier instead of harder," Ash says out of one side of his mouth.

She's back a few minutes later, but doesn't jab the clipboard toward me like I'm expecting.

"I ran out of forms," she says. "Can you stop by the office later?"

"Oooh. I'm not sure." I look at Ash. "Do I have time for that?"

"He's a pretty busy guy," Ash says. "But I think he can squeeze you in around three after strength training."

"Thank you," she mutters the thanks with a great deal of pain in her tone.

At exactly three o'clock, I stop by Anna's office next to Coach's. I'm freshly showered and in street clothes and I don't miss the full-body scan Scarlett takes of me. I take a seat in front of the desk. It's clean and tidy. Pictures of Anna and her family face me. I move one over to get a better view of Scarlett.

"Here you go." She hands me the clipboard. She's scribbled my name on the top line and I like the way it looks in her penmanship.

I take it and lean back in the chair. "Cream and sugar?"

"Excuse me?" She's staring at a laptop and doesn't look up at my question.

"In your coffee. Do you like cream and sugar?"

"It depends."

"On?" I ask, more and more amused at everything that comes out of her mouth.

She sighs and looks up. "If I'm making it, then yes. But I don't trust other people to mess with my coffee."

"Dark roast? Medium?"

"For someone who doesn't like coffee, you have a lot of questions about it."

"I didn't say I don't like coffee. I said I don't drink it. At least not during the season."

I finish the form and set the clipboard on the desk.

"Thank you. One more thing I can cross off the list today." She looks at the clock on the wall. "Crap. Is that the time?"

"Umm…" I glance at it and then my watch. "Yes."

"I have to take that box of signed shirts upstairs to the media department and haul ass to the bar."

"You're still working at the bar too?"

"Once or twice a week when Mike doesn't have any other options." She stands and looks all around, grabs her purse, shuts the laptop, and starts to pick up a large box sitting on the floor.

"Go. I'll take that to the media department."

"You'll make sure it gets there? I promised them I'd have it there by the end of today."

"I promise."

She hesitates as if she's not sure she should trust me.

"Thank you." She takes a few quick steps and pauses, looking at me square on for the first time all day. "See you tomorrow, Leo Lohan."

"See you tomorrow."

I sit there for a few minutes after she's gone, smiling as I think about the small interactions I've had with her today. It's a real twist of fate that she's here, where I can see her face every day. If only for a week or two, I have an opportunity to remind her how good things were between us and figure out how to make this work where Coach doesn't send me packing.

One thing is for sure, I have to make the most of this time because something tells me she isn't going to unblock my number so easily. I pick up the clipboard, take my form and crumble it into a ball.

To making the most of it.

I shoot the ball of paper into the trash can, then grab the box to take upstairs.

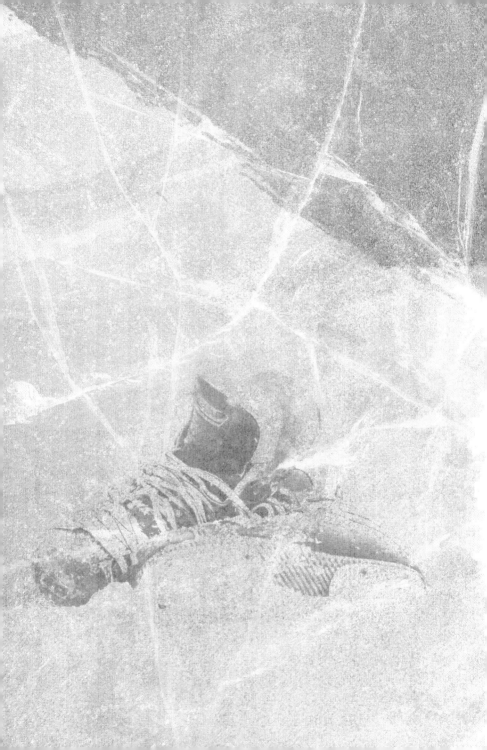

CHAPTER ELEVEN

SCARLETT

THE BEST SEX OF YOUR LIFE

Wednesday morning I get to the arena even before my father. I set three alarms and laid out my outfit last night like I'm a preschooler. I also promised myself I'd stop at Starbucks, but I pressed snooze one too many times, and here I am, coffeeless as I flip on the light to Anna's office.

My dad's assistant is organization goals. Once I got into her file system yesterday, I was blown away. She even has a checklist of her tasks every morning, which includes making coffee. She did not include the steps to make said coffee because I guess she just assumed any adult could figure out a coffee maker. Any adult but me.

"I've got this," I say to myself as I enter the break room. "Filter, coffee packet, water. Filter, coffee packet, water. Filter, coffee—"

The smell of fresh, hot coffee fills the air. I inhale and my gaze goes to the carafe that is on and full of coffee. A yellow sticky note is stuck to the top. I pull it off and read the messy scrawl, *Turn off the burner, turn on the warmer, look to your left.*

I follow his instructions, knowing who wrote it even before I see the Starbucks coffee cup with my name on it. Nicely done, Leo Lohan. Nicely done.

I hold onto those pleasant feelings until Dad asks me to take the forms the players filled out yesterday to the equipment manager. I count through them one more time to make sure I have them all, but come up one short. Ah, Leo's. But when I look at the clipboard, it isn't there either. Weird. I watched him fill it out. I go through the forms three more times until I'm certain I'm losing my mind.

Anna's desk is immaculate so there's nowhere for it to be hiding. I get up and look around the room anyway. Somewhere near insanity, it hits me like a jolt of lightning. He wouldn't. Though even as I try to convince myself that Leo wouldn't have taken the paper just to make my life more difficult, I find myself in Dad's office, asking where I can find the players.

"Everything okay?"

"Yeah, perfect," I say. "One of the guys forgot to fill out a few things."

"Check the therapy room. Just past the locker room." He smiles, glasses perched on his nose. "And, before you give the forms to Lewis, fill out the travel preferences for yourself too, just in case you need to come to any of the games."

"Need?" He's already mentioned that Anna rarely travels with the team.

"Okay fine. In case I want you to. I like having you close. It's nice seeing you everyday again."

I have no plans to travel with the team, but I smile and agree to fill out the form anyway.

I stop off in the bathroom to give myself a pep talk and reapply my lipstick. I go with a fiery red and lean against the counter. "He's just a guy. An insanely hot guy who was the best sex of your life. But that doesn't matter because he lied and he didn't call you."

Laughter snaps me out of my pep talk, and I look up to find Lindsey smiling at me. "Bad combination."

"No kidding." I turn away from the mirror and rest a hip against the sink. "You survived picture day."

"Just barely." She adjusts her stubby blonde ponytail while looking in the mirror. "Thanks again for your help."

"Are you kidding? It was the highlight of my week. I was actually hoping we could chat sometime. I'd love to hear about how you got here. I'm thinking of taking some classes or workshops."

"Absolutely. I heard you were helping out your dad until Anna comes back."

I nod.

"If you have time, come up to our office one day and I'll show you around and answer any questions you have. Maybe I can convince you to take a few photos too."

"I would love that."

When we both fall quiet, I stand tall. "Well, I guess I better go. I need to confront a boy before I lose my nerve."

Her lips twist into a grin. "Good luck."

On my way to the therapy room, I silently go through my pep talk one more time. He's just another guy. Just another guy. Just another guy. Just another… holy shit. When I spot him getting out of the ice bath, my mouth goes as dry as the Sahara. He doesn't see me and I have several seconds to take in the glory that is Leo Lohan naked from the waist up, water dripping off him, muscles contracted, black shorts molded to his thighs.

I'm transported to that night in the pool and the hot tub and on the couch. His back yard saw a lot of action. My body heats and desire pools between my thighs. I might not be interested in a repeat, but erasing the memory of him is proving difficult.

I storm forward, ignoring the race of my pulse. When he finally sees me, he pauses, and a slow smile turns up his lips. A smile that tells me he knows exactly why I'm here.

"Scarlett. Good to see you today."

"Cut the crap, Lohan. What did you do with the form?"

"The form?" His brows pull together, and I'd almost believe he was innocent if it weren't for the smile that doesn't falter.

He sits on a nearby bench and wipes a towel over his chest. Several players are back here. A few in the ice baths, others on massage tables. Ash lifts his head from where he lies on his stomach while a pretty brunette massages his back. He smiles when he sees me talking to his friend.

I have an irrational flare of jealousy, wondering if Leo gets massaged by her. I don't want him, but the idea someone else touches him makes me want to scream. That's totally normal and rational behavior, right?

"The form you filled out yesterday when you came to my office."

"I left it in your office."

"Then how come I can't find it?"

He tilts his head to the side. "Couldn't say. How was your coffee this morning?"

I wish I hadn't drank it now. No, that's a lie. It was delicious. "I poured it down the drain."

He grins like he knows I'd never do that.

"The form, Leo. I need your form."

"What are you doing for lunch?"

"Lunch?" Exasperation makes me snap at him.

"Yeah, that meal in the middle of the day. I have a break then so maybe we could meet up, I'll buy you lunch and fill out the form you misplaced."

"Or I could bring you another right now."

He stands and takes a step into my space. I tilt my head up to keep my glare locked on his. His eyes drop to my red lips.

"Can't," he says, then lifts his gaze. "Busy until lunch. Twelve-thirty okay?"

He brushes past me, taking his amazing body and the smell of ice and fire with him. "I'll swing by your office to pick you up."

At twelve-thirty, I'm ready to go. I have two forms in my hand when he appears in the doorway. Athletic pants and a T-shirt shouldn't look so good. The ends of his hair are damp and the smell of his soap is divine.

I slap the blank form down on the desk.

"Bring it with us. I'll sign it after I eat. I'm starving," he says and motions for me to come closer.

Rolling my eyes, I hold the other up in the air. "I thought you might say that, so I took the liberty of filling out one on your behalf."

He takes it from me, laughing as he reads it. "Under food allergies, you put all."

"Can't be too careful." I take it back. "This is what I'm sending if you don't fill out this form by the end of lunch. You'll be eating cardboard all season."

"Fine," he says. "Let me feed you first. All that wit and charm you're hitting me with must be exhausting."

I assume we're going to the cafeteria upstairs, but he exits out the back of the building and starts toward his car in the parking lot.

"I'm not getting in that thing." My steps falter.

"That *thing*?"

"Your car." My cheeks warm. The last time I was in it, he had one big hand on my thigh the entire drive and the promise of sex hung around us so thick I was drunk on it.

"I promise to return you in one piece." He opens the passenger door for me.

"Fine." I get in the car, ignoring how having his scent surrounding me makes my breaths come in quick shallow gulps. "But I need to be back in forty-five minutes."

CHAPTER TWELVE

LEO

ONE NIGHT OF FUN

I let Scarlett pick the restaurant. She chooses McDonald's and then stares at me, daring me to tell her no. Ash is going to give me so much shit. Especially after he joked about taking her to get an extra value meal for our second date.

It's hard to care right now though as she sits across from me dunking a chicken nugget into honey mustard sauce and casually glancing at the form she placed on the table between us.

Bad news for her: even when she's glaring at me, I like being around her.

I pop a fry in my mouth and lean back in the booth. "Sooo, photography?"

Her gaze narrows.

"I heard you talking to Lindsey yesterday. You didn't mention it the other night."

"We didn't mention a lot of things."

"Fair enough. Do you have your camera with you?"

"Yeah, why?"

"Can I see some of your pictures?"

"There isn't a lot to show. I'm just practicing and doing favors for friends."

"What about the ones you take just for you?" I keep staring at her until she rolls her eyes and relents. She pulls her camera from her purse and then comes over to sit beside me. I hadn't realized asking to see her photos would get her closer, but I'm high-fiving myself as her hair tickles my shoulder.

She powers it on and holds the display where I can see. She skips through a dozen images of Mike's bar, finally stopping on one of Jade smiling, eyes downcast, hand up to her face, tucking her hair behind one ear.

"She was tired of posing for me at the end, but it ended up being my favorite. She looks so sweet and innocent." Scarlett snorts like Jade being innocent is funny, then looks over and our eyes lock. Her gaze darts to my mouth and she licks her strawberry red lips. "She's a chameleon like that. Sweet and polite one minute and ready to hop on the bar and dance the next."

"Beautiful."

She looks away first. "She is."

I meant Scarlett, but something tells me she knows exactly who I was talking about.

"Anyway." She moves back across from me. "How's hockey? Ready for the first game?"

I chuckle at how quickly she's put space between us—both physically and emotionally. "It's great, and I'm always ready."

"Of course you are. I bet you spend the entire off-season counting down the days."

"Something like that."

She raises both brows pointedly.

"What's that look?"

"Nothing." She sets her empty nugget container on the tray and then pushes the form toward me with one pink nail.

"All right. All right. A deal's a deal." I fill out the form and she takes it fast, like she's afraid I'm going to do something with it. I guess I can't blame her.

"Tell me what the look was about. Is counting down the days for hockey that bad of a sin?" I take our trash and dump it, then hold open the door for her.

"I've known guys like you. Your whole world revolves around the sport and everything else is second. At least you're honest about it."

Is that me? Hockey is my job, so yeah, it's important. I love it, too, which makes it easy to focus on. But Scarlett doesn't know me well enough to be making a judgment call like that, which tells me this isn't about me.

"Your ex?"

"He is a Formula One driver."

I nod slowly as I try to picture her with someone else. I don't like it. "You came second to his career?"

"It was better for his image if I stayed out of the picture."

She's quiet, and I'm sorry I pushed her to talk to me. I didn't mean to poke at old wounds, and I definitely didn't want to end this date with her thinking of some other guy.

The ride to the arena is silent. I kill the engine, and she immediately goes for the door.

"Wait." I place a hand on her thigh. Heat travels up my arm. She looks at my hand and I remove it. "You deserve to come first. Always. You're right not to settle for less. I'm sorry if I made you feel that way."

"No." She shakes her head. "You didn't. It was just one night of fun with a stranger, right?"

I nod, but can't seem to make the word come out of my mouth. It doesn't feel like an accurate assessment at all.

After our afternoon practice, coach asks me to hang back.

"The A looks good on you," he says.

"Thanks, Coach. It feels good." And it does. We're finding a rhythm with the new guys and I think we've got a great team that can win some games this year.

"I don't know how to say this delicately, so I'm just going to shoot straight with you."

I gulp. Oh shit. My first thought is he knows I slept with his daughter, but then I realize he's far too calm.

He places both hands on his hips. "We're looking good out here. Everyone is focused and excited."

"But?"

One side of his mouth hitches up. "We're in the pre-season bubble where everyone is dedicated and working hard, but soon enough that will fade. Last season was one drama after the other. The thing with Declan and the intern, then Ash getting a sex injury and missing two games."

I almost laugh, but it's clear coach is really worried.

"We had some unfortunate setbacks," I say. "No one wants to win more than us."

"You guys are young. I don't expect you to be on all the time. I know you have lives outside of hockey, but when those things impact the team, I worry. Especially when it feels like we have something special here. This is maybe the most talented team I've ever worked with."

A spark of pride fills my chest. I love playing hockey, but knowing you're part of a team that has a chance to do big things is something special. "What can I do to help?"

"Look out for the guys. You're steady and reliable."

"You make me sound like a used car." One corner of my mouth pulls up into a half-smile.

"You're a good guy, Leo. Your head is on straight. Be a leader, on and off the ice, that's all I'm asking." He slaps me on the shoulder and squeezes. "If only they could all be as scandal-free as you."

Nervous laughter escapes my lips as the weight of what he's asking settles on my shoulders. He thinks he can trust me and he can—on the ice.

"See you tomorrow," Coach says as he skates off, leaving me feeling like the biggest jerk of all time for having his trust and respect when I'm secretly lusting after his daughter.

Ash rode to the arena with me today and he's waiting for me in the locker room.

"What's wrong with you?" he asks when he sees me.

"Nothing. Tired, I guess." I can't get Coach's words out of my head. I know I should have already had these feelings of guilt, but they were drowned out by the excitement of having Scarlett so close. I've been too focused on her to really think about what it'd mean for my relationship with Coach if he knew what happened. And what I want to keep happening.

"Bullshit. You looked energetic as hell five minutes ago when you were scoring on Mikey like he wasn't there."

I pull off my practice jersey and sit in my stall. "First road trip of the season. Do you think the guys are ready for it?"

"Nice dodge. Fine. I won't press." He stretches his legs out and crosses one ankle over the other. "Yeah, I think we're ready. You know as well as I do that nothing gets rookies going like those first few games. It'll be a chance to see how we play as a unit and work out kinks. Loosen up. It's just the pre-season."

"Yeah, you're right."

"Cheer up, Romeo." He laughs. "Your dream girl works here now and tomorrow we're flying to Vegas." He waggles his brows.

"Yeah, about that. Coach wants me to keep an eye on the team and make sure everyone stays out of trouble and that there's no drama on our first trip."

"They'll be fine."

"What about you? He's also worried you're going to break your dick again."

He grimaces and curls into himself protecting his crotch. "Me too."

Ash had an unfortunate sexperience that resulted in a trip to the emergency room with a penile fracture. That's an injury I hope to never have.

"Not to worry, though. I invited the guys over tonight so they can get it out of their system and are focused when we leave tomorrow."

I groan.

"Ah come on. I ordered food—all healthy shit. I picked up a small amount of booze, invited all the guys, a few girls; it'll be very chill. Hey, hot tub clean for later?"

"That's not happening."

"Fine. Fine." He grins so I know he's fucking with me. "No hot tub, but at least come hang out. This will be good for the rookies, and for you."

"Good for me?" I prefer a quiet night in before games and he knows it.

"Yeah, we'll go good cop, bad cop on them together tonight and let you clear your conscience, and then we can all avoid your pep talks when we get to Vegas. Everybody wins."

A FEW HOURS later, I'm on Ash's couch playing Xbox with Tyler. He's coming from the juniors league, where he put up some impressive numbers. He's on the chopping block to make the final roster, so I know I don't need to waste my breath on giving him a pep talk. His ass is on the line.

I'm not a fun-hater, contrary to Ash poking fun at me about not wanting to party tonight. Unfortunately, we've been friends long enough that I know he's usually right. So I'm trusting that getting the guys together to hang and let loose will be good and not result in things escalating and a bunch of hungover guys showing up to the plane tomorrow.

My phone buzzes in my pocket and I reach to get it while trying to keep up with the game one-handed. But when I see Scarlett's name on my phone, I forget all about the controller and the game in front of me.

"Sorry, man. I have to take this." All those good intentions to back off from pursuing Scarlett after Coach's talk earlier, take a flying leap out the nearest window.

I toss the controller, and answer as I weave my way toward the front door. "Hello?"

"Hey, Leo. I'm sorry to call."

"Nah, don't be. It's good to hear from you." My heart's racing as I step out into the driveway.

"I think I forgot the form in your car."

I'm silent. Her voice has made me temporarily stupid, and I can't process her words.

"The form with your travel preferences," she clarifies.

"Right, uh, let me check." I walk across the street and open the garage.

On the floorboard of the passenger side of my car, the form sits partially under the seat. "Found it. Do you want me to email it to you or…?"

"Can I swing by and get it? I'm already halfway there, and if I don't get it to the equipment manager in an hour, my own father might fire me."

I chuckle. "Doubtful."

"Yeah, well, I'd rather the thought not cross his mind. I should be there in about ten minutes. Are you home?"

"Yep. I'm here."

"Great. I'll be there soon if I can remember how to get there."

"I'll text you my address." I do and then bring the form inside with me. While I wait, I pick up the living room and kitchen. She knocks as I'm lighting a vanilla-scented candle. Overboard? Probably.

I hustle to the door and pull it open. I'm smiling even before I lay eyes on her, but when I do a once, fuck who am I kidding, a thrice-over, my jaw drops.

She's changed since work and the dress she's wearing molds to her small curves, pushes her boobs up, and shows a lot of smooth, tan leg. Fuck me.

"Leo?"

"Yep." My voice is tight and squeaks like I'm going through

puberty.

"Do you have the form?"

"Say what now?"

She laughs and brushes past me. I pickup my jaw and close the door.

"I can't believe I missed this the first time I was here," Scarlett says as she walks through my house for the second time.

She runs a hand along the framed jerseys on the wall and picks up a hockey stick lying in the entry way between the garage and kitchen.

I take it from her and set it against the wall. "You were distracted by the pool."

"Among other things," she says quietly.

I nod toward the form on the kitchen counter.

She picks it up and reads it. "Perfect. Thank you."

"Welcome."

Awkward silence hangs between us. Damn I want her, but I can't shake the feeling of disappointing my team and screwing up my relationship with Coach. Without that, I'm as good as done.

She takes a step back. "I need to get this to the arena."

I want her to stay, but I keep my mouth shut. She's my coach's daughter. I'm the one he expects to stop any drama and keep the guys from losing their heads. But right now? I'm struggling to keep myself in check.

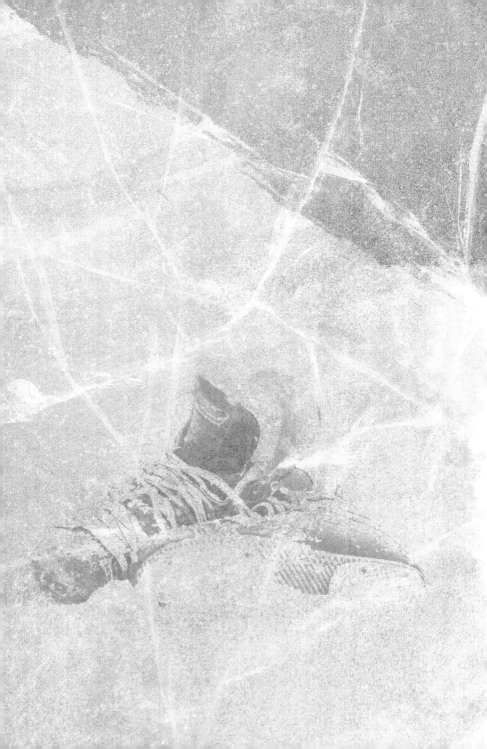

CHAPTER THIRTEEN

SCARLETT

IT LOOKS LIKE YOU'RE GOING TO A FUNERAL

I let out a long breath when I get to my car. I wave to Leo watching me from his doorway and slide into the driver's seat. Memories from the last time I was here whack me over the head.

My hands are shaking as I start the ignition. I'm already running late for my date and now I need to stop by the arena to drop off the form.

When I try to put the car in reverse, nothing happens. Head swimming in a pool of Leo-induced thoughts, it takes me a few seconds to notice all the warning lights are on. I try the ignition again, but nothing.

Ugh. I drop my head to the steering wheel. Not now. I comb through all possible scenarios. I do not want to walk back inside and ask Leo for help. But even if I call a tow, he's going to notice me sitting outside like a stalker before they get here.

I bring my purse and phone with me and knock on his front door for the second time tonight.

He answers, phone to his ear, but when he sees me, he pauses.

"I have to call you back," he says and ends the call without a goodbye. "Everything okay?"

"My car won't start. I'm going to call a tow, but is it okay if it sits in your driveway for awhile?"

He starts outside without answering. "I can take a look."

"That's okay," I say, but it falls on deaf ears.

After a few minutes of staring under the hood of my car and having me try to start it again, he shakes his head. He pulls his phone from his pocket and puts it to his ear. "Hey, Frankie. It's Leo. Can you get a tow out to my house tonight?"

"That's not necessary," I whisper.

He ignores me. Again. "Yeah. I think it's the timing belt. No, not the Jag. It's a friend's car." His eyes bore into mine, and I get butterflies in my stomach. Friend. Is that what we're calling it? "Thanks."

"We can take my car to the arena." He takes off without giving me a chance to speak. I hustle to keep up with him in my heels.

He opens the garage door and gets in his car, starting it. I open the passenger side door, but don't get in. "This isn't necessary. I can call an Uber."

"You need to get the form to the arena in the next thirty minutes, yeah?"

I check the time on my phone. Crap.

"Get in, Scarlett."

He's quiet as we back out of the drive and head out of his neighborhood.

"Sorry for ruining your plans tonight. Looks like Ash is having a party." Cars line his driveway and down the street.

"Eh. We were just hanging out, getting to know the new guys a little more." He glances over at me. "Where were you headed? A funeral?"

"What?"

"The dress. It looks like you're going to a funeral."

Laughing, I tug on the short, black dress showing way more thigh than would be appropriate for mourning. "I look like I'm going to a funeral?"

He mutters under his breath. Something about the dress being the death of him.

"I have a date. Or I did. I'm not sure he's still going to be waiting for me by the time I get there." I sent Chad a text to let him know what happened. In a way, I'm hoping he decides he doesn't want to wait an extra thirty minutes for me. I only accepted the date because Jade vouched for him. And also—I wanted a distraction from the guy sitting beside me.

It all sounded fine until an hour ago when it hit me that it was really going to happen. I'm nervous about putting myself out there. And now I'm going to have to Uber to and from the restaurant. Just my freaking luck.

"Who's the guy?" The car seems to speed up and the muscle in Leo's cheek flexes.

"A friend of Jade's boyfriend."

"A college guy?"

"Yes." A nervous laugh bubbles in my chest. "What's with the third degree?"

"Just making polite conversation." His tone still has a hard edge.

We make it to the arena in half the amount of time it would have taken me. I fling the door open. "Well, thanks for the ride. You'll let me know where they towed my car, so I can get it?"

"I'll have him drop it off at the arena tomorrow."

"Wow. He can fix it that fast?"

"Frankie's a friend," he says simply. "Is Lewis expecting you?"

"Yeah. He's still here."

"How are you getting to your date?"

He knows exactly how I plan to get there; he is so not driving me to a date...with another guy.

"Thank you for the ride and for working your Leo Lohan magic on my car service, but I can take it from here."

His brows raise defensively. "It's no problem, Scarlett. I'll wait."

I consider arguing, but doubt he'll listen anyway.

The arena is mostly empty at this hour and my heels clack on the floor as I navigate the quiet halls. After I drop off the form with Lewis, I turn back around, heart racing faster with each step closer to the parking lot. Leo is still parked at the curb, staring straight ahead with a frustrated scowl.

I told him I had it from here. I don't know why he keeps insisting to help, if he's going to be all pissy about it.

"Look," I say when I take a seat inside the car and he doesn't make any move to go. "I think it's best if—"

Whatever protest I was about to make dies on my lips as Leo wraps a hand around the back of my neck, pulls me closer, and covers my mouth with his.

Shock makes me slow to respond, but when his tongue slips past my lips, I press my mouth to his harder and give into the crazy desire I feel every time he's near. His kisses are all-consuming and the only thought in my head is more.

I might not like the idea of dating another professional athlete like Leo, but I do like him. Especially when he's kissing me.

He pulls back too soon, leaving me breathless.

"Sorry." His voice is gruff. "Fuck. I'm sorry."

I press shaky fingers to my swollen lips. Wow. I forgot what that felt like. No. That's a lie. I remember, I'd just been pushing it way down past the frustration and heartbreak of Rhyse and finding out Leo is another selfish athlete.

Though, the more I get to know him, the less I believe that. It may have just been a team get-together he left, but he did drop everything to help me tonight.

He starts the car. "Where am I taking you?"

"What?"

"Your date or whatever. Where is it?" His scowl returns, and he refuses to look at me while he waits for my answer.

And just like that, frustration burns. Seriously? His mood swings are giving me whiplash. Whatever. He wants me to date someone else, then great, glad we're on the same page.

I tell him the address and sit back in the seat, silently fuming as he drives. His hands wrap around the steering wheel at ten and two and he stares straight ahead.

Even if Chad is gone, I'm going to the bar, ordering a drink, and hitting on every cute guy I see. Take that, Leo Lohan. What kind of game is he playing?

He pulls in front of the restaurant, and before I can flee, he hits the lock button, keeping me inside.

"I'm sorry, okay? I shouldn't have done that."

My cheeks flame with anger and humiliation. "It's fine." I try the handle. "Let me out."

"I like you," he says.

"Yeah, obviously."

"It's just—"

I squeeze my eyes shut. I physically cannot hear another word. "Save it. It doesn't matter."

The last thing I need is to listen to more of his words of regret for kissing me right before I walk inside and meet my date for the night. I get out of the car and fidget with my dress. I haven't been on a real first date since before Rhyse, and despite my anger, I need some reassurance right now. "Do I really look like I'm going to a funeral?"

Maybe black was the wrong call.

"Nah." His voice softens. "You look gorgeous."

Seconds pass with only my heartbeat filling the silence between us.

"Thank you for the ride."

He dips his chin in a small nod. "Anytime."

I shut the door, step back, and watch as he pulls away from the curb.

CHAPTER FOURTEEN

LEO

YOU DID WHAT NOW?

I barely remember the drive back to my house.

Sitting in my car, engine off, I run the pad of my thumb along my bottom lip. Scarlett is on a date with another dude. And I freaking kissed her.

I can't seem to stay away and that's messing with my head. I'm a smart guy. I know the ramifications, and still… all I want to do is drive back and get her. She belongs with me.

Crossing the street, I walk into Ash's place, where cars still line the driveway and road.

Chanting from the back of the house leads me to where the guys are all gathered.

"You're back!" Ash juts his chin and yells over the noise. He's at the back of the group. "I thought you ducked out for the night."

"Nah. Just had to take care of something."

Ash raises one brow. "Everything okay?"

"Yeah." *No.* I motion with my head toward the center of the room. "What's going on?"

Instead of answering, he weaves through, leading me to the front where I see what they're all staring at. Or in this case, who. Johnny Maverick is shirtless, doing pushups in the middle of the circle.

Tyler holds up a stopwatch in one hand and counts along with the other guys.

"Should we tell him to save his energy?" Ash asks, knocking my arm with his elbow.

"Nah. Let him wear himself out. Maybe he'll sleep on the plane ride."

"Time," Tyler calls. "One hundred and one."

"Told you I could do a hundred pushups in two minutes." Maverick pops up to his feet. His face is red from exertion, but he's grinning big.

"Only one hundred and one?" Ash scoffs with a playful glint in his eyes. "Lohan here does that every morning before he gets out of bed."

"How would he do them before he gets out of bed?" Tyler asks, brows scrunched in confusion.

"It was a joke, rookie." Ash claps him on the shoulder. "All right, everyone. I think Lohan has a few things he wants to say."

I push forward and kneel down in the same spot Maverick was occupying. "Two minutes. Tell me when."

A beat of silence follows my request. They were expecting a pep talk, but the last thing I want to do right now is give some heartfelt speech on keeping our heads straight while mine is on a Scarlett-driven loop.

"Uhh. Yeah," Tyler lifts the stopwatch. "Go."

Every rep, every burn of my muscles fades away and all I see is Scarlett standing next to my car in that black dress looking uncertain and nervous. All that for some guy who probably doesn't even realize how fucking lucky he is to be in her presence.

And if he does? Fuck, that's even worse.

Is she having fun? Did they decide to skip dinner and go back to his place? The unknown is a total mind fuck.

Tyler's voice cuts through my thoughts. "Time."

I do one more and sit back on my heels. My chest heaves and my pulse races, but I don't know if it's because of the pushups or Scarlett.

"Damn, Lohan." Maverick bows his head and lifts and drops his hands twice before he says, "I'm not worthy."

I stand awkwardly. "How many?"

If they were counting aloud, I didn't hear them.

Laughing, Ash wraps an arm around my neck. "One hundred and nineteen."

"Nice speech," someone yells, and the guys laugh.

"The message was loud and clear: be epic this weekend." Ash drags me into the kitchen and tries to hand me a beer.

I wave him off. "No. I'm good."

With a shake of his head, he says, "You don't seem good. What the hell happened to you in the last hour?"

"I kissed her again."

"Who?"

"Who the hell do you think?"

"Ah, dream girl." He chuckles and crosses his arms over his chest. "And? Is she at your place waiting?"

"And nothing." I rough a hand through my hair. "I dropped her off on a date with some other dude."

"You did what now?"

I give him the quick version of tonight's events concluding with, "It can't happen."

"Go." He points to the door.

"Did you not hear me? It can't happen."

"I heard what you said."

"And you're still kicking me out?"

"Hell yes. It's for your own good."

"What happened to team bonding to get our heads straight?"

"Yours is the only one twisted right now, so go figure it out. There's no way you're flying to Vegas tomorrow ready to play hockey while simultaneously wondering if your dream girl went home with some other dude."

A deep growl vibrates in my throat. I flex my jaw and look around. The mood is fairly chill now, and it seems like things probably won't get out of hand.

"Get the hell out of here," he says. "I'll get everyone else out in the next hour so they're rested."

I take two steps toward the door. I don't know what I'm going to do, but I don't want to be here. "Thanks, man."

"Good luck," he calls after me.

The drive back to the restaurant takes an eternity. I don't have a plan, but at minimum I have to make sure she gets home safely.

Yeah, keep telling yourself that asshole.

I park across the street and jog toward the entrance. Scarlett is exiting as I approach and my heart rate kicks up. She's alone, so I guess that's something.

Pausing on the sidewalk, I wait for her to look my way. When she does, my entire body clenches with panic at her icy stare. She isn't happy to see me. Not that I blame her.

"What are you doing here?"

I take another step toward her. "I wanted to make sure you had a ride."

She glances over her shoulder back into the restaurant. "You can't be here."

"How are you getting home?"

"That's none of your business."

I close the remaining distance between us and slide my hand around the back of her neck. "I want you to be my business."

Her pulse thrums under my touch.

"Are you going home with him?"

She tries to glare but even so her body melts into my touch. Slowly her head shakes side to side. "He's in the bathroom. We're just going to share an Uber."

"Not anymore." I take her hand and lead her to my car. She doesn't resist or speak until I open the passenger side door.

"This really isn't necessary."

I drop my forehead to hers and skim my lips over hers. "Then get in because you want to. Because you can't stop thinking about me and because there's nowhere else you want to be."

I force my feet back and give her room. She stares at me through hooded eyes. Her tongue flicks out to wet her lips and finally she moves into the car.

I don't waste any time once I'm inside, pulling her to me and capturing her mouth.

"This doesn't change anything," she whispers. "I don't date athletes. Especially ones that play for my dad."

The excitement with which she kisses me makes it hard to care about words that don't alter the here and now.

Dropping my hand to her thigh, I slide it up and under the hem of her dress. She whimpers as my fingers brush the delicate material between her legs.

She shifts to give me better access and loops her arms around my neck.

"You're drenched, baby," I murmur against her lips. "This for me?"

Her nod is nearly imperceptible, but when I circle my thumb against her clit, she cries out with relief. I tug until the material gives way and dip two fingers inside of her. She clings to me, nipping at my bottom lip and scraping her blunt nails along my back. The things she mutters are mostly nonsense, but they affirm me. She feels this too. It might be madness, but we're in it together.

I would give up blow jobs for the rest of my life in exchange for watching Scarlett on the brink of bliss. To be clear, I'd like both, but if I have to give up one, it's an easy choice.

Her pussy clenches around my fingers as her orgasm wracks her body and leaves her limp against me. A phone rings, hers or mine I'm not sure. Don't care.

I take her mouth in a soft kiss as my heart hammers with adrenaline.

"That was…" she trails off. "Oh my gosh."

I push back the strands of hair that have fallen forward, blocking her face. "You're beautiful."

"My dad," she says.

Caressing her neck and sweeping two fingers along her delicate skin, I let the smallest bit of the outside world in with my acknowledgment. "I know."

Fuck, I don't have an answer for that, but I know it's going to be messy.

She pulls back. "No. My dad is calling. That's his ringtone."

Her purse is on the floorboard, and she leans down to retrieve it. She casts an apprehensive glance my way. "I should answer. He never calls."

I nod and sit back in my seat. Coach's voice is distant and hard to understand, but it still hits me and coats my insides with guilt.

I roll the window down an inch to get some air to my lungs. Scarlett isn't saying much back, but her bowed head and fingers rubbing at her forehead tell me it isn't good news.

Dammit. What are we going to do?

She sits back and drops her phone to her lap.

"Is everything alright?" I ask.

A soft, brittle laugh leaves her lips and she looks over at me through dark lashes. "Looks like I'm travelling with the team this weekend."

CHAPTER FIFTEEN

SCARLETT

I THINK I HAD A TINY ORGASM

The next morning, I ride with Dad to the arena. I have a small suitcase packed for the weekend. The team has an early practice, so I'm working half the day, and then we leave this afternoon for three exhibition games in three different cities.

The beginning of the season is always hectic. I hate that that knowledge makes me question if Leo really would have texted eventually. I know from Rhyse and from my dad just how consuming pre-season activities are with media, practices, and events. Plus, being here the past week, I've had a glimpse into Leo's schedule.

I still maintain he could have texted, but I get it in a way I didn't before.

In the break room, my coffee is waiting for me, like it's been all week, and my stupid heart flutters in my chest. I can't believe I have to spend the entire weekend traveling with the team. I can't let anything else happen with Leo, but that's easier said than done when he's around.

Dad stops by my office after practice. "Busy?"

"No. I think I have everything ready. Anna took care of most of the travel arrangements before she left."

"Good." He motions with his head. "Come with me."

In the back parking lot, an area has been roped off and people stand in a long line that leads to tables where the players are signing autographs. A local radio station is here playing music, and Wenzel, the Wildcat mascot, is doing cartwheels and high-fiving kids in line. Some of the ice girls are here too in their bright green sequined shorts.

"What is this?" I ask as Dad holds the door open for me.

"One of the pre-game events the Foundation does for members of the Wildcat Leaderboard Club."

I arch a brow.

"The top tier season ticket holders. Throughout the season, there are a number of events they get exclusive access to, including seeing us off before our first game of the season."

"Are you nervous?"

He nods as Blythe power walks up to us.

"Hey, Coach," she says, "the DJ wants to do a quick interview with you."

"I'm ready," he says.

"Hi, Scarlett." Blythe moves that excited and serious stare to me.

"Hey." I wave.

"We need extra hands at the player table to snap photos and keep the line going. Any chance you can help?" She looks to me hopefully.

"Yeah, I can help." My stomach dips as I spot Leo at one end of the table. He smiles at the kid in front of him and then stands and kneels for a photo.

"Have fun," Dad says and shoots me that proud-father smile. That smile is the reason I'm giving up a weekend and traveling with the team. I should have said no, especially after what happened last night in Leo's car. What is it about that car? But I love that my dad wants to share this with me.

"Great," Blythe says. She walks me toward the players. I try to head to the opposite end of the table as Leo, but she points right at him. "Leo stands for every photo, so why don't you help him and see if you can move things along a little faster. We have to wrap it up and get them on the plane in a few hours."

"Got it."

"Thank you. You're a lifesaver."

He looks up as I draw near. Twin girls with mini-matching Lohan jerseys stand in front of his table, looking at him like he is the dreamiest guy they've ever seen. Yeah, I know that look because I gave it to him once. Fine, more than once. And just last night. Groan. How am I going to be around him all weekend and not blush crimson red every time we're in the same space?

"Can we have a picture with you?" one of them asks. Brown eyes widen with hope.

Leo answers enthusiastically, "Of course."

The dad of the twins gives Leo an appreciative smile as he holds up his phone. Leo squats down, and the girls crowd in on either side of him.

"Would you like me to take one with all of you?" I ask the dad.

"That'd be great." He hands over his phone and stands behind his daughters and Leo.

I stare at Leo through the phone. He's dressed casually in a black jacket with his number embroidered on the right side of his chest in green and the Wildcat logo on the left. It dips low enough to reveal the black T-shirt underneath and molds over his shoulders and biceps, showing off his pro-athlete physique.

One I've seen and felt.

His hat is pulled down, not quite as low as he wore it the night at the bar, but enough that it's putting a shadow over his face.

My cheeks flush as I realize this nice family is still waiting for me as I ogle Leo. I take three and then hand the phone back.

Leo immediately sits back down at the table for the next person in line. It's a single guy who thrusts a jersey in front of him, and Leo chats him up while he signs.

I ask the guy if he wants me to take a picture, but he shakes his head and holds out the phone as he leans over the table to snap a selfie with Leo. We have a tiny break in the line. The next group is a large one, and they're still with Ash, one table away.

Leo's smile dims in the absence of fans, and he adjusts his hat. We ended things last night a bit awkwardly, with me telling him it couldn't happen again, then letting him drive me home but making him drop me off a house down in case my dad was up. I might have kissed him again before I got out of the car, too.

What a mess.

He's looking anywhere but at me when he asks, "How was your date last night?"

I don't know if he's really asking or trying to remind me that he fingered me in his car right after said date. Instead of answering, I step closer and quietly say, "You should turn your hat around."

"What?" His brows pinch together, and he pins his hazel eyes on me.

"Turn your hat backward. That way in the photos, they'll be able to see your face."

He nods slowly, grips the bill of his hat, and twists it backward.

I didn't realize what I was asking for. Holy hell. Leo in a hat is sexy; Leo without a hat is even sexier, but Leo in a backward hat... I think I had a tiny orgasm.

The big group of girls finishes with Ash and starts our way. I step out of their path, which, thanks to the number of people now crowded in front of him, pushes me behind the table.

They each take a selfie with him, then several group photos. Leo takes it all in with a smile, even when one girl begs him to sign her stomach. I'm glad when they move along.

And so it continues. He's humble and polite and either a really good actor or genuinely excited to interact with fans.

He spends almost ten minutes with an old man who won't stop talking, and even as I intervene, giving Leo an out and trying to move things along for the people patiently waiting their turn, Leo refuses to walk away until the man pats him on the back and wishes him a good season.

We're playing catch up for the next half-hour. The end of the line is in view, and I shift on my feet, wishing I'd worn different shoes today. Leo, who doesn't miss anything, glances at me, and a smile pulls at his lips. He signs a foam finger, takes a photo, and then pauses on his way to his chair.

"Sit," he says and motions to his seat.

"I'm fine."

"We have a few minutes. That's Ash's girlfriend and her friends." He pulls the chair out. "Sit."

My pride would really like for me to insist on standing, but my toes are pleading for mercy.

I sit, take off my heels, and let out a groan. "Thank you."

"Welcome." He fidgets with a Sharpie.

If I'm going to be on a four-day road trip with him, I need to clear the air and make sure it won't be awkward. Or less awkward, anyway.

No matter how much I want to dislike him or be angry at him for not telling me who he was that first night, or for kissing me and then leaving and then coming back and kissing me again, one thing is clear – Leo is a nice guy. It would be so much easier to forget about him if he wasn't.

I decide to give him a peace offering. "He had food stuck in his teeth for an hour."

"What?" Leo cocks his head to the side to look at me.

"My date last night. I couldn't decide if I should tell him or not. Normally, I would, but first date, you know? I debated for too long, and I got really uncomfortable and nervous. I couldn't even look at him. For thirty minutes, I probably didn't hear anything he said."

Leo laughs. It starts light and grows into a hearty, rich sound that breaks the uneasiness between us.

"That isn't even the worst part," I say.

He crosses his arms over his chest and waits for the rest.

"We sat at the bar after dinner, chatting and drinking. At one point, he leaned in like he was going to kiss me, and that's when I finally decided to tell him. I held up my hand like this and cringed." I reenact it, making a cross with my fingers like I'm warding off a dark spirit. "He recoiled back, and before I could explain, he'd paid our bill and called us an Uber."

Leo is full-out laughing now, head thrown back.

"I don't think I'll be hearing from him again." Not that I really want to. We didn't really seem to connect, food-in-teeth disaster aside.

Movement beside us catches my eye. The line is moving again, so I stand and step into my shoes. Leo moves closer and takes my hand as I wobble.

His touch sends goosebumps racing up my arm. After I'm steady with my feet squeezed back into my heels, neither of us moves. It feels like there are a lot of unsaid things hanging between us, but neither of us speaks as I hold tight to his hand.

"Leo!" Someone calls to him, and I pull away and let out a long breath.

For the rest of the line, I keep my distance and take a dozen more photos of Leo with fans.

When the final person is through, Blythe thanks the guys, and Assistant Coach Peters lets them know they need to be at the plane in two hours.

"Busy day," I say as we head back into the building.

"Yeah."

The awkwardness has crept back in, and I don't know what to say.

"Your car should be here by lunch."

"Oh right. Thank you. I assume I can call and make a payment?"

He makes a non-committal hum. Not his problem. He's done enough. I can figure out how to pay for it. I really hope it doesn't wipe out my savings.

"Okay, well, guess I'll see you later." I swivel around to head toward my office.

"I'm glad," he says from behind me.

I glance over my shoulder. Leo sidesteps down the hallway, eyes on me.

"What?"

His nice-guy smile morphs into something far cockier. "I know it makes me an ass, but I'm really glad your date was a disaster."

Our first stop is Vegas. I sit next to my dad at the front of the plane and sleep most of the way there. It's dark by the time we get to the hotel. The guys are in meetings or resting for their game tomorrow, which means I'm alone in my room and all too aware that Leo is somewhere not far away.

I call Jade to entertain me and to fill her in on my new weekend plans.

"Go out and have fun. You're in Vegas." She's working at the bar and somehow waits on customers while also holding the phone out to FaceTime.

"By myself? I don't think so."

"Maybe ask Leo." Her smirk is obnoxious, and I flip her off.

Mike comes into view next to Jade.

"Distracting my employee even when you aren't here. Impressive." He gives me a playful wink.

"Sorry, Mike. It was an emergency."

"She's in Vegas with a bunch of hockey players and bored. Can you imagine?"

"You're a hockey fan?" Mike asks.

"Kind of," I answer.

"Her dad is the coach of the Wildcats," Jade fills him in. "She's travelling with them this weekend."

"No way." Mike looks from me to Jade for confirmation.

"Yep."

"You know, we've had a few players come into the bar in the past."

"You don't say?" My tone is all sarcasm, but apparently Mike didn't recognize Leo Lohan either because he proceeds to tell me about the time Declan Sato stopped in, and another time some guy I've never heard of bought the entire bar drinks.

"No one else?" Jade asks. "Like Leo Lohan maybe?"

Mike crosses his arms. "No, don't think Lohan has ever been here, but he's a great player."

Jade and I exchange a secret smile, but Mike gets called by a customer wanting another drink and walks off before we can tell him that Leo Lohan has, in fact, been there.

"Well, at least I'm not the only one that didn't recognize him," I say.

"How was the date last night?"

"Fine."

"Sam said Chad was home by eleven." She places a hand on her hip.

"He wasn't really my type."

"Your age, cute, nice, not a jock. He's exactly the kind of guy you said you were looking for." The smug smile on her face makes me narrow my gaze at her.

"Yes, yes. I know what I said."

"It wouldn't have anything to do with a charming hockey player who brings you coffee every day, would it?"

I stare down at the strip lit up below me. "I hate you."

She laughs, a big, belly laugh that makes me smile despite myself.

Eventually, I climb into bed and flip through the channels on the TV. My eyes are finally starting to droop when my phone pings on the nightstand.

I grab it and freeze at the name on the screen. *Leo Lohan.*

I smile, then pull my mouth into a thin line. No, I'm not getting excited that the man figured out how to work his phone.

That lasts until I click on the text and read his words. *Trying out this texting thing. Am I doing it right?*

CHAPTER SIXTEEN

LEO

GAME ON

Ash drops onto his bed in our hotel room with a groan. He lifts the phone. "I'm going to request a wake-up call. Two hours *good*?"

We had a light skate this morning, and most of the guys will nap or relax in their rooms until we go back to the arena for tonight's game.

"No nap for me today. I need to finish an assignment for class and take a test." I grab my laptop and phone. "Enjoy, sleeping beauty."

In the lobby downstairs, I sit in a big, pleather armchair. Tyler is coming out of the hotel's restaurant with a to-go box.

"Hey," I say as he takes a seat across from me. "Heading upstairs to rest before the game?"

"No." He flips the lid and pulls out a club sandwich. "I don't nap, and Maverick is talking to his wife in our room. What about you?"

"I have an assignment and test due tomorrow."

He nods as he bites into his sandwich.

I'm reading over my notes, but I'm struggling to concentrate. I look up at Tyler. "Why is coming up with something to text a girl harder than financial modeling? I could ace this test, but I have no idea what to say to her."

"Coach Miller's daughter?" There's a slight smirk on his lips.

"You heard, huh?" Despite her being somewhere in this hotel, I haven't seen her since we got here last night.

"I'm a rookie, but I'm not stupid." His grin pulls wider. "You're still talking to her then?"

"Sort of."

"Damn. I owe Jack fifty bucks. I thought for sure you'd stay as far away as possible once you found out who she was."

Yeah, that would be the sane thing to do, but Scarlett makes all rational thought leave my brain.

He holds out his box to offer me a chip. "Why sort of?"

I shake off the food. "I'm texting her, but I think she might still have me blocked."

Either that or she's getting them and making me sweat it out as punishment for not texting her sooner. I tell him how I promised to call after the first time we hung out and then let a week go by.

I pull up the message I sent last night. I thought it was funny, but maybe I should have gone with another apology.

"Let me see." He motions with a hand, and since I have nothing to lose at this point, I give Tyler my phone.

He snorts. "Funny. That's it? One text."

"I didn't know what to say when she didn't respond."

Ty tosses the phone back. "Try asking how her day is. Better yet, go find her and ask her in person."

"It's safer to text."

"Yeah, Coach is going to kill you."

He might not be wrong.

I stare down at the screen. "Just… hey, how's your day?"

"You don't have to use those words exactly, but yeah. Ask her a direct question about herself. Show her you're thinking about her and not just trying to prove that you're not an asshole who can't work a phone."

Fuck. That's exactly what I'd been doing.

"Here goes nothing." I tap out the text, asking her about her day, and send it before I can overthink it.

"I changed my mind. I need something to do with my hands." I reach for the food container, and he extends it, so I can grab a few chips. I've just tossed them in my mouth when my phone vibrates. My eyes widen.

"Is that her?" Tyler asks.

I nod and open the text, smiling as I read it because I can hear her in the single word. *Good.*

"Now what?"

"Ask her another question. What she's doing tonight or what color shirt she's wearing. Always follow up with a question, and if she asks you one back, make sure you answer it in detail. Nothing pisses off a girl faster than responding with "K.""

"I know what she's doing tonight," I say.

"Right." He chuckles. "Ask her if she's ever been to Vegas before."

"How are you so good at this?"

"I did the long-distance thing for a while when I was playing juniors. Pretty much lived with my phone in my hand. You get the hang of reading the other person's responses and figuring out how to keep the conversation going. Right now, she's pissed and making you work for it."

"'Did' as in the relationship didn't work out or it isn't long-distance anymore?"

He gives his head a shake. "It didn't work out, but it wasn't because of the distance." He stands. Guess that isn't a conversation he wants to deep dive into. "Good luck."

"Thanks."

I lean back in the chair and tap out another text, *Ever been to Vegas?*

Her response is quick and concise. *Yes.*

I smile. She wants me to work for it? Game on.

WE GET OFF to a slow start against Vegas. Jack and Ash are both sitting this one out. Our pre-season games are a chance for the rookies to get ice time, but it's frustrating without our usual lines.

Coach Miller steps closer to me behind the bench. "Let them hear you out there, Lohan." He claps his hands three times as our line skates onto the ice. "Let's go now. Let's have some fun."

I push hard, calling to Maverick for the puck as two defenders close him in on the opposite wall. He sends it sailing in my direction, and I move to the middle of the ice, taking the puck straight down the middle toward the net.

I flick it to Tyler on the wing, and he sends it right back as I line up and shoot. The goalpost lights up, and Tyler and Maverick huddle around me. Declan joins in, giving my helmet a tap before I skate by the bench to fist bump all my teammates.

My goal shifts the momentum, and we win three to two. I'm walking on air as we get to the team plane.

I look around for Scarlett. She sat behind the bench at the game, but I still haven't had a chance to talk to her, and I don't see her now. Is she not coming with us to the next game? Damn, disappointment hits me hard, and I sit forward, eyes glued to the door as the last of our team and staff arrive. Minutes before takeoff, she finally gets on the plane and slides into a seat across from Coach.

I sit back in my seat and let out a long breath. Ash chuckles, drawing my attention. A quick glance around tells me all the guys around us noticed too.

I power on my phone and get the usual barrage of notifications from my parents and sister, congratulating me on the game and my goal.

But the cherry on top is a new text from Scarlett. Two words instead of one, *Nice goal.*

"What are you grinning about?" Ash asks beside me.

"She finally texted me."

"Ah, I know that look. I miss that look. I haven't been excited about a girl since..." He shakes his head as if he's trying to think back. "College."

"You had a girlfriend in college?"

He points to my phone. "What did our dream girl say?"

"Our?" I chuckle and slide my phone where he can read it.

After he does, his gaze lifts to mine, and he smiles. "How sweet. I guess she was paying attention tonight."

"Not like she had a choice."

"Take the win." He leans his chair back, then lifts his wrist for me to tap.

He's right. It's an opening, however small.

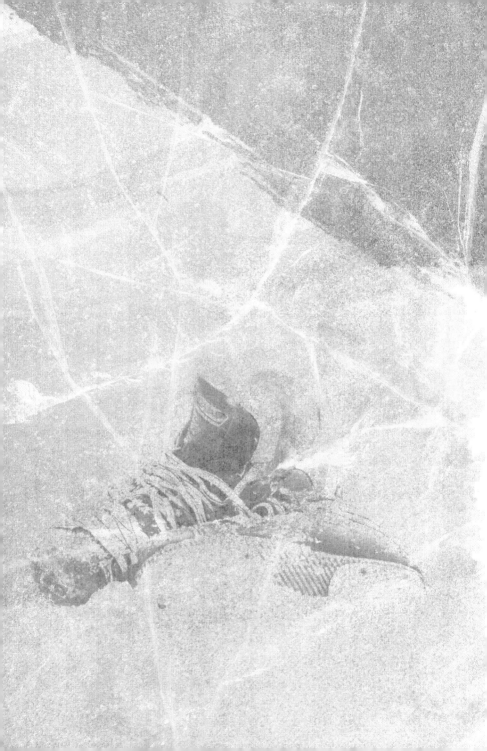

CHAPTER SEVENTEEN

SCARLETT

BALLSY, LEO LOHAN

In Arizona, one of the girls on the media team gets sick, and I fill in with the pre and post-game interview setup and teardown. Even doing the grunt work, it's amazing to see everything that goes into it. The only downside is that I miss a lot of the game, including a goal by Leo.

We're staying in Arizona again tonight and heading to the final game on this road trip in the morning. My phone rings as I'm getting out of the shower, and the name on the screen makes my heart race.

On the third ring, I swipe it and answer hesitantly, "Hello?"

"Hey." Leo's deep voice answers. "Did I wake you?"

"No, you just caught me off guard by calling. Ballsy, Leo Lohan."

"I was afraid I'd fall asleep mid-text."

I can hear the exhaustion in that deep rasp. "Maybe you should sleep then."

"I'm not playing tomorrow. Besides, I wanted to hear you congratulate me on my goal tonight."

"Wow," I say with a laugh. His responding deep chuckle makes me smile. "Congratulations. I saw a replay."

"I heard they had you in the interview room. Man, I hate that room. Though, if I'd known you were working it tonight, I might have offered myself up."

I'm silent, unsure what to say, and a little scared to fall into easy conversation so quickly. This can't happen, and talking to him is just going to make it harder.

"What room are you in?" he asks.

"I'm not telling you that." I pull on shorts and a T-shirt while holding the phone to my ear.

"I'm not going to break in. I might want to bring coffee in the morning."

My stomach flutters. "I have a coffee machine in my room."

"It isn't the same."

He's right about that. "Room three oh three."

"We're on the same floor. I'm in three forty two."

He's so close.

"My dad is next door."

"Right," he says, then falls quiet.

"You must be tired." I fake a yawn. "I know I am."

He emits a low, quiet chuckle. "Kicking me off the phone already?"

I don't answer.

"What are you doing when we get back tomorrow night?"

"Sleeping." We're not set to arrive back in Minnesota until midnight.

"Monday?"

"I'm working."

"You don't get the day off with the rest of us?"

"I'm not working at the arena."

"Oh. The bar?"

"Sort of. Mike has a liquor rep that needed someone to do a promotion for a new flavored vodka. It's just for a few hours at this new paintball bar downtown." I think he feels bad for not giving me more hours at the bar. Regardless, I appreciate it.

"I've heard of that place. Sounds awesome. What about after?"

"You have a game Tuesday."

"Keeping track of my schedule?"

"Your schedule is my job."

His laughter makes me giddy.

"Go out with me Monday night."

"I don't think so."

"Why not? I used my phone and everything."

"Because I don't date athletes."

"What about college guys who play hockey to pay the bills?" A quiet knock on my door follows his question.

My pulse races as I pad to the door and open it a crack. There he is. Phone to his ear, Leo rests his free hand on the wall and stares at me with a breathtaking look that makes goosebumps dot my arm.

I drop my phone and open the door wider. "You can't be here."

"I know," he says. "I just wanted to say good night in person."

My heart lurches as he takes my hand and interlaces our fingers.

"Leo, I—" I start, then swallow. "This isn't a good idea."

"I know." A pained expression crosses his face. He runs his thumb along my index finger. "Night, Scarlett."

"Night, Leo."

In the morning, there's coffee waiting outside my door.

THE LAST DAY of our trip is uneventful. I hate myself a little for admitting this, but it isn't nearly as exciting to watch the team when Leo isn't playing. We get back late Sunday, and I don't hear from Leo again via text or phone call.

Monday afternoon, I get to the paintball bar fifteen minutes early with two army-sized duffel bags. One is filled with bottles of vodka, and the other has shirts, hats, buttons, and other merchandise.

The bar is an old warehouse and just opened this summer. Inside, people are playing paintball on the right side, beyond a metal wall. The sound of playful screams and laughter drifts out. Music plays on the left in the bar area, and there's a patio behind that.

After I find the manager and she points me to a table outside on the patio where I can set up, I get to work. I have everything out and ready to go and am digging for the uniform, if we can call it that—black spandex shorts and a tight tank top with the logo splashed across the front.

I start toward the bathroom only to find a CLOSED FOR CLEANING sign and a woman inside talking on the phone while she mops the floor. She speaks in Spanish, I think. I don't understand her words, but the shooing motion she makes with her hand is crystal clear.

With a sigh, I glance down at my skirt and T-shirt.

Leo steps into my path as I'm deciding between going back out to my car or doing some quick under/over changing maneuvers right here in the bar.

My breath catches, and I freeze in my spot. "What are you doing here?"

"Thought I'd come try the…" He squints. "What kind of vodka did you say you were promoting?"

"I didn't say."

"Are you already done?"

"No." I shake my head. "I'm just getting started if I can find somewhere to change."

This is surreal. Leo Lohan tracked me down at my job.

"Well, come on. You can grab some free merch before it gets busy."

He follows me outside and looks over the table. He holds up a bottle. "Caramel apple vodka? That sounds disgusting."

It really, really does.

"Better keep those thoughts to yourself." I take one of the hats and plop it on his head. It's a really ugly hat, but on him, it doesn't look bad at all. "Make yourself useful and keep lookout."

I shimmy the black spandex up and under my skirt. Leo's brows rise. "You're changing out here?" He looks around.

"The bathroom is closed." I unzip the skirt and push it down my legs. Leo keeps looking at me. "You're a terrible lookout."

"I think I misunderstood what a lookout does."

Laughing, I pull off my T-shirt and toss it in Leo's face, then tug the tank down over my boobs. It's so tight it's squishing the girls. I pull the material down over my stomach and then reach in and rearrange my boobs, so they peek out over the top.

"Okay. Ready." I look at Leo and find his gaze on my chest.

"That's what you're wearing? You look… naked." His voice is low and thick. He reaches over and tries to pull up the tank, but the power of cleavage and a great pushup bra is no match for the cotton material.

"I'm selling flavored vodka at a paintball bar. Looking like this is the whole point."

I pour him a small shot and offer it to him. He sniffs, makes a face, but then drinks it. "Not awesome."

"You have the day off?" I ask. Dad wasn't home when I left, so I assume there's something happening at the arena today, even though he told me not to worry about coming in.

The team has their first home game tomorrow. Mom calls the week of camp, and those next few weeks after it, blackout month because that's how little we see my father at home. Even when practices are over, and the team is in town, he spends long days and late nights at the office.

"Sort of." He checks the time on his watch. "I have until six, and then I need to get back to the arena for a meeting with Coach—"

"My dad?"

He smiles. "Yeah."

It's early still, that awkward time after lunch and before happy hour. Leo hangs by my side and even helps me hand out the free merchandise. He pulls the hat down low over his eyes like he wore it the other night.

We wander around passing out free shots, but that doesn't take very long since the bar is so empty, and I find myself outside alone with Leo Lohan.

"Not a bad gig."

"I'm just filling in. The girl who usually does it had something come up and needed a few hours of coverage. I still need to find something with more hours."

"What about your photography? Any jobs there?"

"I'm not ready for that. I still have so much to learn. I signed up for a free online class, and I'm practicing when I can. Last weekend I went to Owlsen Park and shot photos of a dog birthday party." I don't know why I'm telling him all of this, but being with him like this—just the two of us—makes me nervous and babble, apparently.

He nods, crosses one leg over the other, and leans against the building. "I went to a wedding there last summer."

"It's beautiful, and there's always something going on there. Birthday parties, weddings, families hanging out. It's great for working with different lightings and elements."

"Sounds nice."

"How do you spend Saturdays?"

"Playing hockey, getting ready to play hockey, or on the road somewhere to play hockey."

I roll my eyes and sample the caramel apple vodka. Interesting, but not as bad as I expected. "What about in the off-season?"

He's struggling to come up with an answer, twisting his face up and bouncing his head side to side.

"This is truly pathetic. Do you like to do anything that doesn't revolve around hockey?"

His heated gaze falls over my cleavage and down past my skimpy shorts. I would love to pretend I'm unaffected by it, by him, but I'm not. He places a hand at my hip. His fingers brush underneath the tank onto my stomach.

"You should get out more, broaden your horizons." I pull away from Leo's grasp. "Funny thing happened this morning."

He slides his hands in his pockets. "Oh yeah?"

"Yeah, I went to pay for my car, and someone had already taken care of it."

His lips twitch with a smile he doesn't let free.

"You wouldn't know anything about that, would you?"

"Nah. Frankie loves working on Hondas, though."

I roll my eyes. "Thank you. It wasn't necessary, but thank you."

He dips his head. "Welcome."

A group of guys wander outside. Fresh from paintball, some of them are still covered in it.

"Free shots?" I ask, holding up the bottle.

They crowd around, and I pour sample sizes into the small, plastic shot cups. They're good sports, trying it even though they all agree it sounds awful.

"It's like Halloween in my mouth," one of them says and goes for a second.

"Is that a good thing?" I ask and look to Leo. He's inched back, and I realize too late why he's suddenly gone shy.

The closest guy is staring straight at him with wide eyes. "No way. Leo Lohan. What are you doing here? Are you endorsing the booze?"

"Uhh." He looks to me for help.

"No," I say, quickly, "I saw him and begged him for an autograph. Does anyone have a marker?"

"I bet someone at the bar does," one of the guys says as he walks backward. "I'll go check. I want one too."

In seconds, someone has a Sharpie, and they gather around Leo to get him to sign autographs. It would do me well to remember this is who he is—not my hot Leo that I met at a bar, but Leo Lohan, star hockey player.

The bar starts to pick up, and I hand out more samples while the crowd around Leo refuses to let him go. When Lanie, the girl I'm covering for, shows up, I'm ready to leave, but Leo's still stuck in the same group of guys, except more have joined. I slide between them and wrap my hand around his arm.

"Sorry, guys. I need to get my autograph before I leave." I pull him without waiting for a response.

Inside, I finally stop and check him over. My dad will be pissed at me if I get one of his players hurt right before the season. "Are you okay?"

"I'm fine." He laughs it off.

"That happens a lot?"

"Often enough."

"I wasn't thinking. Sorry."

"I'm a big boy. I can handle myself."

"Are you sure about that?"

He narrows his gaze. "What are you up to, Scarlett Miller?"

I tug him backward toward the paintball room. "Broadening your horizons."

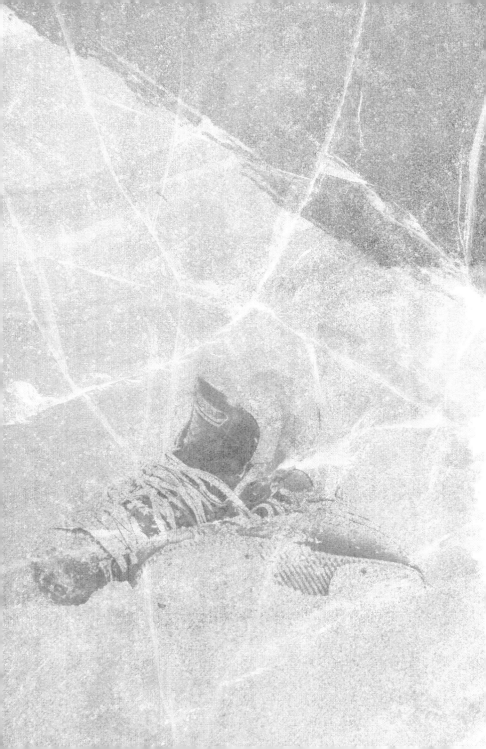

CHAPTER EIGHTEEN

LEO

BODY ODOR AND PAINT THINNER

A bigger group lets us join in on their paintball game.

We're divided into teams of five. Scarlett and I get on the same one, and we move with the rest of our teammates to one side of the large room, as the other team heads to the other side. Tires and other structures divide us and offer hiding spots. When the game starts, our three teammates take off hustling to find the enemy. Scarlett and I hang back.

"This sounded like a better idea from afar. Is it too late to be a spectator?"

"Afraid so." I smile at her nervousness. "Probably got a couple of minutes before they find us. What shall we do with the time?"

I let my gaze flick over her body and then back up to those plump lips I can't stop thinking about.

"How can you possibly be checking me out in this hideous outfit?" She stares down at her clothing. "It smells like body odor and paint thinner."

She's right about that. These clothes could use a spin in the washing machine. Even so, she's sexy as hell in her camouflage overalls and face mask.

"You forget, I know what's underneath."

She looks away and adjusts the goggles on her face. "Is that never speaking of it again?"

"Which time are we never speaking of again?" I ask, and she raises her brows with a playful smirk on her lips I want to kiss off.

The sounds of battle in front of us indicate some of the players have found one another.

"Come over after."

"What?" She laughs lightly. "You have a meeting."

"I know, but I want to spend more time with you. You can clean up at my place, and then hang out if you want while I go to my meeting. Shouldn't take long and we can do something later. Watch a movie or…" I trail off because all the other ideas jumping to mind are dirty.

"Clean up? I don't have a drop of paint on me. I don't know about you, but I plan to leave this game without being splattered in paint. We'll just hide out here and—"

I fire the gun at my shoe and then wipe my hand on the yellow paint.

"Oh no," she says as I reach toward her.

I stalk forward, watching her beautiful eyes widen.

"Leo," she warns and backs away from me. She's so worried about me that she doesn't notice that we're out in the open. Neither do I until a barrage of pink, blue, and green paint pelts us. A blue blob hits the side of her glasses and streaks down her hair, but her smile doesn't falter. And neither does mine.

After a brutal loss, we shuck the overalls, and I walk Scarlett out to her car. "I don't know how to tell you this," I say as I lean into her, brushing a hand along the curve of her neck. "But you stink."

She tucks a piece of hair behind her ear as laughter spills from her lips. "Yeah, well, you don't smell so great either."

I drop my mouth until it's an inch from hers. Just a hint of caramel apple vodka lingers on her breath. I gotta say, I prefer it a lot more this way.

"Come back to my place," I ask again.

"I can't."

"Can't or don't want to?"

She doesn't answer. Instead, she opens her car door. "Thanks for the game, Leo Lohan."

"Just out of curiosity, what's with calling me by my full name?" I ask as I watch her slide behind the wheel.

"Do you have a problem with that, Leo Lohan?"

"Sure don't, *Scarlett Miller*. Just wondering why?"

"It reminds me who you are."

The way she says it like this is a terrible idea, doesn't phase me. I'm in too deep.

I hold her stare. "I'm just me. Awesome paintball player, exceptional date, and vodka tasting assistant."

"You're a professional athlete and you play for my dad," she fires back. "Bye, Leo Lohan."

I GO TO the arena for my meeting with coach.

"Come in. Come in," he calls from behind his desk with a scowl. "Have a seat."

That glower deepens when I fall into the chair. He rummages

through a few papers on the top and then opens and closes every drawer.

"Everything okay?"

"I can't find my phone. I know I left it in here." The stack of papers falls to the ground as he continues moving things around.

"I got it," I offer and squat down to pick up the papers. I stand and set them on a corner of his desk. Finally, he lifts his laptop bag, and the phone appears.

We take our seats again.

"I was supposed to make reservations for tonight and it slipped my mind," he says as he taps out something on the phone. "Just one second. I need to send an SOS text to my wife and see if she can bail me out. After almost thirty years, I think she's probably expecting it at this point."

"No problem." I pick up a framed photo on his desk. It's a black and white of him smiling from the bench. He's younger here, taken some time before he came to The Wildcats, but I recognize the smile. It's a victory smile—one I hope we get to see frequently this year.

"My daughter took that years ago after the junior's team I was coaching won the division title," he says when he notices me looking at the picture.

His daughter. Scarlett.

"It's a great photo." I set it back on the desk.

"She's talented," he says, staring at it like he's seeing it again for the first time. "One year for her birthday, she must've only been five or six, she asked for a camera. We got her the cheapest digital camera we could find, fully expecting that she'd lose it or break it in the first week." He shakes his head lost in the memory. "She had it for years. Brought it with her everywhere. I think most of our family photos over the years were taken on that thing. Lasted well into her teen years before it broke. By that time, I would have gladly bought her a nicer, newer one, but she only wanted to use that old cheap one, so then we had to find someone to fix it."

"Does she still have it?" I'm smiling at the glimpse into a young Scarlett and her stubbornness, not thinking about how asking private details might seem odd.

"Nah. She has this big, fancy thing now with lots of buttons and detachable lenses." He waves a hand dismissively. I know that camera, but I like the image of her with an old cheap one because it's another piece to the puzzle that is Scarlett. I'm eager for any details he might toss out, but he changes the subject.

"Any grumbling in the locker room about the line switches for tomorrow night?"

"No, sir. We're ready." The first regular season game is tomorrow, and the only chatter is how much we want to win. There are a lot of people who have already discounted us because we're young and we want to prove them wrong.

"Good. I saw some nice things on the road. Let's use these next few games to let everyone feel out where they're comfortable and where they fit best. You've been a consistently strong player for us, Leo. I've switched your line maybe more than anyone else. It isn't because I'm trying to figure out where to put you. It's because you make each group better."

It hadn't occurred to me that when he was asking about the guys grumbling, he really wanted to know if I was silently fuming about the lineup for tomorrow. Would I love to be on the first line with Jack and Ash? Hell yes. That's where I was last season and we read each other so well it was almost easy. But Coach's been trying me at center with

Tyler and Maverick. We're not quite at that same comfort level as I was with Jack and Ash, but they're great players, and I have no doubt we'll work well together.

"All that's important is we win."

"That's what I needed to hear." He smiles and stands. "Thanks for swinging by. I won't keep you. I'm sure you have plans of your own tonight. Girlfriend?" He squints like he's trying to think if he's ever seen me with a woman.

"Not currently," I say around a lump in my throat. My palms sweat as I slowly back out of the room. The only woman I'm interested in might earn me a permanent spot on the bench. Or worse.

CHAPTER NINETEEN

SCARLETT

HOLY PUCKING SHIT

I'm sitting in the dark of the kitchen eating a bowl of cereal when Dad comes in. He flips on the light before he sees me.

A tired smile pulls at the corners of his mouth. "You couldn't sleep either, huh?"

I shake my head. Meeting up in the middle of the night for a snack used to be our thing, and I'm happy that after being gone for two years, we still have something that's just ours.

He grabs a bowl and sits in the chair next to me.

"The Raisin Bran is in the pantry," I say as he dumps my Fruity Pebbles in his bowl.

"I missed these. Your mom never bought them when you were gone." He settles in beside me and spoons a heap of the colorful candy cereal into his mouth.

"Are you nervous about the game tomorrow?"

"Always," he says. "They're a talented group. Maybe the most talented I've ever coached."

"Shouldn't that make you less nervous than normal?" He never sleeps the night before the first home game. As far back as I can remember.

He laughs softly. "Probably."

"I get it. It's like when I'm taking pictures of something really beautiful or special and the light is perfect, I expect the quality of my photography skills to be better, too."

"Taken anything recently I can see?"

"You mean like when I forced you to look at an hour worth of my study abroad pictures and you fell asleep?" I sent pictures while I was gone, of course, but I held back all my favorites to see their reactions in person. Dad was out after ten minutes. To be fair, there were a lot and most of them were buildings and churches. The other half had Rhyse in them.

"I'm mostly doing favors for friends and trying to come up with a portfolio before I apply for photographer positions."

He nods his approval. "I know why I'm up burning the midnight oil, but why are you?"

"I told Mom that I dropped my classes." She was giving me the third-degree on missing classes to travel with the team and I couldn't take it anymore.

"Ah." His eyes briefly widen. "That explains why she's up there with her sleep machine on listening to the soothing sounds of the ocean."

I'd bet a month's salary she also has on her gel sleep mask, slipped into silk pajamas, painted her nails, and journaled before bed. My mother drowns herself in self-care when she gets stressed. I'm not hating on her methods, but they're a sure warning sign for the rest of us to give her space to decompress when she's going through her ritual. It makes being the one to cause it that much more miserable to see her in that state.

"She'll come around. We both want to see you happy."

"I am," I say. Or I'm getting there, anyway.

THE NEXT NIGHT I ride to the first home game with Mom. Her nail game is on point and her face has the dewy glow of a day at the spa. She hasn't mentioned school or photography, but I noticed she restocked the Fruity Pebbles.

At the arena, we get drinks and popcorn and find our seats. We're so close to the ice, I could toss popcorn over the plexi glass onto the Wildcats bench.

Dad, as if he has some sort of sixth sense alerting him to our arrival, turns as we're sitting down and waves. He looks handsome in a navy suit with a striped navy, white, and green tie.

"Did you pick out that suit and tie combo?" I ask as I wave back to Dad. He flashes his same old dad smile and then turns back and slips right back into Coach Miller mode.

"I told you, last year he was voted the worst dressed coach in the league. I took the necessary precautions to make sure that doesn't happen again."

"How did you get rid of all of the baggy polyester blends he's been trying to bring back since he wore them in the nineties?"

She grins. The proud grin of a woman who has outsmarted her man. "I refused to take them to the dry cleaner."

Why does it not surprise me that my dad would rather buy new suits and ensure that my mom continues to run his errands than make weekly trips to the dry cleaner himself? He's all about efficiency.

The players are on the ice warming up. I scan, looking for Leo. He texted earlier to make sure I was still coming tonight and to invite me out after. I gave him a noncommittal, *We'll see.*

I had fun with him yesterday, but he's a star hockey player and I'm...rebuilding. Or maybe it's just building, since I haven't successfully made anything of myself yet.

I'm confident in me. I'm awesome. I just liked him better when I thought he was in the same stage of life as me. And before I knew he was a Wildcat.

When I find him, he's already got that dark gaze aimed at me. One long leg is up on the wall next to the bench, stretching. Ash is next to him, his longer hair a shade lighter than Leo's. He talks and Leo nods like he's listening, but he keeps staring at me.

Mom nudges me. "Scar?"

"Yeah." I snap my attention to her and my cheeks warm.

Laughing, she says, "I asked how working with your dad was going?"

I glance back at Leo. He's no longer in the same spot, but I find him by the back of his jersey. Lohan, number fourteen. "It's been good, actually. I missed him while I was gone."

I talked to my mom almost every day on the phone, but rarely my dad. Mom would fill me in on what he was up to and that somehow felt good enough at the time.

"And, there's this photographer Lindsey that works for the Wildcats. She's incredible and she offered to talk with me and tell me about how she worked her way up without a degree."

Mom frowns. I've broken the happy truce by inadvertently mentioning school.

Her mouth opens and closes. I've rarely rendered her speechless.

Before she can find her words and get deep into lecture mode, I place a hand over hers. "I know it isn't what you wanted, but I want to be a photographer and I think I'm pretty good at it."

"You could still be a photographer and get a degree. Just in case."

"Just in case what? I can't find a job or pay my bills? I'd rather make less money and have a job I love than fall back on some career that makes me miserable."

She sighs. That deep, disheartened sigh that mothers perfect over the years.

"I'm sorry if you're disappointed, but I'm not. I'm going to find a job and save up so I can move out and start my own business or I might like to work for a newspaper or a real estate company. I don't know yet, but that's the point of taking time and doing all of these favors."

The buzzer sounds and the players from both teams head for their respective benches.

"I don't have it all figured out," I confess. "But I know this is right for me."

We stand for the national anthem. I find number fourteen on the bench facing the flag, stick in hand, swaying side to side like he's too amped up to hold still.

Mom hums along, a quirky trait that used to embarrass me when I was younger. Tonight, I join in. She glances over and smiles, and I know everything is going to be okay with us. She might not agree with me, but she'll still cheer me on.

We take our seats as the teams get ready for the puck drop.

"So, you aren't pregnant then?" she asks as the first lines skate out.

"What?" I ask a little louder than I intended, causing several people nearby to cast a curious glance. Only for a second though because the action starts.

"I didn't think so. Especially after seeing Cadence. That girl is lit up like a Christmas tree with that pregnancy glow. But I knew something was up with you. You haven't been acting like yourself since the breakup with Rhyse."

"I'm not pregnant," I whisper.

"Will you at least consider finishing your degree? Not because I think you'll fail and need a fallback plan, but as an insurance policy. A lot of companies won't even let you through the door if you don't have a degree in something. I'm not saying it's right, but it's the way it is. If you have a degree, then you'll always know that you have options."

It's a more reasonable request than I was expecting, so I nod. "Yes, Mom, I will think about it."

My uncle joins us halfway through the first period. Mom turns her chatter toward him, and I finally get to focus my full attention on the game. Or more accurately on Leo.

Either I forgot how exciting hockey can be on home ice or Leo is winning me over. He races down the ice, a determined and eager look on his face. I know another time that Leo Lohan had that same expression, and it was naked with me.

Sweat makes the ends of his hair darker and curl up at the back of his helmet. His shift ends and he comes off the ice, chest heaving. We lock eyes and for several seconds, I think I stop breathing.

Holy pucking shit. If I thought I was going to watch him play all season and be completely unaffected, I was seriously mistaken.

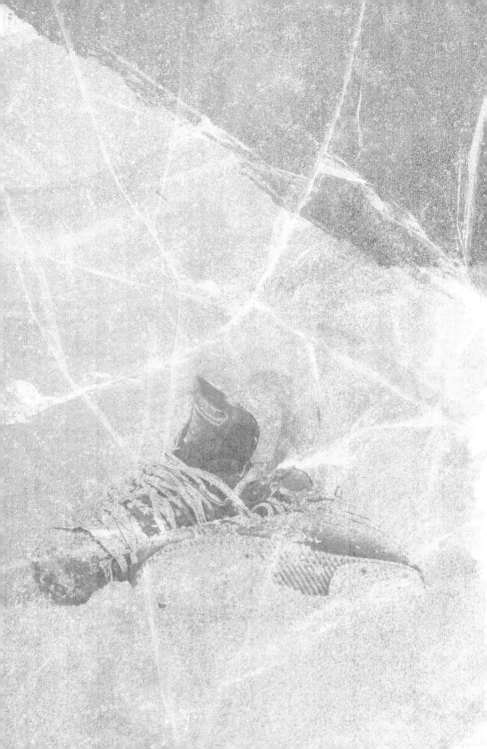

CHAPTER TWENTY

SCARLETT

DON'T BRING YOUR LOGIC AND REASON TO THE PARTY

After the game is over, I tell my mom I'm meeting up with some friends from work and say bye to her and my uncle. I hang out in the lobby, trying to decide if I'm really going to go out with Leo.

The Wildcats won, five to zero, thanks to a little help from Leo with one goal and an assist, so I think there's a very good chance he'll be celebrating. If not, or if I decide against this insanity, I'll be taking a very spendy Uber ride home or hoping I can find Dad before he leaves.

I'm pacing the marble floor when a text pops up from Leo, *Still here? Want to hang out with a bunch of **awesome** hockey players?*

Oh god. I can't seem to help the big smile on my lips. *Awesome is debatable. I'm here.*

I don't directly answer his question, but the excitement and anticipation I feel waiting for his reply is a clear signal that I'm doing this. Bring on the insanity.

When the lobby is starting to thin out, my phone pings again, and I read the text with an ear-to-ear smile on my face, *Meet you outside on the southwest corner (opposite direction of the parking garage).*

I know which way is southwest, I fire back. Or I think I do. I would have found him.

I head outside, hugging my arms to my stomach. A jacket didn't go with the outfit.

On the corner, I wait, clutching my phone in my hand. It's much quieter on this side of the arena, and I'm a woman in a midriff shirt standing alone. Not your best laid plan, Leo.

No sooner than I curse him, a black truck with tinted windows pulls to the curb. The window rolls down and Ash smiles from the driver's side.

"Miller, nice to see you. Couldn't get enough of us?" He revs the engine.

Leo leans over from the passenger seat. "He's mostly safe. Hop in."

The new car smell hits me as I slide into the back seat. Ash pulls away from the arena, going the opposite direction of the popular bar.

"I thought we were going to Wilds."

"Jack is having a party at his place." Leo glances over his shoulder to meet my gaze. "You cool with that?"

"Wild's will be packed tonight. Always is after the first game of the season," Ash says from the driver's seat.

"I have to drop off something, but we can go somewhere else after that if you want," Leo reassures me.

"Sure. I'm game for whatever." As the coach's daughter, I have a feeling I'm much safer in a house full of Wildcats than at some bar.

My phone pings with a text from Leo, *You look gorgeous.*

"So, Scarlett," Ash says and glances in the rearview mirror. "I heard you just got back from London."

"Yeah, that's right. I lived there for two years right after high school."

"That's dope, although unfortunate that you made my boy here wait two years to meet you." His attention turns to Leo. "That was what, your second year with the team when Coach Miller became the head coach?"

"Oh, I never would have dated him two years ago," I say before Leo has a chance to answer.

Ash busts up laughing and Leo's mouth falls open.

"That was in my skinny, drugged-out, rocker guy phase," I tell him with a small lift and fall of one shoulder.

"Sounds… hardcore," Ash says, still laughing.

"Not really. Most of them were wannabes that drank hard seltzer and dabbled in E while living in big apartments their parents paid for. Not exactly the sex, drugs, and rock-n-roll lifestyle the Internet sold me."

"I think I like you." Ash shakes his head.

He drives us to Leo's house, except he pulls into a house across the street. The garage door opens and Ash parks inside a massive four-car garage. Most of the space is filled with workout equipment, but there's a killer Mercedes SUV and a golf cart.

"Is there a golf course nearby?" I ask as I step out of the truck.

"Nah, it's just for driving around the neighborhood," Ash says. "I'm going to drop my stuff inside. I'll see you guys at Jack's."

Leo meets me at the back of the truck and tilts his head in the direction of his house. "Ready?"

He takes my hand as we cross the street. I wasn't sure what agreeing to hang out tonight meant for us, but I know I like the feel of his strong fingers clasped around mine.

"I assume there's no roommate?"

"Nope. Just me." He punches in the code on the garage opener, and it comes alive with a hum. His Jag is parked inside, but Leo hops into the driver's seat of a golf cart that looks identical to Ash's.

"We're taking this to the party?"

"Jack lives up the street."

"Of course, you all live next door to one another." I sit on the bench seat next to him. A hula dancer bobble head is stuck to the dash. I glance in the back, where several cases of beer and a box of wine and liquor are loaded up and strapped in. "We're in charge of bringing the booze?"

He starts out of the garage and makes a right, taking us farther into the neighborhood.

"Yeah it's my unofficial duty as the newest alternate captain." He grins and pulls into the circle drive of a house that's so big it makes Leo's look like a shack.

"Wow."

As soon as it's parked, he reaches over and grips the back of my neck, pulling me closer while he leans in to cover my mouth with his. His thumb strokes my neck as his tongue seeks entrance. He deepens the kiss, and his other hand frames the side of my face.

It seems he's always pulling back sooner than I want, but I realize why this time when headlights pull up behind us.

"We don't have to stay long," he says.

Two guys emerge from the SUV.

He calls to them, "Hey, rookies, little help."

They come closer and I recognize Johnny Maverick and Tyler Sharp.

"No way Coach Miller's daughter is partying with us tonight?"

Johnny asks. He's got this likable, genuine smile and a lot of ink.

"I am."

Tyler is quieter, though something tells me it's easy to be the quiet one around this group of guys. He says hello and offers a shy wave. They each grab a case, and Leo picks up the box of liquor and wine and carries it with one arm on his hip while holding my hand as we walk inside.

A man at the door is collecting phones and making people sign NDAs, but we move right through with a nod in his direction.

"How come I don't have to sign away my silence?"

"It's sort of assumed you being Coach's daughter and all," Leo says quietly.

"How does he know who I am?"

"That's Jack's agent, James. He makes it his business to know everyone."

Leo drops the box on the counter in the kitchen. There's already a healthy amount of liquor bottles to choose from.

"What do you want to drink?" Leo asks as he grabs a beer from the fridge.

"That looks good."

He hands me his and gets another.

"I hesitate to show you Jack's back yard." Leo moves toward an open door that leads outside, where I can see people are gathered around a patio. The music that plays gets louder as I step back out into the night.

"Why's that?"

"Because it's better than mine." He places a hand on my lower back as he guides me.

Heaters are set up around the patio, surrounding a whole lot of outdoor furniture where people sit, while others stand all around the giant yard.

Leo's not wrong. This is amazing. Everything is bigger and more extravagant. The same pool setup but larger. It has a lane roped off for laps, there's a waterfall in one corner and a swim-up bar.

We wander over to a group of his teammates standing in the side yard in front of a smaller guest house. French doors are open, and I can see inside, where another kitchen is filled with booze.

Leo introduces me to everyone, though most of them I've interacted with in some way over the past two weeks. Jack is the only Wildcat I knew by name and face before I started working with my dad. Dad mentioned him in passing and he's in a few commercials and advertisements that make him sort of impossible not to know.

"Fuuuuck. For real?" The captain waves the beer in his hand, motioning between us. "This is really happening?"

Uhhh. I look to Leo. Neither of us finds our words before Jack does.

"Does Coach know?" His question is directed at Leo.

"That I'm at a party with his players?" I cross my arms and step forward. "Because anything else would be none of his or anyone else's business."

"Just trying to look out for the team." Jack holds his hands up defensively. He takes one last look at Leo and then walks off.

The rest of the group falls silent.

Crap. I worried about what my dad would think of me seeing Leo, but not what might happen to Leo or how his teammates might feel about it.

"I should probably go," I tell him.

"No, don't. Jack is just being Jack. He never stops thinking about work."

"Stay," Johnny says.

"Yeah, stay." Ash steps up beside Leo. "What'd I miss? Drama already?"

"Jack being an ass," Leo bites out.

I glance around. I catch the eye of more than one player as I scan the yard.

"He has a point. Besides, even if my dad knew and was cool about it, I don't want the guys to feel like I'm Coach's eyes and ears."

Ash nods. "Then what better way for everyone to see you're cool than to hang out and be chill? You'll blend in, in no time."

Leo's fingers take mine. "What do you say? We can go back to my place or somewhere else."

"Yeah, I'd bet you'd like to take her back to your place again," Ash says under his breath.

Leo keeps his gaze on me as he flings an arm out to smack his buddy on the chest.

"Again?" Johnny asks, then his eyes go wide. "Ooooh. This is dream girl?"

"That's her," Ash confirms.

Leo's eyes scrunch up adorably. "I didn't mean go back to my house to hook up. We can hang out, swim, talk."

The group of guys gathered around all look to me for my answer.

"We can stay," I say, and I swear they all grin.

"Yes!" Ash is the first to voice his enthusiasm. "Let's play some pong."

Leo and I team up against Ash and Tyler. Tyler isn't as quiet as I first assumed, but he's more reserved than the rest of the guys. Possibly because I'm here. He crushes us all at pong and then Ash spends a few minutes trying to convince more people to play Flip Cup Races, which I assume is just flip cup, but as it turns out, it is a variation of the game that involves racing silver and red remote controlled cars between flips.

I sit out the first game and am glad I do, because these guys aren't messing around with these cars. Boys and their toys. Miniature cars— ones that look way fancier and go way faster than those I've seen little kids play with—speed down the road toward Leo and Ash's houses, cutting each other off at the turnaround mark.

Ash's shiny silver car makes it back first. He pumps a fist and calls to me, "Get your ass over here, Miller. You're on my team. I need you to distract your boy."

Leo and I line up in the last spot. There's a playful glint in his eye.

"Do I even want to know how much those cars cost?" I ask

"More than my first real car," Tyler says.

Leo grins. "We tried racing on foot a couple of times, but people were puking left and right. We improvised. Jack loves these things."

"Gross." The visual is not pretty. "Don't you guys have practice tomorrow?"

"Spoken like the coach's daughter," Leo teases me.

"Spoken like anyone with an ounce of logic."

"Aw, Miller, don't bring your logic and reason to the party." Ash boos and then all the other guys join in.

"Okay. Okay." I laugh "Let's do this."

We're in teams of four. Ash and Johnny are the first to go. Johnny finishes his drink faster but is slower to get the remote car going. The guys that have done this more have an obvious advantage, and Ash catches him about halfway down to the turnaround point. The silver and red cars nearly avoid crashing into one another when Johnny swerves in front of him, taking the lead.

Next up is a guy they call Morris and Declan. Then it's Tyler and a girl that's been hanging on Morris.

"Sorry in advance for kicking your butt." Leo winks. He's hovering over his cup of beer, waiting for the car to return.

"Dream on, Leo Lohan."

The second Tyler moves our car past the finish line, I chug the lukewarm beer. It sits heavy in my stomach as I hurry to grab the remote from him. Yeah, running right now would be bad.

Leo fumbles the remote, but I think he might be letting me catch up. Oh, how sweet, he's trying to take it easy on me. Unfortunately for him, I'm playing to win.

"Hey, Lohan," I say as his car races after mine.

He glances up from the road, and I flash him. I have on a bra, so it isn't like he's seeing my boobs, but it's enough to distract him and send his car off into someone's yard.

The guys are cheering behind us. Someone yells, "Nice rack!"

"Oh, you're so going to pay for that," Leo says. He steps closer and maneuvers his car back onto the road. He's gaining on me and I'm grinning like an idiot as this small silver car races toward the turnaround mark. I cut the wheel early, giving myself a bigger lead.

It's close, but my car crosses the finish line first, and Ash hugs me and lifts me off the ground.

"Miller! Miller!" he chants.

The guys lift their beers to me, and a few chant along with Ash.

I wait for Leo to call me on not going past the turnaround point, but he doesn't. Ash puts me on the ground in front of Leo. "Your girl is awesome."

"She's also a cheater," Leo says so only I can hear.

"I have no idea what you're talking about."

"Mhmm." He takes my hand. Warmth spreads up my arm. "Take a ride with me."

"Sure you don't want me to drive?" I ask as he hops into his golf cart.

He laughs and pulls out of the driveway, hops the curb and drives down the grass. There's a path where I can see others have come this way before. He guides us behind Jack's property. There's a lake and several other golf carts are already parked near the bank. A few people are sitting on blankets, others stand. Someone's playing music, but it's quieter than at the house.

I'm surprised when Jack is among those here. He's sitting on the blanket with a pretty girl perched between his legs, her back resting on his chest.

"Is this all Jack's?" As far as I can see, it's an open field and the lake is a decent size.

Leo chuckles and leans back in his seat. We're close enough I can hear the quite murmur of others talking, but far enough away, it feels like we have a little privacy.

"Is this like bougie parking?" I ask when I see a couple making out. "You can't just take a girl to an abandoned parking lot and make a move, you bring her here." I wave a hand to the lake. The moon is full and glows down on the water.

"Told you his back yard was better."

"I don't know how I feel about hanging around with someone who's so… together."

His brows lift.

"I'm serious. My life is a mess."

"You think I have my life together?" He throws his head back and laughs.

"I've seen your house. I watched twenty thousand fans scream their hearts out for you earlier tonight, and you drive a golf cart around your neighborhood."

"Professionally, yes, I'm in a good spot. But everything else?"

When I don't buy it, he arches back and unbuttons his jeans.

"Uhh... I don't think this is the place to show me your penis to prove some point about how you're below average in some areas."

He scoffs. "Below average? Please."

He's not wrong, and I get butterflies in my stomach remembering just how not average he is. Instead of whipping out said well-above-average dick, he tugs on the band of his underwear. Boxers, cheap cotton with hearts all over them. They look like something someone might have bought him for Valentine's Day a long time ago. "These were all I could find today."

Based on the one other time I saw him in his skivvies, I think he prefers boxer briefs.

"Time to do laundry?"

"Seems so." He stares down at them and grins. "Though these kind of set the mood, am I right?"

"Ridiculous boxers do not mean your life is a mess."

He thinks for a second. "The milk in my fridge is expired. I can't remember the last time I changed the air filters in my house, and you just watched me race a remote controlled car down the street."

I laugh quietly, and he rests a hand on my shoulder, brushing his fingers along my neck. I super dig his hands. They're big and just look strong somehow. The callouses against my smooth skin send a shiver up my spine. I lean forward.

"You know," he says as he brings his mouth closer to mine, "I've never had to down talk myself to get a girl."

"Is that what you're doing? Trying to get a girl?"

"Is that not obvious?" He chuckles. "Fuck, I need to up my game."

CHAPTER TWENTY-ONE

LEO

YOUR DAD LIKES ME

She rests her arms on my shoulders. "I had fun tonight, but I should get home. It's late."

With a hand at her hip, I pull her to me and drop my lips to hers. "Don't go, dream girl."

Her laughter spills into my mouth. "You did not call me that."

"Actually, Ash is who started it, but he's not wrong. I like you. You're fun and so sexy." I slip a hand under her shirt in the back and glide it over her warm skin.

"I should still go."

I lift her shirt and duck my head to kiss the top of her tits above her bra. I can't believe she flashed me earlier. Wildcat. It fits her just as well as dream girl.

"If this isn't going to be another one-night stand, then we should take a beat because Jack made some good points earlier. I don't want to cause trouble."

"I'll be fine. Your dad likes me," I say automatically, because I'm an inch away from having her nipple between my teeth, and I could care less about the consequences.

She lifts my head. "I just told my parents that I dropped out of college. Maybe I should give them a few days before I drop another bomb on them."

"So we just can't see each other?"

"That would probably be the smart decision."

"Seems pretty dumb to me."

"Let's just take a few days. You're going to be on the road a lot over the next week. When you come back, if you still want to do this, then we'll talk to my dad."

I run a hand through my hair. "Okay. If that's what you want, but Scarlett? A week isn't going to change my mind."

She smiles and brings her lips to mine. "Then you better hope my dad likes you as much as you think he does."

WE HAVE FIVE games on the road over the next week and a half. We fly to Los Angeles for two games, then to Canada, cross back into the states and hit New Jersey, and our last game is in Pittsburgh.

I don't mind travelling. A lot of the guys get cranky being away for so long, but it doesn't bother me.

We're in the hotel in Winnipeg with some downtime before the game tonight. I'm working on an assignment for class while Ash and Tyler play video games in our room.

My phone lights up on the desk in front of me. Scarlett's name flashes with a text, *Good luck tonight!*

I've been giving her space, but this text opens the door, and I jump right through.

4 days, dream girl, I fire back.

Until what?

Oh, she wants to play it like that. *Until I take you out on a real date.*

Is that a request or a command? I swear I can almost hear the sass in her text.

Which one do you want it to be? And then I add, *Will you go out with me?*

It's several minutes before she responds, *Ask me again when you get back.*

WE WIN THREE of the five games on the road. The amount of interviews and game wrap-ups I have to do now that I'm an alternate captain has increased, but Blythe has prepped me, and I focus on saying as little as possible while still answering their questions.

We're heading back to Minnesota, pretty happy with how we're playing but dog tired.

Even though it's late when we touch down Wednesday night. I text Scarlett as soon as we land, *Just got back. Wanna go out tomorrow night? Or I'm free in fifteen.*

I have no ability to play it cool with this girl.

Coach stands at the front of the plane. "Rest up tomorrow. I'll see you all back Friday morning. We have St. Louis at home Saturday."

Ash catches me in the parking lot. "Tyler and I are thinking about heading up to the lake. Spend tomorrow on the water, breathe in a little lake air. You in?"

"Maybe. I'll text you."

Inside my car, I check my phone. Scarlett's responded. *It's almost midnight. I'm in bed.*

I hit the call button as I drive.

"Helloooo?" she draws out the word.

"Hi, dream girl."

Her sweet laughter crackles over the speakers.

"Entertain me. I'm driving home, and I am beat."

"And yet you wanted to go out tonight."

"Still do if you've changed your mind. I will tap into those energy reserves for you, dream girl."

"You have got to stop calling me that."

Which, of course, only makes me want to call her that even more. "What are you doing tomorrow? Do you have to go to the arena?"

She yawns. "No. Dad is taking a rare day off. But, I need to practice taking some photos outside for an engagement shoot I'm doing next week, and I should probably continue the job hunt. Anna will be back soon."

"Come to the lake with me. Ash has a place on Laurie Lake. A nice house right on the water."

"I don't know."

"Bring your camera. You can get some great shots there. I will personally guarantee it."

She hesitates for a few seconds longer. "Okay."

I pump my fist. "Awesome. I'll pick you up at six."

"In the morning?!" She screeches. "What about nine or ten? I need sleep. You won't like me uncaffeinated and tired. I am not a pleasant morning person."

"Nothing I haven't seen before. I'll take my chances. Night, dream girl."

I PULL UP outside of the Miller's residence at six on the dot. Coach's Tahoe sits in the driveway next to Scarlett's car.

Outside, I text her as I watch for any movement at the door or windows. I did not think this through. Are we telling Coach? Because

I'm not sure rolling up at the break of dawn after a long road trip to tell him I'm dating his daughter was my best-laid plan.

And if we're not telling him, what are the chances he's up and looks outside? Will he know it's me based on my car? It isn't as flashy as Declan's Ferrari or Jack's Lambo, but my Jaguar has a custom paint job and sick wheels that are just memorable enough he might know it's me without seeing through the tinted windows.

Luckily, when the front door opens, it's Scarlett that steps out. Alone. Her hair is pulled up in a high ponytail that swings around her head with every groggy step. I laugh at the grimace on her face as she approaches the car with a small bag slung over her shoulder.

I hop out to open her door. I'm nervous about getting caught, but I'm still a fucking gentleman.

"Are you crazy? My dad is up. He could see you."

Okay, so not telling him right now. Got it.

"Morning," I say, biting back a huge grin at how adorably grumpy she looks. She thought this would scare me off? The opposite actually. It just made my whole day, and it's just getting started.

She slides into the passenger seat, and I shut her in before rounding the car to hop back in.

"Coffee is in the cup holder, Sleeping Beauty."

She grunts but grabs it and holds it between her hands, closes her eyes, and leans her head back on the seat.

"Does your dad know?"

Her eyes open. "I'm not telling him until I decide I like you fully-clothed."

I bark out a laugh and pull away from her house. "Fair enough."

CHAPTER TWENTY-TWO

SCARLETT

THIS IS HAPPENING

The drive to Lake Laurie takes two hours. Enough time for me to feel human. The coffee helped. So did breakfast about an hour back.

Leo has one hand on the wheel, the other drums along his thigh absently to the beat of the music. He pulls into the driveway of a brick home. It's serene. Trees line the property, and I can imagine how green and pretty it must be in the summertime with all the landscaping.

"This is nice," I say as I step out.

Leo comes around and takes my bag. I hold tight to my camera equipment.

"He stays here during the offseason."

"You don't have a matching one down the street?"

His lips curl up. "Not yet. Wanna help me pick one out?"

This guy. He's too freaking much.

I follow him to the front door where he knocks and waits a beat before going right in. "They're probably out back."

He sets my bag on the couch in the living room and leads me out the back door, where we're throwing distance to the lake. It's overcast and windy, but it's still breathtaking.

"You made it," Ash calls. He and Tyler are sitting at a table with plates of food in front of them.

"There's more inside if you're hungry," Ash says, around a mouthful.

"We ate on the way up." Leo pulls out two chairs, and we sit with them.

"You missed a hell of a run this morning. I took Tyler down our summer trail."

These two already went for a run on their day off? Upon closer inspection, they're in workout clothes and sweaty.

"I got a quick five in before we hit the road." Leo leans back and laces his fingers together at his waist.

"You did?" I need some of his energy. He couldn't have slept more than four or five hours tops.

"He's a morning person," Ash says and lifts his brows like it's an awful thing to be. He's not wrong.

"Gross. Really?"

"I'm a morning person, a day person, a night person. I don't need a lot of sleep."

"Wow. It just gets worse and worse. Well, thanks for a great time." I place my hands on the table like I'm going to stand.

"Okay wise-ass," Leo says. His foot finds mine under the table. He looks to Ash. "Are you taking the fishing boat out today?"

"Yeah. We already got the cooler and gear loaded up. Do you fish?" Ash asks me.

"I have before."

"Not an outdoorswoman, eh?"

"I like the outdoors just fine, but I prefer activities where I can photograph along the way."

"You can do that from the boat," he says.

"The four of us won't fit in that boat," Leo says. "Not comfortably anyway."

"It'll be cozy."

Leo looks to me. "We can go on the boat or walk around and explore. What do you say?"

I do enjoy being out on the water, even if fishing isn't my favorite thing, but spending time with Leo alone is far more enticing.

"I'd like to take some photos along the water and maybe some in the wooded area." The weather isn't the best for pictures, but I need to practice in all conditions.

Ash and Tyler stand with their empty plates. "We'll be back in a few hours. Hopefully we can have fish for lunch."

Once we're alone, Leo leans closer. "Are you ready? Need to grab anything?"

"Just my camera."

He dons a hat and sunglasses, and I get my camera before we head out. Leo guides us from Ash's house down to the beach. The lake is quiet today. The wind comes in gusts that make me thankful we're not on the choppy water. I do not need to spend the morning with my head hanging over the side puking.

"What'd you get up to while I was gone?" he asks as we walk along at a slow pace.

"I worked another promotion for Mike, hung out with Jade. I even sang some Backstreet for you at karaoke last weekend."

He holds both hands over his heart. "Dream girl."

I roll my eyes, but secretly love it when he calls me that.

We come up on a wooded area that has a path heading away from the lake. The trees help shield us from the wind, but my nose and fingers are cold.

I snap a few pictures looking back at the water, and then we move off the path, and I play around, shooting all the various fall colors displayed proudly on the leaves. Even with the clouds, the trees this time of year are beautiful and vibrant shades of yellow, orange, and red.

Leo is quiet beside me.

"Sorry. I'm not very good at shooting and talking."

"I don't mind." He pulls his hoodie over his head and holds it out to me. He has only a T-shirt on underneath.

"I'm fine."

"Your cheeks match the color of that tree," he says, pointing toward a nearby tree with reddish-orange leaves.

I place a hand to my face, but my fingers are cold too.

"Now you'll be cold."

"Nah, I'm used to it. I spend a lot of time in the cold." He continues to hold out the sweatshirt toward me.

"Thank you." His scent and warmth envelop me as I put it on. He comes forward and lifts the hood up over my head. Nobody looks sexy in a hoodie. Nobody. But the way he looks at me, the butterflies in my stomach refuse to believe that.

We walk the path and then backtrack along the beach again. I'm not sure how much time has gone by, but I can see a lone boat out in the distance.

"Is that Ash?"

"Yeah, looks like it. There'll be more people out this afternoon when it warms up a little."

"You've been here a lot then?"

We sit together on the grass just beyond the beach.

"Yeah." He shrugs. "I guess I have. Ash and I go way back. We both went to college in the northeast and played against each other, then came to the Wildcats."

"And now you're BFFs who buy homes in the same neighborhood and vacation together?"

That sexy smile graces his face. "Jack started it. He bought a house in that neighborhood first."

"It is a nice neighborhood. Neighbors are questionable." I aim my camera at him and snap.

"Oh no." He holds up a hand. "You don't want to break that thing."

I look at the picture on the display. His eyes are half-closed. Laughing, I show him.

"I told you. I have never taken a good picture."

"Never?"

"I mean, they're varying degrees of bad. From acceptable to flat-out awful."

I turn the camera around to take a selfie. He grimaces.

"Smile," I instruct. "Actually, maybe don't. One, two, pretend I'm flashing you." I click the button and then bring my camera to my lap to see it.

"You're looking at my boobs!"

"You said pretend I'm flashing you."

I set my camera down, and we stare out at the water. He rests one palm on the ground behind me, angling himself so my shoulder brushes his chest.

"I forgot how much I love it here."

"The lake?"

"Minnesota." I lean into him. "We left when I was in middle school. Dad got a coaching job in Maryland."

"You didn't like it?"

"It was fine. We were only there for two years before he got a job in Michigan. We were there for three years, and then we came back here."

"How come you decided to go to London?"

"Sounded fun."

He laughs.

"My high school boyfriend broke up with me about a month before graduation."

"I'm sorry."

"We never would have worked. I know that now, but I was heartbroken and wanted to do something drastic."

"Were your parents supportive?"

"Yeah. Mom did a gap year, and she always talked about how it changed her life."

"Did it change your life?" He uses the strings on his hoodie to tug me closer.

"Mhmmm. I learned to trust myself and be independent. It was easier there. Since I've been back, I feel like everyone is watching and waiting for me to get my life together."

My eyes dart to his lips. He's so close now I can feel his breath. My pulse kicks up a notch, and my stomach is doing somersaults. I wasn't kidding when I told him I wanted to make sure that I liked him fully clothed (aka not naked and kissing me) before we told my dad. I convinced myself that I'd imagined the chemistry between us. Maybe I wanted to protect myself or him, but I've dated enough to know that what I'm feeling is rare, and it's absolutely real.

"You couldn't have just been a regular guy."

He chuckles. "Sorry."

I reach out and cup his cheek. It's rough with a day or two's worth of stubble. "Don't be."

I make the first move this time. That dimple on the left side of his mouth appears as my lips drop to his. Somehow he's warm, even though I'm wearing his sweatshirt. He wraps his arm around my waist and pulls me against him. I might have started the kiss, but he takes over.

And I give in. Not just to his kiss, but to him.

This is happening.

WE SPEND THE rest of the day at Ash's house. He and Tyler come back from fishing, and the four of us sit outside, enjoying the sunshine that finally came out. We play bags (which Ash and Leo insist on calling corn hole), and as the afternoon fades into evening, we get ready to head back.

I walk down to the lake one more time to capture the late sun over the lake. Leo comes with me, but stands off to the side while I snap a dozen or more photos. I glance back to find him watching me.

"I'm almost done. I promise. I just need to get one more shot."

"No rush." His smile is easy, stance relaxed and unhurried.

I bring up my camera and take the photo before he realizes what I'm doing.

"Are my eyes closed? Am I holding my mouth weird? Sometimes I pull my bottom lip behind my teeth. Not a great look in photos." He walks toward me.

"See for yourself?" I hold it out for him to look.

"I'll be damned." He clears his throat. "I'm going to need a copy of that."

"You're serious?" I ask through laughter when he doesn't break a smile.

"Hell yeah, I'm serious. It's a one in a million shot."

"You just needed the right photographer." I smash my cheek to his and extend the camera out in front of him, taking one more of the two of us just for me.

CHAPTER TWENTY-THREE

SCARLETT

READY FOR ROUND TWO?

Saturday night Jade and I are working a promotion at Wild's, the bar next to the arena. I thought it would be quiet in here until after the game, but it seems that anyone who didn't get tickets to see the Wildcats play St. Louis came here to watch instead.

I'm standing behind our promotion table while Jade makes rounds around the bar. She's so much better at this than me.

"I'm so glad you're here," I say when she comes back with her tray empty.

"Only for another hour. I have to get to Whittaker for my shift at the bar."

A group of girls approach our table, and I fill shots for them. One good thing about it being so busy in here is that people don't stay and chat, which means I can catch up with Jade.

"How much longer until you're done?"

"I told Mike I'd cover any weekend shifts until he finds someone else."

There's cheering at the bar, and I look up to see the Wildcats scored. The guys on the ice gather around Jack.

"I wish you could stay and hang out." Leo and some of his teammates are coming here after the game. I'm giddy with anticipation. "He invited me to stay at his house tonight, so we could spend more time together before he leaves for Arizona tomorrow afternoon."

Jade grins. "When are you telling *Coach* Miller?"

I elbow her. "I'm not sure. I don't want to make a mess of things for nothing."

"You want to make sure you like him first?" she asks. "That makes sense."

I nod, and that is what I told Leo, but I already know the answer to that question. I like him. A lot.

Jade has to take off before the game is over. I tear down our promotion table and take what's left of the free merchandise to the bar for people to grab throughout the night.

I change in the bathroom, then get a pitcher of beer and luck out when a table in the back becomes available.

Leo texts to say he'll be here as soon as he can, and I occupy myself with my phone and the commentary on the TV from the game.

I look up when a shadow falls over the table. Smiling, I expect Leo, but instead, it's some guy with a shy grin.

"Hey." He's holding a half-empty glass of beer and motions to the empty chair across from me. "Want some company?"

He slides into the chair before I can answer. He doesn't seem threatening, more like clueless.

"I'd offer to buy you a drink, but it looks like you've got that covered. Did your friends ditch you?"

"No, they just haven't shown up yet."

"I'm Cory."

"Scarlett."

"Nice to meet you."

"Were you at the game?" I ask, pointing to his Wildcats jersey. Leo's in fact. I can't see the back, but the number fourteen is on both sleeves

"Yeah. Great game. Are you a Wildcats fan?"

"Something like that."

"The team is looking great this year." He starts talking about their current record and upcoming games. Three guys walk up to the edge of the table as Cory continues rambling about the Wildcats. He glances quickly at the men without stopping talking but then does a double-take.

Leo gives the two of us a curious look.

"Holy fuck. You're Leo Lohan." Cory sits tall.

"Hey, man." Leo slides in next to me and drops a quick kiss on my lips.

"Ash Kelly. Tyler Sharp." Cory stares at the two remaining men.

"Mind if we have a seat?" Ash asks.

Cory jumps up with a wide-eyed, starstruck expression on his face. "These are your friends?"

"Umm… sort of," I say.

"Sort of?" Leo scoffs.

"It's a polyamorous thing," Ash tells Cory as he and Tyler sit across from us. "One guy just isn't enough for her."

Leo kicks him under the table.

I can't help but laugh at Cory's stunned expression. He blinks slowly as he takes in the four of us.

"Nice to meet you guys." He ambles off.

"If tomorrow's gossip includes my name with the word

polyamorous in it, I'm going to kill you," Leo says.

"Relax," Ash says as he pours a beer from the pitcher. "So, where are we heading tonight? Jack's not partying. My house? Yours?"

"I think it's going to be an early night for us," Leo says. His hand finds my thigh under the table. "Scarlett's had a long day."

I love how he's the one that just played hockey for three hours, but he thinks I've had the long day because I handed out free liquor to drunk people for three hours.

"Early to bed or early to sleep?" Ash asks.

Leo's grin is the only response Ash gets.

"Ty?" Ash looks to his buddy.

He shrugs. "I might call it early tonight too."

Ash shakes his head. "You all suck. We get to sleep in tomorrow. At least humor me with a game of darts?"

The four of us move to the dart boards in the back corner. We play in teams—me and Leo against Ash and Tyler.

While Tyler takes his turn, Leo sits on a stool, and I stand close, but not as close as I'd like. There are a lot of eyes in here. Leo's hand brushes against my back. I lean into his touch just as he moves it away. When he stands to take his turn, he places both hands on my hips as he moves past me. They're little, unnecessary caresses and they're driving me wild.

A game of darts has never felt more like foreplay. The only downfall is that I'm too distracted to pay attention to anything but Leo. Ash and Tyler easily beat us. Not that either me or Leo care.

"We're taking off," Leo says, gliding his hand along the band of my jeans and letting his pinky and ring finger slide under the denim material in the back. "See you boys tomorrow."

I wave bye to Ash and Tyler and let Leo haul me out of Wild's like a man on a mission, which he very much seems to be.

His car is parked in the lot across the street, and when we make it there, he pins me against the passenger side door. Both hands frame my face as he kisses me with all the pent-up frustration of the past hour.

My heart races and heat courses through me.

He breaks the kiss, pulls me against him in a tight hug, and rests his chin on the top of my head. "Ready for a slumber party?"

I nod. I'm ready. So very ready.

AT HIS HOUSE, Leo parks in the garage and takes my hand as he leads me inside. The place is dark and quiet. Neither of us speaks as he ascends the stairs with my fingers still entwined with his. At the top of the staircase is a hallway with rooms in either direction. He makes a left and pulls me through the doorway of the last room.

"I'll give you the full tour tomorrow," he says as an arm wraps around my back. He brings his mouth to mine slowly, gazing into my eyes.

I lunge for him, heart punching against my chest. He scoops me up, and we tumble onto the bed together. He rolls me onto my back and hovers over me. I'm overwhelmed by the scent of him in the bed and on top of me.

Leo undoes my jeans and pushes them down my legs. Then he's back kissing me as he strokes one hand down my bare skin. Over my hip, down my thigh, calf, and ankle. He's gentle yet strong and confident in his touches. Every move is with intent. I forgot how good he is at this. And how thrilling it feels to have his attention totally devoted to me.

So thrilling that I forget for a few seconds how great his body is and how much I'd like to see it again. I grip the hem of his T-shirt and tug upward. He leans back and pulls it over his head, then captures my mouth with renewed urgency.

My shirt comes off, bra and panties, too. I fumble with his jeans, unzipping them and pushing them down as far as I can. Eventually, he stands beside the bed to finish undressing. His hazel eyes are dark and hooded. My breaths come in quick and shallow gulps.

"Damn. I forgot how sexy you are."

With that declaration, he grabs a condom from a drawer in his nightstand and rolls it over his long, thick erection.

He drops kisses onto my stomach and chest as he climbs on top of me. His biceps flex as he holds himself up, and I slide my hands up his arms and around his neck to pull him down onto me.

There will be time for more foreplay later. Right now, I want him like I've never wanted anyone.

With a deep groan, he pushes inside. My breath catches, and my eyes flutter closed. Inch by inch, he fills me.

"So sexy," he murmurs against my jaw. "We fit together so perfectly."

Every compliment that spills from his gorgeous mouth makes me light up. He moves slowly inside of me.

"Are you okay?"

I open my eyes. "Perfect."

He chuckles, and the mood shifts between us. It's still hot and sexy, but it's playful too. He licks the side of my face, and I squeal and retaliate by biting his neck. It's like that for a while, but teasing and fun eventually bring out Leo's domineering side. He pins my arms above my head with one large hand wrapped around my wrist. His mouth crushes mine, hips driving me closer and closer to orgasm.

"Dream girl," he whispers, and it's my undoing. I fall apart around him, and he picks up the pace as he chases his own release.

He's beautiful as pleasure and bliss wash over him. His head drops and the loud, ragged breaths coming from him match mine. It's the only sound for several moments. When he lifts his head and locks his stare on me, that playful side returns.

His mouth lifts on one side and then the other, as if he's fighting his smile. "Ready for round two?"

"Wow. You weren't kidding. This really is the worst driver's license photo I've ever seen." It's Sunday morning, and I haven't left Leo's house yet. What can I say? I like the house. I like him too.

He reaches for the license, but I lean away from him on the couch and keep staring at it. His eyes are half-closed, making him look like he's either high or half asleep, and there's some sort of weird shadow going on that gives him a mustache.

He grabs me by the waist and hauls me close to him, then snatches it from my fingers. "I told you. I'm incapable of taking a good photo."

"That's not true. I got some good ones at the lake."

His mouth pulls up into that half-smile that makes my stomach flip.

"Are you close with your parents?"

"Yeah." He nods. They're both retired now, so they travel a little, and I don't see them as much as I'd like, but they make a few games each season.

"Do you go back home to visit them?"

"Not really," he admits. "I was better about it when my sister still lived at home."

"A sister. Just one sibling?"

"Yeah, just one. Mindy. She lives in San Francisco with her girlfriend. And you have one older sister, Cadence, right?"

"Good memory."

"Yeah, after I was blindsided finding out you were my coach's daughter, I did a little digging. I researched all of the coaches' families. No more surprises."

The front door opens, and a woman with dark hair pulled back in a long braid shuffles in carrying a stack of casserole dishes and dry cleaning over one arm.

Leo jumps up to help her. "Morning, Pam. This is Scarlett."

Leo tips his head toward me, and I lift a hand awkwardly.

Pam waves after Leo takes the casseroles from her. "Nice to meet you, Scarlett. That's a pretty name."

"Pam keeps this place from looking like my college dorm room," Leo says, falling back beside her. "She makes the best casseroles, and she picks up groceries and essentials for me, too. Hey, Pam?" he calls. "Can you get an extra toothbrush for Scarlett, so she'll leave mine alone?"

My cheeks heat. Totally busted. I give him a murderous look. "Not necessary. I'm never staying over again."

Leo wraps his arms around my waist and drops a kiss on my flaming hot cheek. "She absolutely is."

An amused smile twists her lips as Pam heads upstairs.

"How did you know I used your toothbrush?" I ask with a sheepish grin. "I dried it off and everything."

"It was on the wrong side of the counter." He lifts his left hand.

"I'm left-handed, babe."

"I'm sorry, but you really should have spares lying around for this type of situation."

"*This* type of situation?" He smirks like he has no idea what I'm talking about. *Please.*

"Girls staying over."

"There really haven't been any girls in a while," he says. "At least not any I'd let borrow my toothbrush." He brushes his lips against mine, and I can taste the minty toothpaste. He used it after me. "For the record, you can use my toothbrush any time. After last night, I don't think there's anything of mine your mouth hasn't touched."

"Noted. What time do you have to leave?" The fun is coming to an end. Or at least a pause. The team leaves for another road game today.

"Soon. Ash will be here any minute. You're welcome to stay and hang out as long as you want."

"I need to go home and show my face."

There's a knock at the front door, and Ash walks in. He smiles at me and tips his head. "Good morning, Miller."

I lift the fingers around my mug. "Good and morning are oxymorons."

Ash chuckles and looks at Leo. "You're right. She's a bundle of sunshine in the mornings."

I flip him off, which makes them both laugh harder.

"Ready to go?" Ash asks Leo.

"Yeah, I'll meet you in the car."

I take my coffee mug into the kitchen, rinse it, and put it in the dishwasher. "Don't worry. I'm just going to shower before I head out. For real this time." The hour we spent in the shower this morning did not make me any cleaner.

"I'm not worried. Pam's here. She's good at taking out the trash." He circles my waist and presses me into the counter from behind as he teases me.

"Oh my god, you did not just call me trash." I try to swat at him, but he's really strong. He bites my neck and then licks the spot.

"I'm kidding. You know I'm kidding." His attention on my neck continues. "Can I call you later?"

"I don't know," I say pointedly. "Can you?"

"I'm never going to live that down. Am I?"

"Not likely."

Ash beeps the horn outside. "I better go," Leo says, and slants his mouth over mine. His hand slides down the back of my bare legs and lifts me so I'm sitting on the counter, legs spread.

"I thought you had to go." Any protest dies on my lips as he brings his hands around to cup my boobs.

"Ash can wait a few more minutes."

"You're starting something you won't be able to finish," I tell him.

"Can't help it." His fingers brush the side of my panties as Ash lays on the horn again.

Leo chuckles and steps back. "Bye, dream girl. To be continued."

CHAPTER TWENTY-FOUR

LEO

A GOOD FRIEND

A s soon as we return from our road trip, I convince Scarlett to come back to my place and hang out for the day. I have homework, a massage scheduled, and a meeting with my agent, and she has editing to do for some photos she took, but I want her in my space, even if we can't be doing the same things.

I'm pacing the living room and talking to Daria while Scarlett sits on the couch with her laptop in front of her.

"Your new roster photo is a definite upgrade," she says, humor laced in her tone. "Not that it could get much worse."

"Glad you approve."

"Don't get ahead of yourself. I have a long list of gripes."

I laugh and shake my head. I love that about Daria. She isn't afraid to bust my balls. While she tries to convince me to do a few more interviews or appearances by going through the list of events I've been invited to, I walk around behind Scarlett and lean down to kiss her neck. She smells all girly. Her hair is some sweet floral scent and she has this peach lotion that she's always putting on her hands. I'm never going to be able to see a peach again and not think of Scarlett.

"Earth to Leo," Daria chirps.

"Sorry, Daria. I don't have time for any of those right now."

"An hour tops. Make an appearance, take a photo, bring a date," she says the last thing pointedly.

"I'll think about it."

"I'm sending over my top five. Pick one. And if you need a date, Tiffany Ryan would loooove for you to finally take her up on a joint appearance."

I grumble, which makes her laugh.

"Honestly, you're the only player I manage who isn't jumping to go to all the A-list events. Enjoy your youth."

I nip at Scarlett's neck. "I will. Promise." Just not the way she has in mind. Who needs A-list events or Tiffany when I have my dream girl right here?

I drop the phone and hurdle over the back of the couch, bouncing onto the cushion beside Scarlett.

"Those are good."

She tries to hide the screen with both hands. "Don't look. I'm not finished."

"Come on, let me see." I give her puppy dog eyes until she relents.

It's a picture of a couple embracing outside near a lake. She clicks through several more, all of the same couple. Some are posed, others aren't. They're all really good, as far as I can tell.

"This one is my favorite." She stops on one where they're smiling at one another.

"What kind of photographer do you want to be?"

She shuts her laptop and turns to face me. "The really good kind."

I pull her legs onto my lap. "You know what I mean. Do you want to take pictures of buildings, nature, weddings, events, sports?"

She laughs lightly. "I'm not sure yet. I think events would be fun. I like the idea of capturing candids of people out with friends and family, having a good time, living their best lives. Like those A-list events your agent is trying to get you to attend."

"You heard that, huh?"

"She talks awfully loud."

"I'll tell her you said so."

Her eyes widen. "Don't you dare, Leo Lohan. She's already trying to pawn you off on other women. I need her on my side."

"Uh-oh. Both names." I lean back, taking her with me, so she's lying on top of me. "I must be in trouble."

She hums, then threads her fingers through my hair. I take her mouth and palm her ass—a cheek in each hand. I never considered myself much of an ass man, but Scarlett's is perfect.

"I'm not interested in other women." I bring my hands up so I can slide them under her shirt. Her skin is warm, but she shivers as my fingertips run along her spine. I get her shirt off and jeans unbuttoned before my phone rings again.

I'm so hard and out of my mind for her that I have no plan to stop until Scarlett murmurs, "You should probably see who it is."

"Don't care."

She giggles, pulls away and reaches for my phone. "It's Ash."

"I'll call him back later."

"Answer it," she says. "If you don't, he might show up."

"Good point." I sit up and take the phone, then pull her back on top of me. I answer as I bury my face in her breasts. "Busy. Call you later?"

"Only take a second," he says. "I'm having a few people over later."

Scarlett works on the button of my jeans. I help, and she kneels in front of me and pulls both my pants and boxers down my legs.

"Great. See you then." I suck in a breath as she looks up at me with wet, swollen lips. She wraps a hand around the base of my dick, and I groan.

"Wait," Ash says before I can hang up. "I need to talk to you about something else. It's kind of important." Worst.timing.ever. I tighten my grasp on the phone and close my eyes as Scarlett wraps her mouth around the head of my dick.

"What's up?" I grit out.

"It's Talia. I think I might really be falling for her."

White-hot pleasure courses through me as Scarlett works her lips down, taking me all the way in and sucking hard.

"Really?"

"Yeah."

If this weren't the start of the best blow job of my life, I'd be more hesitant to believe him. His relationship with Talia has always been about convenience and sex. "Awesome, man. Congrats. Let's talk—"

"She's gorgeous and uncomplicated…"

I stop listening somewhere around the third adjective. Scarlett pops off my cock for a quick break and gathers her hair out of her face, pulling it to one side. I take over, holding it for her, and she smirks at me still on the phone. I give her an apologetic shrug, but she doesn't seem to mind because she swallows my dick again.

She licks me from balls to tip, swirling her tongue and then taking me to the back of her throat and sucking until her cheeks hollow. This is heaven.

I'm getting close to coming, and Ash is still going on about how great Talia is.

"That's really great. Happy for you. Call you la—"

Again, he cuts me off. "Yeah, I'm just not sure if I'm ready for a real relationship. You know? What if I screw it up?"

"You won't." I shudder as my balls draw up tight.

He bursts into laughter. "I can't keep this up anymore. I'm sorry, man. You're a good friend. Tell Scarlett hi for me when she gets her mouth off your dick."

Mother fucker.

I end the call and toss the phone. I cup the back of Scarlett's neck and pull her to her feet. I get her jeans and panties off as I kiss the hell out of her. I lie her down on the couch and hook an arm around one leg. "I almost came in your pretty mouth."

She arches into me as I drop my mouth to her pussy. "You should have. I wanted you to."

I push two fingers inside of her as I suck on her clit. When she starts to writhe underneath me, I grab a condom from my pants and cover myself. I help her onto her stomach and lift her ass up into the air.

Damn, there's no better sight. I line my dick up at her entrance and then rub the tip along her sensitive pussy before pushing all the way in.

"Leo," she gasps.

I squeeze her ass in my hands as I drive into her. It's never been like this with anyone. I don't want it to end, but nothing is sexier than watching her fall apart underneath me.

LATER, WE WALK over to Ash's house. When he sees me, he comes over with a big grin and pulls me into a hug.

"I'm sorry," he says. "I couldn't resist, but seriously, you're the best. Know I can always count on you."

"Next time, I'm letting it go to voicemail," I tell him.

"Hey, Miller." Ash hugs Scarlett next. "Glad you two could come up for air long enough to hang out."

"I was promised there would be food and alcohol," she says.

Ash runs a hand through his hair and laughs. "In the kitchen."

I lead Scarlett to the back of the house. A spread of mostly healthy foods is laid out buffet-style. I hand my girl a plate and watch with amusement as she piles it high with so much food I know there's no way she can eat it all.

"What?" she asks when she finds me staring. "I'm ravenous."

I hug her from behind and place a kiss on her neck. "Me too."

"Uh-uh. No more until I'm fed."

Chuckling, I let her go, fill my own plate, and we take them to the living room. Some of the guys are playing video games, a group is playing beer pong, and others are just hanging out in couples like Scarlett and me.

My girl isn't messing around. She doesn't speak for five minutes. She devours the food with little moans of appreciation that have me waiting for the second she's full, so I can drag her somewhere and make out some more.

I'm not sure I've ever been more anxious to get someone naked twenty-four-seven. It's never enough with Scarlett.

She leans back and sighs. "I think I'm going to live."

"Note to self, keep Scarlett fed, or sex is off the table."

She hits me with a playful smile. "You should really keep more food in your fridge."

She's not wrong. Besides the prepared meals I get from Pam, my refrigerator is pretty bare. It's just easier during the season, and it ensures I'm eating enough. Pam will be pleased to stock it with something besides her casseroles.

"Why is Daria trying to get you to go to more events?"

"All publicity is good publicity or some such nonsense," I say. "My contract is up after this year, and she thinks the more I'm seen out enjoying Minnesota, the better my chances are of getting a lucrative deal that will keep me here. In addition to playing stellar hockey, of course."

"Of course." She leans back against me so that her shoulder rests on mine. "Do you want to stay in Minnesota?"

"Yeah." I move my arm around her and pull her farther into my chest. "Minnesota is looking pretty fine."

She rolls her eyes and laughs. "Then I guess you better go to some A-list events."

"Will you come with me?"

Shifting so she can better look me in the eye, she says, "I'm not sure. People would know we're… whatever."

"Whatever?" I ask, grinning at her inability to define us. Whatever isn't the term I'd use.

"Dating, hooking up, whatever."

"I'm okay with that. Are you?"

We haven't talked about it, but I know we're reaching that point that we need to tell her dad before he finds out from someone else. I'd be lying if I said I wasn't nervous about that conversation.

She closes the space between us and presses her lips to mine. "I guess I am, Leo Lohan."

CHAPTER TWENTY-FIVE

SCARLETT

PLUS ONE

Jade comes to have lunch with me at work on Thursday. We take our food to the ice where the team is doing skills work—lunch and a show.

"How much longer until Anna is back?" she asks as she fishes out another chip from the bag in her hand and tosses it in her mouth.

"Not long at all. Another couple of days. A week at most."

"Then what?"

"Well…" I start and then sneak a glance at Leo on the ice. "I was thinking of applying for some entry-level photography jobs, working as an assistant or apprentice."

My best friend smiles. "Damn, he's good."

"Who?" I look around and then take a bite of my pizza.

"Leo fucking Lohan, that's who. He really did fuck the confidence back in you."

I smother a laugh with my arm as I chew and don't bother denying it. I didn't even realize how I was holding myself back until I wasn't. None of it was intentional, but I guess I wasn't willing to put myself out there professionally, so I didn't have to worry about another possible blow.

I swallow and take a long drink of water. "He's pretty great."

"I'm happy for you, babe." She squeezes my knee. "Truly. I've got my eye on him, but I'm happy for you."

"Thank you." I laugh. Honestly, he's so different than Rhyse, my early fears of dating him because he's a professional athlete are gone.

"So... are we telling Coach Miller any time soon?" She looks out at the action on the ice. Dad is skating around the perimeter, calling out orders every few seconds.

"We haven't talked about it, but yeah, I think we're going to have no other choice. We're spending so much time together, sneaking time during the day when we're both free and hanging out at night when he's not traveling. Mom knows I'm dating someone. She sniffed that out real quick, but I told her it wasn't serious, and I promised to bring him for Sunday dinner if that changed."

"Now, that's a dinner I want an invite to." She stands. "I have to get back to work. I got my first real writing assignment."

"Ooooh. Is it about bridezillas? Please say bridezillas."

"No." She smiles and gives her head a shake. "I'm writing about wedding cake. Specifically, the most sought out wedding cakes in the state."

"Ooooh, cake." I place a hand on my stomach. My appetite is like no other lately.

Her face lights up. "It's a short online piece about this amazing local wedding cake business. I go Saturday to meet the owners and sample some cake."

"Wow. Best job ever."

"You should come," she says and then nods her head. "Yeah. The magazine told me to grab a couple of photos while I'm there."

"Don't they have staff photographers for that kind of thing?"

"Only for the print edition. The online articles are a lot more casual." She sticks out her bottom lip. "Please? What's the perk of having a photographer bestie if she won't sample cake in exchange for a few photos?"

"I'm in," I agree. "Any excuse for cake."

AFTER WORK, LEO is waiting for me in the parking lot. My pulse races at the sight of him leaning against his Jaguar, arms crossed over his chest. He's in gray slacks and a white T-shirt, somehow dressed up yet still casual, and he smells divine.

"Hi," I say and move into his space, allowing the slightest body contact, knowing there are eyes everywhere around here. "You look nice. Hot date?"

He grins with a devilish glint in his hazel eyes. "Hope so."

He pushes off the side of his car and opens the passenger door.

I glance around before sliding into the seat, and he shuts me in. He rounds the car and hops in.

"Where are we going?"

"Dinner and a surprise."

I don't ask any more questions as he rests one hand on my thigh and drives away from the arena. He takes me to a little Italian place, where we sit side by side in a big booth.

"We're totally one of those obnoxious couples," I say, as the waiter flashes an amused smirk while dropping off the check.

"Don't care," he says as he briefly removes his hand to scribble his name on the receipt and pocket his card. When his hand returns, my nerve endings light up. "It's the only way I get to touch you."

His palm slides higher, and my stomach dips.

"Is the surprise going back to your place?" I ask hopefully.

Quiet laughter presses against my temple. He kisses me and then helps me up. "One more stop, and then you can take me home and ravage me."

We walk down the street, hand in hand. It's chilly out, and I left my jacket in the car.

I nuzzle against him.

He wraps an arm around my lower back. "This way."

We head down a side street and into a parking lot that runs along the back of the businesses. "I wasn't sure how you felt about being photographed with me, so we're sneaking in the back."

He holds open a door for me. I step inside tentatively. The warmth greets me, and noise from the building trickles into the backroom. There are shipping containers and cases of wine. Leo watches me as I take it all in. He grabs my hand and pulls me down a short hallway and into a sizable open space. Large black and white photographs are hung on the white walls, and people walk around and stand in front of them.

"Oh my gosh," I shriek a little too loudly for this type of event, then lower my voice. "A photography exhibit? That's what you chose as your A-list event?"

He shrugs it off. "I thought you might enjoy it."

I pause and raise up on my toes to kiss him. "Thank you."

"Welcome." He brushes his lips across my lips for a second kiss. "I have to go out front and make sure someone takes my photo to appease Daria. You'll be okay in here?"

"More than okay." I glance around at all the large photographs. I can't wait to inspect them closer.

"I'll be back in a minute," he promises.

I grab a flyer and a glass of champagne. I'm giddy as I walk around. The exhibit is called *Found Things*, and each photograph features an object or thing found in an unexpected place. A shoe hanging from a stoplight. A letter shoved in the jamb of a door. A soccer ball in the ocean.

Leo's back before I make it all the way around the exhibit.

"Sorry. That took longer than I expected." He rests a hand on my lower back.

"Did you do Daria proud?"

"Yeah. For now. I'm sure she'll be on my case again in a week or two."

"I'm having a hard time feeling sorry for you." I lift my champagne flute.

He takes it from me and sips it, then brings his mouth to mine. The sweet liquid mixed with his minty taste makes my body light up. It feels so much more intimate to be out in public with him, kissing and holding his hand, after being so careful at the arena.

"I mind them a lot less when you come with me," he says when he pulls back and looks into my eyes.

"Well, if they're all like this, I don't think I mind so much either."

"I'm serious," he says, interlacing our fingers. "Wanna be my plus one?"

"Like…" I'm slow to put words in his mouth. We've been spending a lot of time together, but it's still so new.

"I'm not dating anyone else. I don't want to date anyone else. Be my girlfriend, dream girl?"

"What about my dad and the team?"

"We'll tell him together." He leans in. "That is if you've decided you like me with my clothes on."

"I definitely prefer you naked," I say, resting a hand on his chest.

"The feeling is very mutual." He kisses me again. This PDA thing is addicting. "A buddy of mine is here with his wife. I want to introduce you."

"Okay." I hold his arm as we circle around the room. His buddy is a retired hockey player, Maxwell Smith. He's well-known enough that even I've heard his name.

Leo keeps his arm around my waist the entire time. I feel a surge of happiness that he so possessively keeps me by his side, but I'm anxious at being in public with him. We need to tell my dad soon because it's clear we aren't going to be able to keep this a secret for much longer.

We look at art, we run into more people he knows, and he continues to introduce me as his girlfriend. I'm practically humming with happiness from it all.

He hands me a second glass of champagne, and we find ourselves alone in front of one of the photographs.

"This was the best date I've ever been on." I drape my arms around his shoulders, balancing my flute carefully. "I might have to start calling you dream guy."

CHAPTER TWENTY-SIX

LEO

NAKED CELEBRATION

The following day, I arrive at the arena with Scarlett's coffee as usual. I stop in the break room, but the coffee is already made. Someone got here early. I'm smiling as I head to her office, thinking of last night. Daria already texted late after I got home to give me the thumbs up. I was tagged in a bunch of photos outside of the exhibit and I got bonus points because one of Maxwell and me blew up. He's been retired for two years, but the people of Minnesota still love him.

I head to Scarlett's office to deliver her coffee, but when I step into the doorway, my steps falter at the sight of Anna. She looks up from her desk and smiles. "Hi, Leo!"

"You're back." I've never been more disappointed to see Coach's assistant.

"Yeah. Just this morning." She blows out a breath and looks around frazzled. "I feel like I've been gone for a million years. Did you need anything? I haven't checked emails yet."

I take a step backward, retreating from her office. "No. I didn't need anything. I just saw the light on. Welcome back."

I can't believe how disappointed I am. I guess the good news is that I'll still see Scarlett, but with the season in full swing, it was nice to catch little glimpses of her during the day and steal kisses over breaks.

She's waiting for me outside of the locker room, coffee cup in hand. A smile spreads across my face at the sight of her. Damn, I'm going to miss seeing her every morning.

"I just stopped by your office," I say when I stop in front of her.

"Was I there being fabulously efficient?"

"Sadly no." I lean in and inhale her fruity-smelling shampoo. "There's an imposter in my dream girl's office."

I pull back at her soft laughter.

"I found out last night when I got home."

"I guess you'll have to get your own coffee from now on." I point to the cup in her hand.

"Oh, no. This is for you." She holds it out. "I thought it being my last day and all, I'd bring you a morning drink for a change. A small repayment. Plus, I wanted an excuse to see you."

"You never need an excuse." I take it but don't make any move to drink it.

"It's tea." She rolls her eyes. "I had a real moral dilemma ordering it, too."

I hand over hers. She reads the side where I had the barista write *Girlfriend* instead of her name. The guy looked at me like I was an idiot, but the smile on Scarlett's face makes it totally worth it.

"Where are you heading today?" I put a foot of distance between us when a couple of teammates appear in the hallway.

"I'm not sure, but I'll be at the game tonight, *boyfriend*." She brushes her fingers against mine and starts down the hall. "Do me proud."

We have a light practice, and then I go home to nap before the game. Ash stops by when it's time to go to the arena.

"Knock, knock," he says as he walks through the front door. "Ready?"

"Yeah. One more minute." I set the vase of roses on the kitchen table. The entire first floor is romance central—candles and flowers on every surface.

"What in god's name happened in here?" Ash looks horrified as he takes in my attempt at romance and seduction.

"Scarlett's staying over tonight after the game. Too much?"

"It's… intense." His brows climb up toward his hairline.

I may have gone overboard. "We made things official last night. I wanted to do something big for her."

"Congrats. You sealed the deal with your dream girl." He claps me on the shoulder. "I'm happy for you."

"Okay." I step back and scan the room one last time. She's either going to be pleasantly surprised or run out the door. Here's hoping she's wearing heels, so I can catch her if she chooses the second option.

Ash and I are both due in the media room before the game. As much as I dread interviews, the best time is always before the game when I can wax poetic strategy and optimism.

We're playing Pittsburgh tonight. We've tinkered with the lines enough that we're starting to get into a rhythm. Those early season nerves and worries are abating, and it's just pure excitement rushing through my veins during warmups.

As I stretch near the bench, I scan the seats Scarlett sat in last game with her mom, but they're empty. A ping of disappointment hits me, but then I see her making her way down the aisle with a drink in one hand, popcorn in the other. Jade is a step behind her. Warmth spreads through my chest, and another dose of adrenaline floods my bloodstream.

She looks up and catches me staring. Two fingers around her drink lift in a small wave, and my heart beats faster.

My family doesn't come to my games that often anymore. They're supportive, and I know they're proud, but we weren't a hockey family growing up. In fact, my family wasn't really into sports at all.

Having Scarlett here for me feels nice. I forgot what it was like to look up in the crowd and have people there just for you.

I don't have time to bask in it for long. The game is a full-out war. We lost to Pittsburgh in the playoffs last year and the hard set of Ash and Declan's jaws during the first period tells me I'm not the only one out for redemption.

At the first intermission, we're up by one and head to the locker room. I glance up at Scarlett, and she winks at me. Yeah, I think I could get used to this.

We pull out a victory, and after cooling down and showering, I'm the first dressed and ready to go. I don't have any after-game media tonight, so I slip out and text Scarlett.

She replies back with a selfie of her standing next to my car. Hell yeah.

Ash stops me before I leave. "Wild's tonight?"

"Got plans," I say with a grin.

"Right. The fiery seduction. Don't burn the place down. I'll call you tomorrow."

I make a beeline for the parking lot. Before Scarlett can see me, I hit the unlock on my car, and she jumps back.

She looks up, smiles, and jogs toward me. I let my bag fall to the ground and catch her.

"First one out. Impressive." Her breath is visible in the night air. "I missed you all day."

"I had incentive." I place a quick kiss to her mouth. "Missed you too."

"What are we doing tonight?"

"The guys are going to Wild's, but I was thinking we could celebrate by ourselves at my place?"

"Love that idea." She drops down and tries to pick up my bag. It weighs about as much as she does.

Laughing, I scoop her up, bag and all, and deposit them both in my car. When we get to my place, I do the same, picking her up and carrying her inside.

"I thought we were celebrating." She laughs as I strip out of my T-shirt and jeans in the entryway.

"Yeah." I pause, boxers still on. "A naked celebration. Was that not clear?"

A sexy, husky laugh sounds from her lips, and she pushes the only remaining clothing down over my hips. My dick springs up, happy to see her. She kisses the head of my cock, just as I remember I have a whole setup for this.

"Hold that thought, dream girl."

She shoots me a confused look as she pops off.

"Close your eyes," I instruct as I haul her into the living room. I light all the candles, then turn back to her. She's still fully clothed, but damn, if she isn't the sexiest girl I've ever seen. "Okay."

Her dark lashes flutter open, and she inhales sharply. "Leo Lohan."

"That's the first time you've said my full name, and I don't feel like I'm in trouble."

She shakes her head. "Definitely not in trouble. You did all this for me? Why?"

"I haven't had a girlfriend in…" I trail off. I don't even know how long. "That's not the point. The point is, I'm in this. All in. I really like you. I want to celebrate this." I motion between us.

I don't think I've ever said those words to someone. Definitely not naked.

Slowly, she pulls her shirt over her head. She kicks off her shoes as she unbuttons her jeans. There's a look on her face that tells me not to move, so I stare at her as she strips down in front of me in the glow of the candlelight.

She glances at my dick like she might be thinking of dropping to her knees again.

"I need to be inside of you," I say. "Condoms are upstairs."

"I'm on birth control," she says.

"I'm clean. I was tested last month, and I haven't been with anyone else."

My chest rises and falls in anticipation as she nods. Lust and excitement hang heavy in the air around us.

I set the stage for romance, but I fuck her hard against the wall the first time, too pent up and eager to hold back. I'm so into her. My living room is a scene straight out of a cheesy, romantic comedy, and I'm already thinking of all the other crazy shit like this I can do for her.

The second time is slow on the floor in front of the fireplace— the one thing I didn't light. When we're temporarily satiated, I grab blankets from the couch for us to lie on.

"You really haven't had a girlfriend recently?" Scarlett asks as she curls into my side. She runs a finger down my chest and over my stomach.

"No, not since college."

"Why not?"

"Uhh…" I try to think of a nice way to put that I was busy sleeping my way through puck bunnies for the first year.

She smirks like she can read the thoughts in my head.

"I let all of it get to me—the girls, the money, the attention."

"What changed? I mean, you haven't been in the league that long."

"At the end of my first year, we were in Boston for a three-game series. It was the first time I'd been back since I left college. After the second game, I went to a party at my college to catch up with some buddies. It was nuts." I still remember walking in and people calling out to me, and the girls—damn, the girls. I got attention from girls in college, but this was different. They were unabashedly down to fuck, and they let me know it by pulling me into a room where five girls fed me shots, and we did just that. Yeah, not my finest moment.

"I showed up late to practice the next day. I was so hungover." I shudder at the memory. "Coach Drew, my coach before your dad, took one look at me, benched my ass, and as soon as we got back to Minnesota, he kept me at the rink all-night skating and yelling until he was convinced I learned my lesson."

"And did you?"

"Yeah, definitely. And the photos that surfaced of that night a few days later only confirmed it."

She makes a face. "Ouch."

"Yeah. So, I focused on hockey. I've dated a little, but I guess you're the first girl I've really wanted more with."

She grins. That finger trailing along my chest lifts to the dimple in my cheek. "You know what this means, right?"

That I'm a goner? Totally head over heels for this chick? I shake my head. "What?"

She hops up and takes my hand to help pull me to my feet. "It's time to tell my dad."

CHAPTER TWENTY-SEVEN

SCARLETT

CONSEQUENCES BE DAMNED

I go over to Jade's apartment the next day after the cake testing, and we view all the photos I took, so she can finish her article.

"These are amazing," she squeals as we look through them together.

The storefront was tucked away on a side street, and the signage was almost non-existent. It's one of those places you could drive by every day and not know it's there. I took way more photos than she needed, but the way her face lights up makes me glad I did. She goes through them several times before picking out a handful she thinks she can use in the article.

"What are you doing this weekend?" I ask her after she's picked her favorites.

"Sam's frat is having a party."

"Is it weird going to frat parties now that you've graduated?"

"So weird." She sighs. "I think it might be time to break up with him."

"You said that two months ago, and then you moved in with him,"

I remind her. I never expected Jade to date him as long as she has. He's a nice guy, but they don't really have anything in common. When Jade was working at the bar, it was convenient to date someone who also worked at night, so their schedules lined up, but she's moving on, and he's still very much enjoying the college life.

"Who am I to talk," I say. "I am dating a hockey player after swearing I'd never date another professional athlete."

"Leo is not Rhyse."

I murmur my agreement. She's right about that.

"We're going to tell my parents on Sunday."

"Really?" A smile takes over her face.

"Yeah. He's so nervous. It's adorable."

"Are you kidding?" Jade snorts. "I'd be nervous to tell Coach Miller I was sexing his daughter on the regular, too."

I roll my eyes, but I'd be lying if I said I didn't feel a little apprehension about it myself. "It'll be fine. Leo's a good one."

"Yeah." She bobs her head, and the body language and tone of her voice tell me she isn't saying everything she's thinking.

"What?"

"It's nothing."

I slump forward and meet her gaze. "Don't hold out on me."

"You're right. From everything you've told me about Leo, it sounds like he's a good one."

"But?" My stomach clenches in warning. Is the other shoe about to drop?

"I don't want to see you get hurt again."

"Where is this coming from? You were the one pushing me toward him."

"As a hookup, yeah." She pulls out her phone, scrolls until she finds what she's looking for, and then holds it out to me. It's Leo the night of the photography exhibit, looking fine and smiling out front of the building. "Where were you in this photo or the dozen others from that night?"

"Inside," I say, slowly connecting the dots. "It isn't the same thing as Rhyse. We went in through the back because he wasn't sure if I wanted to be seen with him since we haven't told my dad. He went out front to get a few photos to make his agent happy. That's all."

Jade stays silent. I hand her phone back and repeat, "It isn't the same thing."

"Okay. You know the situation better than I do." She squeezes my knee. "You deserve someone who wants to show you off. That's all I'm saying."

I head back home a little while later, unable to shake Jade's concerns. It isn't the same, one side of my brain says, but the other can't stop worrying that I'm making excuses because I've fallen hard for Leo. I want this time to be different.

I open Instagram, and the first post on my feed is of Rhyse. The universe is obviously fucking with me. I give it the usual scan, but it doesn't hurt the same way it did in the past. He's no longer the guy I want to be with.

When we first started dating, I specifically avoided searching Leo's social media, so I wouldn't have to know the number or quality of his past relationships. We weren't there yet. Until the past couple of days, we'd only briefly talked about those things, and I didn't want to have it in the back of my head while I was spending time getting to know him. But now, with Rhyse popping up and reminding me why I didn't want to date Leo in the first place, I decide to Google him.

How bad can it be?

The first thing that pops up is a news article dated today that makes a cold sweat break out over my entire body. *Wildcats Leo Lohan in a New Relationship?*

Under the headline, there's a photo of the two of us at the photography exhibit. To anyone that knows me, it's clearly me, but whoever wrote this article has no clue. In the small write-up, it states only that Leo was spotted with an unknown woman looking cozy, and then the article proceeds to detail out his dating history. Here it is, everything I wanted to know laid out in chronological order: Leo's entire dating history.

It starts with the awful college scandal he told me about. A younger Leo, shirtless, with a girl on either side of him, stares at the camera with a hazy expression. That's the tamest of the pictures from that night.

I skip past to see who else he's dated since. He said none of them were serious, but that hasn't stopped him from dating. And the girls he's been paired with in the past two years are as stunning as I feared. Models, college girls, blondes, brunettes, redheads, all as beautiful as the next. The gorgeous blonde sports reporter his agent has been trying to get him to go out with is the latest woman he's been cited as dating.

I groan, but now that I've ripped off the Band-Aid, I can't stop. I type in his name and scroll through pictures of him at various events with dates. I skip over any sports-related news and go right for the trashy tabloids. I suddenly need to know it all. My stomach twists. Here he is with all of these women he said meant nothing, and I'm an unknown in a blurry photo that will probably be forgotten tomorrow.

I should be glad, but the irrational part of me that wants to be his in a way that these girls weren't, wants the whole world to know—

consequences be damned.

I get ready for the game. Leo has a standard pre-game routine, and I know if I text him and warn him, there's a good chance it'll screw with his game, so I don't.

Still, I know that as soon as the game is over, I need to tell him about the article, and then we need to have an awkward conversation with my dad. I can't wait for Sunday. If that's the only reason he doesn't want to be pictured with me, then I'll know.

And I *need* to know.

CHAPTER TWENTY-EIGHT

LEO

JUST FRIENDS

When the final buzzer sounds, denoting the end of the game, I skate off the ice and follow my team down the tunnel. Losing always sucks, but never more than when you know you're the better team.

Tampa Bay should have been an easy win. Three of their top players are out with injuries, and they've struggled to patch together a line that can get anything going. Until tonight.

Coach is grim-faced and quiet in the locker room after yelling for fifteen-minutes straight. He attempts a smile and tells us to keep our heads up. I cool down and then get summoned with Jack and Ash to the media room.

I pull on a Wildcats T-shirt and shorts and run through the things Blythe told me to say during interviews if I was stuck. I shouldn't need to say a lot. The media loves Jack, and he'll be happy to answer whatever they throw at him, but if I'm going to be a leader on this team, or any team, I need to be prepared.

The three of us take our seats behind the microphones placed along a row of tables, facing reporters and cameras. Coach comes in last and takes a seat next to me. He starts us off, fielding a few questions on what went wrong and how we move forward.

I'm starting to tune it all out when someone calls my name. I sit forward, so my mouth is near the microphone.

Tiffany Ryan, not her real name, stands. There's no need to stand other than she wants all eyes on her. I squirm. Tiffany is the reporter from camp who scoped me out during an interview. You know, the one everyone thinks I slept with because I was staring down—NOT at her tits. I knew it was only a matter of time before I ran into her again.

I have prepared for this moment. *Do not look anywhere but at her face. Do NOT look anywhere but at her face.* I repeat it over and over in my head.

"Leo, you appeared distracted tonight." She pauses to give me time to respond, but like Blythe taught me, I stay silent until she asks an actual question. She's fishing right now, and I'm not taking the bait.

Her dark red lips pull into a devious smile. "Is your new relationship with Coach Miller's daughter causing tension between you and the rest of the team?"

"My relationship with…" I gulp, look at Coach, then Ash and Jack, like they might be able to bail me out, then back to Tiffany.

"Scarlett Miller." Her brows furrow in fake confusion. She holds up a phone, and even from eight feet, I can tell it's her. "This isn't you and Scarlett Miller at a photo exhibit earlier this week?"

"We're friends," I say confidently. Fuck, it's hot in here. "And no, it has not caused tension between the team and me." At least not until this moment. "Tonight Tampa came ready to play, and we didn't."

Her gaze flicks back to the phone. "Just friends?"

I nod. A small dip of my chin that feels like a wrecking ball. Yeah,

yeah, we look like more than friends. We are more than friends, but this isn't exactly the time or place to announce it. Dammit, Tiffany.

"Next question," Coach asks, with a side-eye in my direction.

I don't hear anything after that, thanks to the ringing in my ears. Oh fuck, this isn't good. Did I really call Scarlett my friend in front of... I count the number of cameras aimed at the front of the room and feel like throwing up.

As soon as the press conference is over, I bolt.

"Slow your roll, Lohan." Jack presses a hand to my chest. He juts his chin behind me. Right, Coach. Fuck. I don't know which conversation I'm dreading more.

We file out into the hallway, and I wait for Coach to catch up. Head lowered and voice quiet, he says, "Be in my office tomorrow at eight. We'll talk about the photo then."

"Coach, I'm—"

He holds up his hand like he physically can't handle me saying one more word. "Tomorrow. First thing."

In the locker room, Ash is sitting at his stall next to mine.

"And the award for the first scandal of the season goes to..." He holds out both hands in my direction dramatically.

"Damn." I drop onto the bench. "I really fucked this up."

"What'd Coach say?"

"Nothing. He told me to be in his office first thing tomorrow."

He inhales sharply, teeth clenched so that it makes a whistling noise.

I pull my phone from my pocket. I have texts and voicemails from everyone but the person I was hoping.

"What the hell am I going to say to her?"

"You mean to your *friend*, Scarlett?"

"We were supposed to tell her dad together. I froze. I didn't know what to say." I fumble through excuses, and they all suck.

The look Ash gives me tells me as much.

I shove everything in my bag as fast as I can. "I gotta go. Text you later."

"Good luck, buddy."

I head out to my car and text Scarlett to find out where she is. I don't know if she's seen the interview yet, but I know it won't be long if she hasn't.

She responds back to let me know she's at my place and that's where I head, as fast as I can.

She's waiting in her car when I pull up. I can tell the instant I get a glimpse of her face that she saw.

"I'm so sorry," I say. "They caught me totally off guard."

She lets me hug her. "I know. I saw the article this afternoon. I wanted to give you a heads-up, but there wasn't time."

I nod slowly. Yeah, a heads-up definitely would have been nice. "Did your dad already know too?"

"I don't think so. The article referred to me as an unknown. I guess they figured it out sometime during the game."

"Should we talk to your dad tonight?"

"I'll talk to him. He's going to be upset I didn't tell him before he found out like that."

"I'm pretty sure any anger is going to be directed at me. I'm supposed to report to his office in the morning."

Scarlett gives me a sympathetic face. I take her hand and start to walk inside, but she doesn't budge. "Wait. I need to ask you something."

"Sure. Anything."

Her gaze darts to the ground and then slowly lifts to meet mine. "Was my dad really the only reason you didn't want the media to know about us?"

I replay her words twice in my head. "I don't follow."

"I've been in relationships where we kept things secret, and I don't want to do that again."

"The ex?" I say, slowly piecing together her concern.

"Yes. He kept us a secret for the entirety of our relationship."

"You said you were together for a year?"

"Yeah, an entire year that I was hidden from his public image. It wasn't all his fault; he was following the advice of people he trusted, but Leo, I can't do that again. So, if you aren't ready to be with me, really be with me, then I can't do this."

I cup her face. "I'll call every reporter I know right now if that's what you want, baby."

One side of her mouth pulls up into a smile. "I don't think that's necessary, but I do need to know that I'm not going to be kept separate from your professional life. I don't want to get in the way. I just want to be a part of your whole life. And I don't want to be Leo Lohan's friend."

"You're Leo Lohan's girlfriend, and I promise, no more hiding," I say. "Wherever I go, you go. I want to hold your hand everywhere we go."

"Okay." She lets out a breath. "Good."

She wraps her arms around me and squeezes me tight. I sigh in relief. "Want to go to Wild's? The guys are all there, and I can show you off. A little PDA, and I'm positive we can make the front page of the news."

"Next game for sure," she says. She peers up at me and bites the corner of her lip. "I think tonight I need to go home and talk to my dad."

"Right." Oh man, my palms sweat. "Do you want me to come?"

"I better talk to him first." She smiles. "I'll call you later, boyfriend."

CHAPTER TWENTY-NINE

SCARLETT

BE NICE, DADDY

A s much as I'd like to, I can't stay and hideout at Leo's. I know I
need to talk to my parents, especially my dad.

Mom's already in bed, but Dad is in the kitchen when I get
home. I pull a bowl from the cabinet and take a seat next to him. I
smile at the Fruity Pebbles box.

"How'd you know I was on my way?"

"I didn't," he says and continues spooning the cereal into his
mouth.

"So, uh, I'm dating Leo." I sit beside him.

He chuckles softly. "Little late on the news for that one."

"I'm sorry that you found out from someone else. We wanted to
make sure we really liked each other before we said anything."

"And?" His tired gaze meets mine.

"I really like him."

"He called you his friend and made a spectacle in the media room."

I'm quick to defend him. "He panicked. We were going to tell you
together this weekend."

I get a grumpy, throaty noise in response. Dad finishes his cereal and rests an elbow on the counter. "Are you sure about this?"

"I am. Leo isn't like Rhyse. He wasn't hiding me. We were just trying to decide how much we liked one another before we made a big deal of it."

"That isn't what I meant."

"Then I don't follow."

"Leo is a nice guy, honey. If you were anyone but my daughter, I'd have no problem signing off approval. He has a good head on his shoulders for someone his age."

"I know his life is busy. So is yours, and you and Mom make it work."

"It isn't just that. These guys are under constant scrutiny in the media. Part of me selfishly loved that Rhyse kept you out of all of that. It may not have been his intention, but he shielded you from a lot by keeping you out of the headlines."

"I can handle it," I assure him. The things people said to and about me with Rhyse were so much worse than anything I've seen about Leo or the women he dated.

"I'm not going to try to talk you out of it. I know you're too stubborn for that anyway, but think about it and be careful."

"It'll be fine. I promise."

"Okay." He presses a kiss to my temple. "As long as you're happy."

"I am. You're really okay with this then?"

"If you're happy and he can keep the nonsense away from the ice, then yes." He gets up, puts his bowl in the sink, and starts to leave the kitchen.

I swivel on the bar stool. "Leo said he has a meeting with you tomorrow morning."

Dad grins.

"Be nice, Daddy."

I GO TO the arena the next day after working the early afternoon shift at the bar. Leo has a quick break after practice, and he climbs into my car with a groan. He leans over and somehow manages to lean his big frame over the console and put his head in my lap.

"Rough day?" I thread my fingers through his unruly hair.

"Your dad hates me," he mutters against my thigh.

"That bad, huh?" I knew by the look in Dad's eyes last night that he wasn't going to let Leo off that easily. "I'm sorry."

"I'll survive. Totally worth it." He burrows in between my legs and nips at my inner thigh.

"I brought food. It's in the back seat. How long until you have to be back?" The guys have an away game tomorrow, but they're leaving tonight for Dallas.

He sits up with another groan. "An hour. Factor in an extra fifteen because I can't feel my arms or legs."

"What exactly did he do to you?"

"Pushups. Squats. More pushups."

"Because you're dating me?"

"Because I made a scene in his media room."

"Oh." I pull away from the arena and drive toward my house.

He's quiet in my passenger seat until he realizes where we're going. He sits up and shoots me a panicked look. "Are you trying to get me killed?"

"Relax. Dad never comes home during the day, and Mom is at school for another two hours."

We walk into the house, and I lead Leo straight down to the basement.

"This is me." I drop my purse on the dresser.

"This is nice." He looks around with a smile.

"It's a little cramped." I point to my mom's crafting supplies on one side. "But it's temporary. I have enough saved up to move out, but I want to nail down a job before I commit to a lease."

"Makes sense," he says, walking around taking in every detail. He finally sits on the couch with his food.

He hands over his fries with a smirk, like he knows I really got them for myself.

"My mom took the news much better than Dad," I say, sitting beside him and folding my legs underneath me. "She's already setting a place for you at Thanksgiving."

"Sounds nice." His mouth quirks up into a smile.

"Do you see your family around the holidays?"

He nods. "I go home for a day or two at Christmas when I can."

"They never come here?"

"Nah. My aunts and uncles, cousins, grandparents are all in Boston, so it just makes more sense that I go to them."

"Well, you're welcome here." I realize I might be putting a lot of pressure on something so new, especially considering my dad is his coach, and they're on shaky ground. "You know, assuming I'm not sick of you by then."

"Too late. Your mom's set a place for me. I'm coming."

It's all so easy and natural. Even here in my parents' basement.

"I can't wait. Let's just make sure to sit you *all* the way at the other end of the table from my dad."

He grimaces. "I really thought he liked me."

"He does." I scoot closer, and he steals one of my fries. "He just likes me more."

CHAPTER THIRTY

LEO

SHIT LIST

I get to the plane way, way, *wayyy* early to make sure I'm in my seat ready to go to Dallas before Coach arrives.

He didn't threaten to trade me or bench me, so there's that. He did, however, inform me that if I couldn't keep my head in the game and show up today ready to go, he'd strip me of the A.

And stripping me of the A, essentially demoting me, is the fastest way to get traded next season. I don't want that. Especially now. Scarlett and I are just getting started. I can picture a life in Minnesota.

"You're alive," Ash says as he falls into the seat beside me.

"For now, anyway."

My buddy, soon-to-be former buddy, laughs, then mocking me says, "We're friends. Just friends."

I scratch the side of my face with my middle finger.

His laughter gets louder. "Did you get Daddy Miller's permission to date his daughter or what?"

I bob my head side to side. "He's not thrilled, but as long as I don't let it interfere with the team, then we're cool."

"Well, for what it's worth, if I had a daughter, I'd totally let her date you."

"Yeah?"

"Hell yeah," he says more enthusiastically.

"Thanks."

He rests his elbows on either armrest. "What about me?"

"What about you?" I ask as I stretch out and get comfortable for the flight.

"If you had a daughter, could I date her?"

I haven't given a lot of thought to having kids, but I get a pretty great visual of a dark-headed girl with a smile like Scarlett's.

"Oh, uhh…" I struggle to decide on the right answer. Ash is great. No question about it, but his dating history is a little all over the place.

His mouth falls open, and his eyes widen. "Seriously? I'm not good enough for your daughter?"

His voice carries, and people look our way.

"Can you not draw any attention to us today?" I whisper and duck my head.

"Why not?"

"Because I'm trying to stay off Coach's shit list."

"Not that. Why can't I date your daughter? Maybe she's my dream girl."

I rub my forehead with two fingers. "I don't have a daughter."

He presses me with a hard stare.

"If I did, then I'd let you date her," I relent. I'm proof that when you meet the right girl, the past shit doesn't matter. "But I'd be keeping a close eye on you."

One side of his mouth pulls up into a knowing smile. "Couldn't blame you there."

In Dallas, we go to the arena for a light practice first and then to the hotel.

"Declan's swinging by. We were going to hang and have a drink here, or we can go downstairs," Ash says as I'm about to call Scarlett.

"Whatever." I pull out my headphones. "I'm gonna take a walk and call my girl."

I slip on my headphones and FaceTime her as I leave the room.

Her face fills the screen, and Scarlett hits me with a smile that makes my chest warm.

"Hi, gorgeous."

"Hey. Are you at the hotel or the arena?"

I tilt my phone to show her the hallway of the hotel. "We just got here. What are you doing?"

"Getting ready to go out with Jade."

Jade's head pops into view. "Hey, Leo."

"Hey, Jade. What sort of trouble are you two going to get up to?" I take the stairs down to the first floor and sit in one of the chairs adjacent to the lobby.

Jade disappears as fast as she appears.

"She's saying goodbye to Sam before we leave," Scarlett answers when Jade doesn't.

"You need to go?"

She shakes her head. "Uhh... that was my polite way of saying she's going to give him a blow job. We have a few minutes."

She shifts the phone, and I get a glimpse of the tight green dress wrapped around her.

I bark a laugh. "Fuck, I miss you already. You look nice."

"We're going to this bridal runway show." A slight blush creeps up her face. "It's for Jade's column."

"You better sit far away from the stage then so you don't show up the models."

She rolls her eyes, but her smile doesn't falter.

"A few minutes, huh? I can work with that."

Her eyes darken. "You're in the middle of a hotel."

"But you aren't." My back is to a wall, and I hold my phone closer to me so no one else can see the screen.

With a hesitant smile, she pulls the fabric of her dress down until the black lacy bra she's wearing is the only thing blocking her tits from view. "Damn, baby. You're so gorgeous."

A shadow falls over me, and someone clears their throat. I look up to scowl at whoever has invaded my space and stare straight into Coach Miller's irritated face.

"Coach. Hi," I squeak out, "I was just talking to Scarlett."

"Oh my god," she mumbles. I take a quick glance down to make sure she's righted her dress before I show him the screen.

"Hey, Daddy."

"Hi, honey." His face transforms when he speaks to her, but slips right back to irritated when he speaks to me. "When you finish here, can you grab Maverick and Tyler for a quick line meeting?"

"Absolutely," I say a little too eagerly.

Scarlett laughs. Glad one of us can find the humor in this situation. Damn, that could have been hella awkward.

"I'll call you tomorrow," I say. "Have fun with Jade."

"Good luck."

I don't know if she means with Dallas or her dad.

CHAPTER THIRTY-ONE

SCARLETT

DITTO, BABY

Our first outing as an official couple comes on a Saturday night after a home game. Butterflies flutter in my stomach as we walk in to Wild's, hand in hand.

Ash is the first to see us, and he stands from the bar and hugs Leo, slapping him on the back and smiling at me. "Miller!"

"Hey, Ash."

He rests a hand on his hip and keeps smiling at us. "So happy to see you two out. What do you want to drink? I'm buying."

We grab drinks, and when Tyler and Maverick get up to play pool, we take their seats at the bar.

It's still busy with fans from the game, which means the guys have people coming up to them constantly. Leo takes the attention in stride. He shakes hands and makes small talk with anyone who approaches, but he never turns his back to me.

When we get a moment by ourselves, he runs his hands up my bare thighs and rests them on my hips. I wore his favorite black skirt tonight, and I love the way he can't stop touching me.

"Wanna play darts?" he asks, voice low and husky.

I shake my head.

"Pool?"

"Not unless you do."

His head moves side to side. "Not particularly."

"We sort of got in a routine of celebrating on our own, and now it's all I can think about." Sex… it's my new favorite way to celebrate.

"I promised Ash we'd hang for a bit."

"Okay." I tilt forward and brush my boobs against his shoulder.

His eyes darken. He stands, drains his beer, and pulls me to my feet. "Pool. Let's play some pool."

Laughing, I follow along. If Leo thinks watching him lean over and shoot a pool stick is going to make me want him less, he is mistaken. The man is seriously fine, and he's all mine.

I glance over my shoulder as I line up to take a shot and catch him punching Tyler next to him.

"Eyes off her ass."

"Dude. I wasn't looking," Tyler says with a chuckle but moves off to the side.

"Aww, let them look, baby. I'm only leaving with you."

He grumbles under his breath.

Fully-clothed celebrating isn't so bad either, I suppose. If nothing else, it's delayed gratification for the naked celebration I know is still coming.

And, I enjoy hanging out with the guys. Now that my dad knows they all seem more relaxed around me.

"Is that Ash's girlfriend?" I ask Leo when I see his friend at the bar kissing a pretty girl with legs that never seem to end. Her blue hair is twisted into a braid that falls down to her ass.

"Sort of. They have a mutual interest." Leo's lips twitch.

"Sex?"

"And hockey."

"Hockey or hockey players?" I ask.

"The latter for her." He shrugs. "Her name is Talia. I'll introduce you if they come up for air."

As I look around, I realize very few of the guys have girls with them.

"Does no one have an actual girlfriend?"

"Well, I do," Leo says, getting an eye roll from Tyler. "And Maverick does."

At his name, Maverick looks up and shakes his head. "Nope, not me." He raises his left hand and shows off the wedding band on his left ring finger.

"You're married?" I ask, unable to hide the shock in my voice.

He grins. "Yep. Three months now. She's coming up next weekend."

I did not peg him for the type that's settled down at such a young age. "I'd love to meet her."

"We can probably give up an hour or two of sex." He nods to himself like he's thinking it over. "Yeah, let's do it. Party at my place next Saturday."

Leo and I stay for one more game of pool and then head out. It's cold outside, and the wind is gusty. I pull my coat snug around me, and Leo's big hand shields mine as we hurry to his car.

We make it home, but not all the way inside before Leo takes me in his arms and kisses me hard. He sets me on the hood of his car, and his fingers slide under the hem of my sweater. I shrug out of my coat and then work on his jeans. We might have strung out the delayed gratification a little too long.

"This skirt is my favorite," he says as he steps between my legs. It has buttons up the front, and he loves undoing them. I lean back as he works his way from the bottom up. When he gets high enough to realize I'm not wearing any panties, his gaze snaps up. "Fuuuck, baby. You've been naked under here all night?"

I nod.

"And bending over the pool table?" His eyes are like saucers.

"I didn't bend over that far."

He hooks an arm around my right leg and pushes me back onto the hood of his car. He wastes no time covering my pussy with his mouth. I'm too keyed up, too high on this connection between us. My orgasm builds quickly, and he doesn't let up even when I warn him I'm close. Leo knows exactly how to get me there and exactly what pace my body and soul needs at any given moment.

He takes me over the edge with my heart racing and my body tingling from head to toe. He kisses his way up to my stomach and then pulls back to stare at me.

"Now, this is a fucking vision. You naked on top of my car."

We get in the hot tub next, where I return the favor, bringing him to orgasmic bliss with my mouth. He slides into the water from where he was sitting on the edge, and I sink down in front of him so that my shoulders are under the water. I press my chest to his, and Leo's arms circle my waist.

His hair is messy, and water drips down his chest.

"That first night, I thought about what it would be like to photograph you like this. You are very sexy all wet and naked."

"Ditto, baby."

I wrap my legs around him and place my head against the left side of his chest. I can hear his heart beating at the same rhythm as mine.

Neither of us speaks for a long time; instead, we just hang on to one another.

There's something very reassuring about getting to that point with someone where you don't need to say a word to know you're on the same page. It's too soon to talk about love and forever, but those are my thoughts as he holds me in the dark. For the first time in a long time, I've found someone that I can see a future with. It's exhilarating and absolutely terrifying.

The next day I go with Jade on another writing assignment. She has a meeting with a hotshot wedding planner for an article, and I convinced my sister to join us and do some shopping for the baby.

"I saw photos of my favorite celebrity couple on Instagram this morning," Jade says as she pulls into the parking lot. "I rescind my concerns."

"Not necessary. If it weren't for you, I might not have had the balls to ask him straight up where we stood."

"And is that place you're standing heading toward wedding bells?" Her eyes light up. "I could do a story on you two. It would be epic!"

"Slow your roll there, Katie Couric."

"I'm just saying, Vivian is the wedding planner, so you might want to book her just in case." She pulls into a parking space and cuts the engine.

My phone pings. "Cadence is here."

"Okay. This shouldn't take long. She could only fit me in for thirty minutes. I'll call you when I'm done and catch up. Don't buy too much adorable baby stuff without me." Jade heads off in one direction, and I go the other.

My phone rings before I've reached the door. I stop and move off the sidewalk, expecting Cadence or Jade, but it's Rhyse's number flashing on the screen.

My pulse thrums loudly. I must hold my breath because when I finally exhale, my lungs burn.

I keep staring at his name while it seems that everything else around me ceases to exist. I answer out of sheer curiosity. If I don't, I know I'll wonder. And I don't want to waste any more time wondering about Rhyse.

"Hello?"

"Scarlett." I can hear the smile in his voice. "Hi. Hello. I wasn't sure if you'd answer. How are you?"

"Good. I'm good." I fall silent. This is too weird. The polite thing would be to ask him how he is, but Rhyse and I haven't been on polite, speaking terms in months. Our breakup wasn't exactly messy, but it was final, and neither of us bothered to keep in contact. We were at a stalemate, and there was nothing left to say.

"I'm in the States," he says. "We have a race next weekend."

"Austin?" I ask because, try as I might, I still remember his schedule.

"Yes, but I came early hoping to see you. I'm in Minnesota."

"What?" I look around like his being in the same state makes him visible.

"I'm at the airport. Can I see you?"

"I'm not home, Rhyse. I'm out shopping with Cadence."

"I'll come there. Just give me an address."

"I don't think that's a good idea." The thought of facing him again makes me anxious. Not now. This is all wrong.

"Ten minutes, Scar," he says. "There are things I need to say."

CHAPTER THIRTY-TWO

SCARLETT

THE FEELING IS NOT MUTUAL

For months I dreamt about this moment—Rhyse calling me out of the blue and demanding to see me. In the dream, he'd fall at my feet and tell me how much he missed me, how life isn't the same without me by his side. And then, of course, after playing tough, I'd take him back, and we'd return to our happy bubble, traveling the world together and making love in fancy hotels.

But now that it's at least partially based in reality (he called and is on his way to see me), it feels more like a nightmare.

Cadence tries to distract me with cute baby clothes while I wait for Rhyse to drive from the airport. I try to pretend like I'm going about my day and just meeting up with a friend for a quick, meaningless chat, but I find myself staring toward the door of the baby boutique every time it opens.

"Are you finding out the gender?" I ask as I hold up a tiny tent that covers little boys while you change them so that you don't get peed on.

She "ooohs" like a pee tent is the cutest thing. "Yes, definitely. I want to be prepared."

I toss the tiny pee tents at her, and she laughs. That laughter dies, and my heart stops at the sound of a sports car outside. I know it's him, even before I spot the shiny red Ferrari.

"Are you going to be okay?" Cadence asks.

"Yeah. I'm happy with Leo." Saying it out loud, I realize how true it is, and I straighten my shoulders. "Maybe it'll be good to get closure."

"Good. I really like having you home. We should do this more often."

I don't point out that the reason we don't has more to do with her workaholic schedule than anything else. I have a feeling that when the baby comes she'll get a dose of the work-life balance she's been missing.

My phone lights up with a text from Rhyse saying he's here. I inhale a deep breath and let it out slowly.

"I won't be long."

She squeezes my arm. "Okay. I'm here if you need me."

I text him back and walk outside. It's windy and cold, but the sun is out, offering a little warmth as I sit on the metal bench in front of the store.

My leg bounces with nerves as I watch him cross the street. I focus on breathing and keeping my heart rate under control.

He's as handsome as the last time I saw him. His hair is dark and thick. Curly strands have been wrangled under a hat, boasting his team and sponsor.

His clothing—jeans and a long-sleeved white T-shirt covered with a black leather jacket—are simple, but every eye on the block follows him. He has that something about him that makes people stop and look.

I stand when he approaches. Do I hug him? Do we shake hands? This is so weird. While I'm still deciding, he steps into me with a broad smile and wraps his arms around me.

"Scarlett." He breathes me in as he says my name.

I always liked the way my name sounded with his accent, and his scent is still familiar, as is the way the top of my head rests comfortably under his chin.

I pull back first and take a seat on the bench. He sits close and rests an arm behind me. "You look fantastic. It's so good to see you."

I still haven't quite figured out how to feel, let alone act, but there's no sense in denying it, he looks good too, and I tell him as much.

He nods toward my camera bag. "Are you working as a photographer now?"

"Oh, uh. No. Not yet. I thought I might take a few photos of Cadence buying things for the baby."

"Cadence is pregnant?"

I nod.

He beams at the news. "When is she due?"

"Next April."

"That's exciting. I bet your mom is over the moon."

My stomach is in knots, and my palms are sweaty. I can't make small talk with this man like he didn't crush me just months ago.

"What are you doing here, Rhyse?"

"I miss you."

Three words that I dreamt of coming from his lips so many times.

"Do you miss me?" he asks.

"No." I can tell my response, as well as the hard edge in my tone, catches him off-guard. "I did at first, but I moved on."

"I saw," he says quietly. "The hockey player."

"His name is Leo."

"Right."

"Is that why you're here? You saw that I moved on and decided you suddenly cared that I left?"

"I never stopped caring, Scarlett. You knew I couldn't chase after you."

It's true. I did know that. Still, I hoped he would.

"This is the first chance I've had to see you, and here I am." His smile is crooked and tentative, and it hits me that he's as nervous as I am.

"You shouldn't have. Too much time has passed. I'm happy."

"It's serious then, with you and this Leo?"

I don't answer right away, and Rhyse moves closer. "I love you, Scarlett. If there's any part of you that still loves me too, then give me another chance."

"What will your team say about that?" I ask and cross my arms at my stomach.

"I'll deal with them."

A flash of anger bolts through me, and I curl my hands into fists. Now he'll deal with them? I get that people make mistakes, and maybe my leaving did help him realize what he wanted, but to have him just wave away the biggest reason we didn't work, like it's an easy fix, straight pisses me off. If he'd dealt with them six months ago, we'd still be together.

It's that thought that calms me. I'm not a big believer in things happening for a reason, but if he hadn't broken my heart, I wouldn't be here in Minnesota with my family.

I'm going to be an aunt! One that gets to see my little nephew or niece any time I want. My heart is here. And yeah, Leo's a part of that.

Leo freaking Lohan. The guy I never wanted to fall for, but totally have. I like that he's so quick to apologize when he messes up, that he doesn't make me guess how he's feeling or where his head is at, and most of all, I like who I am with him. Slowly, I've let my guard down, and he's earned my trust.

It's scary, and I have no idea if he's falling as hard for me as I am him, but I want to see where things go.

"I'm happy here, Rhyse. Being in Minnesota close to my family and, yes, with Leo. The breakup was good for both of us."

He nods slowly. "I have to leave for Austin tonight, but I want to see you again before I fly back home."

"Rhyse—"

He cuts off my protest. "Think about everything I said. It will be different this time."

He tucks my hair behind my ear and leans forward to brush a soft kiss on my lips that startles and surprises me.

"What the hell?" Jade's voice has Rhyse pulling back. My best friend glares at him. I lift shaky hands to my lips.

"Hi, Jade. Good to see you." Rhyse stands to greet her.

My best friend is not messing around. "The feeling is not mutual."

Rhyse looks back at me. "I should go."

I get to my feet to say goodbye. He comes in like he's going to kiss me again, and I turn my face, so he kisses my cheek. "I'll leave a ticket for you at will call. Give me another chance."

He starts back down the street. Jade doesn't even wait until he's out of earshot before she starts going off about him.

"What the hell is he doing here?"

"US Grand Prix this weekend." I think I'm in a daze. Did that just happen?

"Okay, well, that doesn't explain why he's *here*."

"Come on," I say. "Let's find Cadence. That way, I only have to answer both of your questions once."

CHAPTER THIRTY-THREE

LEO

INCOMING

Scarlett comes over to my house after practice with an overnight bag slung over one shoulder. The team leaves tomorrow morning for a series of away games. It'll be the longest I've gone without seeing my girl since we started hanging out.

I take her bag and laugh. "Are you going on a week-long trip I don't know about?"

"Ha. Ha." She rolls her eyes as I mock struggle to carry her bag. For real though, it's way too heavy for one night.

"Did you have a good time shopping with Jade and Cadence?"

"Yeah." Her tone is distant and distracted, and she looks away.

"That doesn't sound convincing."

"I'll tell you about it on the way to Maverick's party." She drapes her arms around my neck and leans in to kiss me. "How was practice?"

"Good. Your dad didn't glare at me once."

"See?" She smiles. "You're already back in his good graces."

I make a low humming sound deep in my throat. "Ash and Talia are riding over to Maverick's with us."

"Okay," she says. "I'll get ready. I bought new boots."

I change shirts and wait for Scarlett on the couch. She comes out a few minutes later, holding the end of her hair in a braid. I'm temporarily speechless as I take in said new boots. They come up over her knees and make her legs look about a million miles long. "Have you seen any of my hair ties lying around? I thought I brought one, but now I can't find it."

"No." I stand and look around anyway.

"A rubber band would work too."

"I think I have one of those in my office."

She's a damn sight in those boots and a tight little dress, walking up the stairs to the second floor. She follows me into the office while I look around for a rubber band. I find a little skinny one and hold it up for her approval.

"Yes, that's perfect."

I drop it in her hand and sit back on the edge of the desk while she wraps it around the end of her braid. Who knew watching a girl do her hair was such a turn-on? For the record, everything about Scarlett turns me on.

"You know, you could leave some things here. Or a lot of things." I push off the desk and crowd her space. "It's a health and safety issue if you think about it. You keep lugging that bag back and forth, and you're going to pull something."

With a snort, she places a hand on my chest. "You want me to leave things here?"

"I want you to have fewer reasons to leave, so yeah. You can have a drawer or several drawers, whatever you want." If I weren't afraid of scaring her off altogether, I'd tell her what I really want is for her to move in. I'm not sure how long I have to wait to bring something like that up. I've never lived with a girl before, but something tells me living with Scarlett would be a blast.

"I have to tell you something."

Well that doesn't sound good.

"O-kay."

"I saw my ex-boyfriend today," she blurts out.

I'm quiet for a beat as I let that sink in. "The one that lives in London?"

She nods. "He's here for a race. Well, not here. It's in Austin."

"But he came to Minnesota to see you?"

Another nod.

I rub a pinch in my shoulder while I process this information.

"Nothing happened. I just feel... off." She gives her head a little shake. "I wasn't even going to mention it."

"Nah, I'm glad you did. You can always tell me anything." I hug her against my chest. I know she was still reeling from the breakup when we first met. I'd like to think we're in a good place where she isn't still hanging on to old feelings, but fuck, I don't know.

She melts into me and speaks quietly, "Two drawers. One in your room for clothes and one in the bathroom for all my hair and makeup products. And a spot on the counter for my toothbrush."

"Done." I run my hand along the back of her head and tug on her braid to lift her chin. "Are you sure you're okay?"

"Yeah. I'm good." Her lips curve up slightly.

"We don't have to go out."

"No, I'm excited to go out tonight. I can't wait to meet Maverick's wife."

"Dakota. She's cool." My phone buzzes in my pocket. "That's probably Ash. Ready?"

"So ready."

I sweep her legs out from under her and get the first real smile out of her since she walked in. My worries disappear, at least for now.

Maverick lives in an apartment across from the arena. I lived here my rookie season, as did Ash, so I know the building well.

Music filters out into the hallway when we step out of the elevator onto the eleventh floor.

"Ah, this brings back some memories," Ash says with a hand at Talia's back as we head toward the source of the noise.

The apartment is packed with teammates and other people associated with the Wildcats. Even Hercules, one of our strength trainers, made it.

Tyler's standing near the door with a beer in hand. He lifts it in greeting.

"You're just in time," he says and points toward the living room where Maverick is singing karaoke.

The wild rookie belts out the lyrics to some nineties love ballad, loudly and a little off-key.

"That's his wife, Dakota, in the kitchen," I say to Scarlett.

We weave through the party, stopping to talk to everyone along the way. When Dakota sees me, she smiles. "Leo Lohan. How are you?"

"Good. You?"

"Good." Her gaze flicks to Maverick. He's added hand motions now, waving one arm dramatically toward her. "Thinking about investing in ear plugs, but good."

"Probably wise." I circle an arm around Scarlett's waist. "This is my girlfriend, Scarlett."

"Hi." Dakota smiles. "I've heard a lot about you."

"You have?" my girl asks tentatively.

"Oh yeah. Maverick gossips about the team like a schoolgirl. I've been following along since the night he found out Leo's dream girl was the coach's daughter."

I pull Scarlett tighter into my side and leave my arm wrapped around her waist. She looks up at me with those killer brown eyes, and my heart beats faster.

It's a fun night, letting loose with the team. During the season, nights like this are few and far between. And it seems like everyone is taking full advantage.

The booze is flowing, the karaoke is loud and awful, and I can't stop touching my girl. Though that last thing has little to do with the boozy atmosphere.

We're sitting on the couch: me, Scarlett, Ash, and Talia. The latter is trying to convince Scarlett to sit in the WAG section at the next home game.

"You have to," she says. "It's so much fun."

She looks to me for help.

Before I can tell her to sit wherever she wants, Ash leans over. "I don't know. Do they let *friends* sit in that section?"

I'm gonna kill him.

I hook an arm around his neck and hold him in a headlock.

"Not the hair," he says, while sending an elbow into my ribs.

We're just playing, but Talia gasps beside him.

I let him loose, but when I look over at her, it isn't us she's staring at it.

"Oh my god." Her eyes widen, and she looks up from her phone like it personally accosted her.

"What's up, babe?" Ash asks and tucks his hair behind his ears.

She hands over her phone, and when his face makes a similar shocked expression, an uneasy feeling settles in the pit of my stomach.

"Everything okay?" I ask.

"Yeah." He hands the phone back and whispers something to Talia, then stands. "Lohan, can you help me in the kitchen?"

"Umm… Sure."

Scarlett looks between us, as confused as I am. I shrug and tell her I'll be right back.

Ash grabs two new beers from the fridge and hands me one. "We have a problem."

"Your hair looks fine."

"Of course it does." He fishes his phone out of his pocket, and several long seconds pass before he thrusts it in my direction.

There she is, my dream girl on the front page of some trashy tabloid.

"What the fuck?" I mutter under my breath. I skim the article, but the pictures are what makes my heart pound in my chest. So this is the ex. Or as the headline puts it, Formula 1 Bad Boy Rhyse Fletcher.

She failed to mention that she kissed him. Fuck.

A sick feeling comes over me.

"What are you going to do?" Ash asks me.

"Show her." I hand his phone back. "I'm sure there's an explanation. She told me she saw him today and that nothing happened."

Ash doesn't look convinced, but I owe her an opportunity to explain. Fuck, I hope there's a good explanation.

"Incoming," Ash says behind his beer.

I open my stance as Scarlett steps to my side. "Is everything okay?"

Ash doesn't speak, and Scarlett glances between us.

"Show her," I say.

Her brows pull together as Ash moves closer. I look anywhere but at the phone. I don't need those images burned in my brain again.

I know as soon as she sees it. She inhales sharply, and her hand flies to her mouth. "Oh my gosh."

She swipes his phone and scrolls frantically. I focus on her expression, which is horrified. That seems like a good thing.

"It isn't what it looks like," she says. "He kissed me for a millisecond. I didn't see it coming. You have to believe me."

I nod. "I do."

Or I want to. I can't think of a good reason that she'd lie about it.

"I need to call Rhyse."

"What?" His name on her lips makes white-hot jealousy course through my veins. "Why?"

"This isn't good for him."

It isn't good for anyone.

She starts off, and I follow, gripping her bicep lightly. "Wait."

We move into one of the bedrooms out of earshot. The news must be making the rounds because we have more than one set of eyes on us.

"I should have asked this earlier, but I just assumed I knew the answer. Maybe I don't. Do you still have feelings for him?"

"Not like you mean, but I do care about him, and if he hasn't already seen this, he needs to know."

Shit. Maybe it shouldn't sting that her first reaction is to call up the guy she was photographed kissing today, but it does. I shove my hands in the pocket of my jeans.

Scarlett closes the distance between us. "I am crazy about you. I want to be with you. Seeing him made me more sure of that than ever." She moves before I'm ready to let her go. "I'll only be a few minutes."

I leave her alone and head back out to the living room.

CHAPTER THIRTY-FOUR

SCARLETT

I'M IN DEEP AVOIDANCE

Rhyse has already made it to Austin, and his team is in damage control when I speak to him. Neither me nor Leo are in the mood to party anymore, so we head back to his house. Ash eyes me warily as we say goodbye to him and Talia. Leo might believe me that nothing happened with Rhyse, but it's obvious that Ash isn't so sure.

The time it takes to get back to his place, the Internet has exploded. There are several more articles, and each headline is worse than the last. *Wildcat Head Coach's Daughter in Love Triangle* and my least favorite *Who is Scarlett Miller, The Woman Dating a Wildcat and Pregnant with Formula 1 Driver's Baby?*

Being photographed outside of a baby store was not the most ideal location. My phone starts ringing incessantly, and then Leo's. I knew it was bad when I saw it, but with every call, it gets bigger and bigger.

My mom tells me everything will be fine, and it'll blow over. When I ask how Dad is, she gives me some bullshit answer that tells me he's pissed.

"I'm so sorry," I say as I lean into Leo. He hasn't answered any of his calls. We're sitting on the couch at his place. The TV is on, but neither of us is paying any attention to it. "I wasn't thinking when I agreed to see him."

"You couldn't have known it'd go like this."

His words are exactly what I want to hear, but he's distant.

"I should have. This is how it always went with him."

"What do you mean?" Leo stares down at me with a puzzled expression.

"You already know the reason that Rhyse and I broke up, but the reason we started hiding it in the first place is because of this." I wave a hand toward my open laptop. "It's a long story, but the short of it is that Rhyse's father was a F1 driver too. Rhyse is like racing royalty. He can do no wrong, and there is no woman good enough for him. When we first started dating, we weren't hiding it, and the backlash was awful. His fans came after me like I was stealing their most prized possession."

"Seriously?"

"Yeah. It was crazy. We thought it would blow over, but his team wasn't willing to risk it. They suggested we keep our relationship a secret until the end of the season. They banished all evidence that we'd ever been anything, and after a few weeks, no one questioned it. He had a reputation as the single, bad boy, fun-loving guy, and they just fed into it and made it seem like I was a nobody he once hooked up with."

"Being a couple wasn't good for his image, and I could see that the constant need to defend me was wearing on him. So, I agreed at first. One season became two." I shrug. "I got tired of being hidden. If we went to an event, I had to arrive separately, and we couldn't appear like we were a couple. Sometimes he even had dates to keep up the charade."

"I want to kill him," Leo grumbles. His hand rests behind me and rubs small circles absently on my shoulder.

"I'm sorry they're dragging you into this mess."

"I'm used to ignoring that crap. As long as I play good hockey, no one will care tomorrow. But this…" He motions between us. "This means something to me. I will battle for you, if you'll let me."

"I hate that you feel like you need to."

A yawn escapes me, and my body goes limp against his. It's been a long day.

"We should get some sleep," he says.

"I should go home."

"Tonight? It's after one."

"Yeah. I just want to crawl into my bed, turn off my phone, and avoid the world."

"You can do that here." He stands and pulls me to my feet. When I reach for my phone, he steals it. "We're avoiding the world together."

He takes me to bed and holds me tightly against him. It isn't long before his breathing evens out into a slow rhythm. His grip remains tight, and I lie there staring up at the ceiling, feeling embarrassed and angry and a million other emotions. It's easy to say, ignore it or it'll blow over, but I'm a real person, and the things some people say are awful.

My accounts are already private, thanks to learning this lesson with Rhyse, but that won't stop people from sending me nasty messages any way they can. They know nothing about me, Rhyse, or Leo, but they think they do.

Sleep is fitful, but I doze off at some point and wake to an empty bed. My eyes burn, and my head is fuzzy. I walk toward Leo's voice downstairs. His hair sticks up, and he's running one hand through it as he paces the length of the kitchen.

He smiles when he sees me and pours me a cup of coffee.

"Thank you," I whisper.

He leans down to kiss me and then speaks into the phone, "She just got up. I'll talk to her and let you know. Thanks, Blythe."

"Damage control?" I so hate this for him.

"She called to see if there was anything she could do to help."

I nod toward my phone on the counter. "How bad is it this morning?"

"A few more sites have run articles, but someone must be squashing them because they disappear as quickly as I find them."

"I'm sure Rhyse's team is monitoring any that mention him."

He makes a disapproving sound deep in his throat.

"I'm not their concern." And I don't blame them. At least not anymore.

"Well, you're mine. What can I do?" He runs his hands along my shoulders and down to my elbows and back.

"Nothing. Go play awesome hockey and call me later tonight."

"Done and done. Why don't you come with us?"

"To California?"

"Yeah, or meet us in Phoenix or Seattle," he says, listing the other cities they're traveling to this week.

"Umm, I can't just run away from my life here. I need to get serious about finding a job. Also, I promised Jade I'd go on another wedding adventure with her." I run a hand along the smooth muscles of his chest. "I'll be fine. Promise."

"Okay, but if you change your mind, I'll kick Ash out of our hotel room for you."

"Yeah, I don't think he's my biggest fan right now." I sip the coffee.

"Nah, he knows how the media can twist things." He brushes my messy bedhead hair away from my face. "Blythe said she can help us craft a statement if we want."

"What kind of statement?"

"Something that says we're together. Officially." He shrugs. "It might make the crap news die down faster."

"That's what she thinks is best for you?"

He glances at the ceiling. "Sort of."

"It's best for me. Not for you," I guess.

He lifts one shoulder and lets it fall. I think of my dad and the team and shake my head.

"No. I don't want to drag you any further into this mess. The less you're mentioned, the better." I lean up and place a kiss on his lips. "But thank you."

After Leo leaves for the team plane, I head home. The smell of apple pie greets me, and I smile when I see said pie and the note Mom left for me. *When life hands you lemons, trade them for apples and make pie.*

I eat a slice for breakfast and then shower and go to Jade's apartment. I don't feel like being alone with my thoughts or my phone.

Her boyfriend, Sam, answers the door with a smirk. "You're famous."

"Not cool." Jade glares and shoves at his shoulder. She takes my hand and leads me to the couch as Sam disappears into their bedroom.

Jade wraps her arms around me and squeezes. "Are you okay?"

"Yeah. I'm fine." I hold up my phone, which is still off. "I'm in deep avoidance."

"Me too. Let's stay there together all day."

Now that I'm taking a second to look at my best friend, it's clear something is wrong. Her hair is up in a messy bun, and she has on a baggy sweatshirt. Jade is beautiful no matter what she does to her appearance, but she gets ready every morning—full makeup, hair, outfit—like other people brush their teeth.

"What's going on?"

She frowns. "My editor hated my article on Vivian."

"I thought Vivian was *the* wedding planner?"

"She is. My editor loooved Vivian, but hated my angle. I have to come up with another one, then write it and turn it in by tonight."

"I'm sorry."

"She's not wrong. All of my ideas are tired and have been done a million times before. I have no clue how I'm going to come up with something fresh. What do I know about getting married?"

"And here I am dumping on you when you have a real job to do." I sit forward. "I can grab you coffee and food while you work." I need a task or a thousand to keep my mind occupied today.

She smiles. "Coffee and donuts?"

My stomach growls. It's obviously on board with deep avoidance and more sugar.

"Come on. I can work there. Sam's friends usually end up here by mid-afternoon anyway."

She grabs her stuff, and we head out.

"How's living together going anyway?" It's been two months since he moved in, and honestly, I didn't think they'd last this long.

"I don't have to go to a frat house to see my boyfriend anymore, which is a plus."

"Yeah, definite upgrade."

She huffs a laugh. "It's been an adjustment for sure. I think it'll bring us closer together, though." She sighs.

I think she's in deep avoidance about more than her article.

CHAPTER THIRTY-FIVE

LEO

I'LL TAKE CARE OF YOUR STICK

"**N**ext question," I grumble into the microphone and glare hard at the reporter who showed up here and thought it'd be a good idea to ask me about my mindset going into tonight's game with the rumors floating around about my association with Coach Miller's daughter.

I guess she doesn't even get a name. Not that I want the asshole speaking it.

It's been a long week with the same tired questions every game.

I get out of the pre-game interview without yelling at anyone—just barely.

"They wouldn't be doing their job if they didn't ask," Ash says in the locker room.

I know he's trying to calm me and that on some level, he's right, but it still pisses me off. "Since when did my personal life become any of their business? I came here to play hockey."

My buddy falls silent. The rest of the guys give me a wide berth. When we take the ice for warmups, I roll my neck and focus. When I move over near the bench to stretch, Coach approaches me.

"Is your head on right?"

I nod, but he sees right through me.

"Take it out on the ice, leave it behind for a few hours, whatever you need to do." He runs a hand down his tie. "Are we good to go?"

"Yes, sir." The best way to get everyone to shut up is to skate my ass off tonight. This is my chance to prove all of those assholes wrong.

Seattle is fast. They've been on a losing streak, and it's clear from the start they're hungry to get a win. I do my best to leave all the drama behind, take it out on the ice like Coach said, and I succeed for a little while too. I'm reading my line mates and we're getting opportunities.

It's during a face-off at the beginning of the second period when I see the sign in the crowd. *Lohan, My Dad Isn't the Coach, but I'll Take Care of Your Stick.*

That anger bubbles to the surface, and Seattle's captain, Ryan Moore (an asshole on and off the ice) sneers as he sees my reaction. "Trouble getting a date, Lohan? Had to resort to fucking your coach's daughter?"

"How about you worry less about my sex life and more about helping your team out of a five-game slump, huh?"

The puck drops, and I shove him before going after it. My anger fuels me. The better I play, the rowdier the crowd seems to get. Every second I'm off the ice, my frustration vibrates under the surface.

"Let's keep our heads out there." Coach claps his hands as my line goes in. It's a different kind of adrenaline pumping through my veins tonight. I'm feeling reckless and eager to prove that my personal life doesn't impact the way I play.

I've reined it in as long as I can. The speed and energy are making me sloppy. I know it, and I fight to regain control. Not before I get called for elbowing. I start toward the box, and Moore starts mouthing off, asking if we pass Scarlett around after the games. I see red. I get two good hits in before Declan and Maverick pull me back.

It's a downhill spiral from there. Seattle scores on the power play. I do my time in the box, leg bouncing and rage pulsing.

Coach yells at me when I make it back to the bench, but I barely hear him. Moore continues to sneer at me every chance he gets, but he doesn't say Scarlett's name again, so he gets to live. I know that the more I show how he agitates me, the more he'll do it.

The game comes down to a shoot out, and Seattle gets the win. The locker room is quiet. Coach doesn't come in to talk to us. I guess there isn't anything to say. This game should have been a cakewalk.

I'm not at all surprised when I'm called to the media room. Jack places a hand on my shoulder and stops me before we walk in. "Are you good?"

"I'm fine." I shrug out of his hold.

He moves his big body in front of me. "Do not go in there pissed at the world."

Taking a deep breath, I nod.

Despite feeling like I'm ready to explode, I manage to answer questions and take my part of the responsibility for losing my head and costing the team an early goal.

By the time we get on the plane to head home, I feel like I've aged a hundred years.

"Drink?" Ash pours scotch from a mini bottle into a glass with ice.

"Nah."

"Have a drink," he says and places it in front of me. "You need to chill the fuck out. I can feel the rage radiating off you."

I stretch my legs out and sip the whiskey.

"There you go." He makes himself a drink and reclines his chair back. "What the hell did Moore say to you?"

"Just shit about Scarlett." I keep my voice down. The last thing I want is for Coach to hear.

"You can't rage on every guy that talks shit about her, or it's going to be a very long season."

He's right. Once guys know you have a weak spot, they'll rub against it every chance they get. "I know. I lost my shit. It's been a long couple of days."

"It'll blow over. Somebody else will do something dumb soon enough."

I blow out a long breath. "God, I hope so."

When Ash passes out, I call Scarlett.

"Hey." Her voice is husky and tired, but it still lights me up.

"Did I wake you?"

"Yeah, I guess so." She groans. "I fell asleep on the couch watching the game. Did you win?"

"No. Lost in a shoot out."

"Oh, really? I thought you guys had it. I'm sorry." The genuine sympathy from her end makes me realize she has no idea I got into a fist fight during the game. She'd definitely mention it.

"How are you?" I ask. "What'd you do all day?"

Calm that I haven't felt since I talked to her this morning washes over me. We've barely mentioned her ex or the pictures since I left. I have Blythe and Daria keeping me updated, but Scarlett and I have been carefully skirting the drama and enjoying the few minutes we get to chat every day.

It feels like it's already occupied so much of my week, with everyone else wanting to talk about it. Is it too much to ask to keep all the nonsense from ruining the few minutes I get with her while I'm on the road?

Everything else is bullshit. I just want to talk to my girl.

CHAPTER THIRTY-SIX

SCARLETT

OUR HAPPY COCOON

I crashed hard watching the game, and now after talking to Leo, I can't sleep. I'm in the kitchen eating cereal to make up for the dinner I didn't eat when I hear the garage door open. Dad walks in a few minutes later, looking tired. He sets his bag on the table and looks up to find me sitting at the island.

Silently, he comes over and grabs a bowl, fills it, and sits beside me. We never really talked about the problems Rhyse and I had. That was more Mom's department. But now that my relationship involves one of his players, I'm not sure how to broach the topic. I decide to go with straight hockey talk.

"Tough loss tonight."

He hums around a spoonful of Fruity Pebbles.

"I'm sorry about… well everything, I guess." I don't even know how to describe the media shitstorm I caused.

"Oh, honey, it isn't your fault."

"It feels like it." At least with Rhyse, it didn't directly impact my family.

"I have to ask. Is this the life you want? Living in the public eye, having your every move scrutinized?"

"I really like him."

Dad nods thoughtfully. "And I'm sure he really likes you, but it seems like you're both risking a lot."

"Leo doesn't care about the media."

"Maybe not, but his performance this week made it clear that he can be distracted. Opponents will use that against him, and the reporters will poke and prod, hoping to get a rise out of him."

"Did something happen?"

Dad's mouth pulls into a straight line.

"Tell me."

"He let the crowd and the other team get in his head and use you against him. It cost us the game tonight."

My stomach rolls. Why do people suck so much? "He didn't say anything when I talked to him. I feel awful."

"It isn't the first time, and it won't be the last that people try to get under his skin. He needs to learn to tune it out."

I know on some level Dad is right, but still. "He said we could make some sort of statement together if I wanted, but I told him it would be better to keep it quiet and let it blow over."

"That's good. I think that'll be best for both of you. There's no reason this thing between the two of you needs to be front-page news."

My heart hurts. I don't know what the best thing is anymore.

"He's a talented kid with a bright future. He'll be okay," Dad says. "You both will be."

I wish his reassurances made me feel better.

The next day, I go over to Leo's after he's done at the arena. He answers the door with a sleepy smile and folds me in his arms. "Hey, dream girl."

My insides light up at the endearment. I feel the furthest thing from his dream girl right now. I can't shake the feeling that I'm more trouble than I'm worth. Still, I melt into him—his warmth and his strength.

"How was your day?"

"Better now," he murmurs against the top of my head.

We're supposed to go out tonight, but we go to his room and collapse on the bed. Neither of us slept well, and my eyes are heavy as I feel a peace I haven't since the last time we were together.

I wake up to the sound of his phone ringing. Leo answers, eyes closed. He pinches the bridge of his nose as he murmurs one-word replies.

He hangs up and rolls over, eyes finally opening. "Hey, beautiful."

"Time to leave our happy cocoon?"

"Yeah, I promised Daria I'd go for at least an hour."

We'd made plans to attend together, but now I'm not sure. "Do you still want me to come?"

"Of course I do." He rolls on top of me. "We can skip the grand entrance if you want."

My pride stings. Another event where I'm hidden. I'm so tired of being hidden.

"No, I can handle it."

He searches my face. "Are you sure?"

"Absolutely." I kiss away his hesitation.

The event is at a local brewery. There is really no avoiding making an entrance at this place because everyone is jammed into one large lounge area for the tasting. Leo doesn't drop my hand as we make our way through the crowd to where some of his teammates are standing around a tall table.

A server brings us each a flight of beers, and I try to relax as Leo falls into conversation with Jack and Declan. He hasn't mentioned last night's game or the fight I now know he got into with Seattle's captain. It was all over the sports highlights today.

I see Lindsey among the photographers milling about and wave when she gets close.

"Hey, it's so good to see you." She hugs me, holding her camera in one hand. "I've missed you at the arena."

"It's good to see you too. I didn't know you were working the event."

"My boyfriend owns the brewery." She grins and points to a guy at the bar with red hair and a trendy beard. "I'm free labor."

She steps back and aims her camera toward our table. "Everyone crowd together a little."

We smile as she takes a few. Leo presses me to his side.

I feel more at ease after that. The Wildcats aren't the only local celebrities in attendance, but our table is a constant hub of activity with people coming up to say hello or ask for a picture.

Leo gets pulled into a ton of photos with the guys, and I hang back, admiring how handsome he is and how lucky I am to be here with him. He winks from where he stands, posing between Jack and Declan.

I head off to the bathroom and, on my way out, get stopped by a guy that smiles and waves tentatively.

"Hi," I say and keep walking.

"You're Scarlett Miller, right?"

I freeze. "Umm... yes."

"I thought so. I'm Antonio, Sam's friend. I think we met at a party a couple of months back."

"Oh my gosh. Yes." My shoulders relax as I place him. Jade tried to hook us up the same week I got back from London as a way for me to get over Rhyse.

"Are you here with someone?" He looks past me.

"Yeah." I wave a hand in the general direction of Leo. He's chatting in a group of guys that I think includes some Twins players.

"You?"

"One of my buddies is a bartender tonight. You know him too, I think. Lawrence. We were both pledge brothers with Sam." He tips his head in that direction. "Come say hi."

"Oh, I don't know. I should probably get back."

"It'll take two seconds," he says.

Leo is occupied, so I nod and follow him to the bar. I don't recognize Lawrence, but I smile and say hello. They ask about Jade and Sam, then introduce me to more people. Their names start to blur together, and I'm not really interested in remembering them anyway.

Also, it might be my imagination, but Antonio is standing awfully close. I don't know a lot about him, aside from being a frat brother to Sam. The one night we hung out where Jade tried to hook us up, he got blitzed out of his mind and passed out in the TV room. Hey, I'm not one to judge. Been there, my friend, but he's acting like we're old drinking buddies instead of strangers with a shared acquaintance.

I take a step back at the same time he asks me if I'm still working at Mike's bar.

"Occasionally, I'm filling in, but not really."

We're about the same height, and he leans in closer and rests a hand on my lower back. "That's cool. I bet you make great tips."

Umm, okay, weird. I nod noncommittally and open my stance,

breaking contact as I look for my date.

Leo's scanning the room like he's looking for me too. I stand on my tiptoes and catch his eye. His features soften, then he takes in the guys next to me and starts toward us.

"There you are," Leo says when he reaches me. He drops a kiss to my cheek.

I motion to Antonio and Lawrence. "These guys are friends with Jade's boyfriend."

Leo nods, wraps an arm around my waist, and says hello.

"Leo Lohan," Antonio says. "It's so cool you're here. Stay and have a drink with us, man."

"Sorry, another time," he says, already stepping away and taking me with him.

I wave bye, and Leo ushers us off to the side to a less crowded area.

"Everything okay?" he asks.

"Yeah, I went to the bathroom and ran into him on the way out. You were busy, and I wanted to give you some space."

"Well, don't." He pulls me closer to him and smiles. "I like you all up in my space. Plus, that guy was standing awfully close to my dream girl."

I push up on my toes and kiss him. "Don't worry. If I'm going to leave here tonight with someone else, it's probably Jack."

He smacks my ass, causing me to yelp. I lace my fingers through his, and we go back to our table. The room gets louder as the night wears on. People are getting drunk, and laughter echoes through the warehouse.

Even Leo has a happy buzz going on. He's quicker to chuckle and getting handsier by the second. I bat his fingers away as he slips them under the hem of my dress.

He winks and places his palm over my knee.

"I think it's time for me to get out of here," Declan says and stands. "Does anyone need a ride?"

"Are you ready?" Leo asks me.

"Yeah." I get up, and he stands behind me, hands still roaming all over me.

Jack laughs as he watches us. "Shotgun. I'm not sitting in the back with those two."

Our progress toward the door is slow. Everyone that they talked to earlier in the night stops them to say goodbye.

I'm hanging off to the side, fingers still intertwined with Leo's, even as he chats with other people. Antonio approaches us slowly.

"You're leaving already?"

"Yeah."

"No way," he says. "Stay. Lawrence gets off in an hour, and then we're going to hit the bars downtown."

"Another time, maybe." I press into Leo's side.

"Ready?" I ask Leo. I think getting blitzed might be the norm for Antonio. He reeks of booze, and he sways on his feet.

My boyfriend gives me his attention. His brows furrow when he catches Antonio next to me entirely too close. He looks between us. "Problem?"

"Nah, man. No problem. I was just trying to talk Scarlett into coming out with us. The night is young."

"She has plans." He kisses me hard and possessively.

"All right," Antonio says when we break apart. He lifts his hands in surrender. "I didn't realize she was spoken for."

Leo lifts our joined hands and shoots him a look that would send a smart man running. Of course, that isn't what Antonio does. He nods slowly, and a smile tips up the corners of his mouth. "Another night then."

Leo's grip on my hand tightens.

"No, man. Not another night."

Leo's jealousy is irrational. I'd never go out with this guy, but it eggs on Antonio.

He stumbles. "I just want my turn on the carousel, man."

Shame and humiliation coat my insides, and I can practically see the wall of red in front of Leo as he steps to Antonio.

"What the fuck did you say?"

Antonio laughs. "She's not that hot. Does she have a golden pussy or what?"

Leo spews a string of curses as he swings at Antonio.

"Leo," I gasp as Antonio crumbles, holding his nose and blood dripping down his face.

Jack and Declan grab him on either side, but Leo doesn't make any move to hit the guy again. His face slowly morphs from rage to shock, and he looks down at his hand.

"I think he broke my fucking nose." Antonio has the audacity to look surprised that his words had consequences.

"You're lucky that's all he broke," Declan says.

"We need to get out of here," Jack says quietly. He puts himself between Antonio and us. "Now."

We've attracted an audience, and one of the security guys is making his way toward us. My ears ring, and panic sets in even before they ask Leo to come with them. Jack, Declan, and I follow. I lose track of Antonio, but a few minutes later, the police arrive, and he reappears, pointing at Leo as he holds a wad of gauze to his nose.

The officers pull Leo aside, and I watch on, horrified as they escort him away.

"Oh my god, is he going to jail?" I ask.

"They're just going to talk to him," Jack says. "I'm going to follow and call Daria on the way. Declan, can you get Scarlett home?"

I start in the direction Leo went. "What? No, I want to go with him."

Declan places a hand on my arm to stop me from following. "It's probably better if you meet him at his place. He needs to get this sorted."

Leo's broad back disappears out of view. Declan escorts me outside, and I climb into his sports car feeling numb. He hits the seat heaters and turns down the music. We ride in silence until we get to Leo's neighborhood.

"Is he going to be okay?"

"Yeah." He glances over at me and then tries to sound more convincing. "He'll be okay."

He pulls into the driveway and stops. "Do you want me to stay until he gets here?"

"No." I open the door, then remember I don't have a key or the alarm code. "Except I can't get in. I don't have—"

"A key." He nods, picks up his phone, and within a few seconds, Ash is coming across the street shirtless and shoeless.

"What the hell happened?" Ash looks from me to Declan for answers.

"Let's get her inside, first," Declan says. Ash lets me in and disables the alarm. I've never seen Ash so scared, and it makes me more anxious.

Declan fills him in, leaving out the worst of it. The things Antonio said were awful.

"Fuck." Ash runs a hand through his hair. "First he lost his captain position, now this?"

"What?" I interrupt them. "He lost the A?"

A new kind of anguish settles in the pit of my stomach.

Declan's expression tells me it's true, and I couldn't feel any lower. Being alternate captain meant so much to him. I think I'm going to be sick.

"When?" I look to them for an answer.

Ash answers quietly, "Today."

I squeeze my eyes shut to force the pain and tears back. He lost his A, and now he's in jail. Both because of me.

CHAPTER THIRTY-SEVEN

LEO

MY MASTERPIECE

I've never been so happy to be home. Jack stops the car in the driveway and gives me that captain look that says I'm about to get a pep talk. I'm too tired to fight it.

"Did you hurt your hand?" he asks.

My right hand cradles the busted knuckles of my left. I extend my fingers and then make a fist. "No. I'm good."

"You're sure?"

"I'm fucking sure," I snap, then apologize. "Sorry. It's been a long fucking night. I'm good. Thank you for being there, but I just want to go in and see my girl."

He nods. I can tell he wants to say more, but he doesn't.

I open the car door. "I'll see you in the morning."

Light from the TV streams into the living room. Ash is in the recliner, and Scarlett is curled up on the couch. He sees me first and stands.

"Finally." He comes forward and hugs me, squeezing all the air out of my lungs. "All good? Did you get the charges dropped? Have you talked to Daria or Coach?"

"Everything is fine. Let's talk in the morning, yeah?" I ask as he pulls back. Scarlett sits up but doesn't move toward me.

"Of course." He looks between my girl and me. "Call me when you get up."

"I'll meet you out front for our run at five," I tell him.

"Oh. Okay. Yeah. See you then." He gives me a two-finger salute.

Only when he's out the door does Scarlett stand. I kick off my shoes and pull off my T-shirt. I feel dirty from spending the past two hours at the police station, stewing in disappointment and potential battery charges.

She nuzzles into my chest, and I close my arms around her and breathe her in. Damn, it feels good to be home and with her.

"I'm so sorry," I murmur into the top of her head. I shouldn't have lost my shit. I don't regret hitting the fucker, but I wish it'd been in a dark alley, and she hadn't seen it.

"Don't be. It's all my fault." Her voice is a whisper spoken into the nape of my neck. "Are you in a lot of trouble?"

"Nah. He didn't press charges."

She looks up at me. "Why?"

I'm silent, and she adds, "You paid him."

I swallow down the anger of that fuck getting a dime out of me. "I agreed to pay for his medical bills." And his silence.

"Leo." It's the first time my name has come out of her lips that I haven't liked the tone. It's filled with exhaustion and a hint of disappointment.

I kiss her to stop whatever she's about to say. "It's fine. It was my fault."

"No, it wasn't." She takes a step back. "None of this would have happened if I hadn't been there."

"If we're going down that line of thinking, it never would have happened if I hadn't forced you to come out to some bullshit event to appease Daria. It happened, babe." I frame her face with my hands. "But I'm here now, and everything is okay."

"It doesn't feel okay." She cinches her hold around my waist. "I did a lot of thinking while you were gone. About us and the drama I've brought into your life. It isn't fair to you."

"Shhh, baby. No more talking tonight. I need you." I kiss her again. Slowly, she melts in my arms and gives back everything I need to forget about tonight. I pick her up and start toward my room.

In the dark, I undress her slowly, kissing every inch of skin as I do it. Our movements are unhurried, drinking each other in and soaking in every moment. She runs her hands over my shoulders and down my back, drawing our bodies closer.

If I were a painter, I could use color and brushstrokes to bring her form to life with my eyes closed. If I were a rockstar, I'd sing the fuck out of some heartfelt lyrics that I wrote just for her. If I could take photos like her, I could show her just how beautiful she is. The twinkle in her eye when she's feeling sassy, the color in her cheeks when she's turned on, and that look of pure bliss as she lies naked beneath me.

Scarlett makes me wish I had all sorts of artistic skills. She deserves all that. I can't show her what she means to me in any way other than loving every inch of her.

That's exactly what I do. I make love to her for hours. We don't say a lot, even as we shower afterward and climb into bed together. Sometimes there's nothing to say.

Nah, I'm not an artist, but loving Scarlett feels like my masterpiece and I'm just getting started.

When my alarm goes off for my run, only a few hours later, I groan and roll over to silence it before it wakes Scarlett, but when I open my eyes, she's sitting up beside me, watching me sleep.

"Morning, gorgeous."

"Hey," she says softly.

I sit up and wrap my arms around her, placing a kiss on her shoulder. "What are you doing up already?"

"I need to get home."

"At four forty-five in the morning?"

She gives me a sad smile that makes my heart hammer in my chest without warning. I hold her tighter and glance around. Her bag is already packed and sitting in the doorway.

"Don't hurry off. Let's shower, and I'll make you some coffee." I take her hand and hold it up, interlacing our fingers and placing a kiss on her thumb.

"No, that's okay. Go on your run. I don't want to mess with your routine. I just wanted to say bye before I left."

"I can't send you out into the world without coffee." I stand and pull on a pair of shorts. "It isn't safe for the other people."

She laughs lightly and grabs her bag. "No, really. I have to go."

"Okay. I'll call you after practice. Do you want to grab lunch later?"

She hesitates to respond, and I can see the uncertainty on her face. "Dinner?"

"I don't think it's such a great idea for us to be seen together for a while."

"We can stay in." God, I can't even imagine how she must feel having the media twist her every move. They've been brutal and fucking Rhyse is staying silent.

"Leo, my life is a mess right now and it isn't fair of me to bring you into it. I don't want my drama to make things worse for you."

"If this is because of last night—"

She closes her eyes and shakes her head, sending her brown hair swaying around her shoulders. "It isn't just that. Why didn't you tell me about the fight in Seattle? Or that my dad took your A?"

I clench my left hand. The sting of my broken knuckles makes me want to hit something all over again. "That's on me."

"You didn't tell me because you knew I'd feel guilty. You wanted to protect me. That's all I'm trying to do for you." She takes a deep breath. "I couldn't sleep. I keep going over everything that has happened the past few weeks, trying to make sense of it all and figure out how we get through this."

"We get through it together."

She makes a strangled sound. "You know that is just going to cause more headlines. I won't let them use me to get a rise out of you. I think it's best if we get a little space."

"Space?" I shake my head. "No, that's the opposite of what would be best for me."

"Not forever, just for a little while." She comes closer and places a hand on my chest. "You are the best boyfriend a girl could ask for."

Yeah, so good she doesn't want to be with me anymore. I step back. Rejection stings. It's been so long since I put so much of myself out there like I have with Scarlett. I know things are tough right now, but damn.

"How long? A day? A week? A month?"

"I don't know."

I can see how much she's hurting, and it's the only thing that keeps me from begging her not to go. Maybe she's right in ending things. She deserves more than being raked over the coals for being with me. It's easy for me to shake off the nasty press, but she's the one getting the worst of it. Try as I might, I can't seem to protect her any other way. Some fucking boyfriend.

"Fine. If that's what you want."

She lingers for a moment, like she's not sure what to do now that I've agreed, or maybe just not sure how to say goodbye. Numb, I turn to the counter and make my protein drink.

Eventually, her footsteps move toward the door. "Bye, Leo Lohan."

I stay turned away, and the door closes her on the other side.

Bye, dream girl.

CHAPTER THIRTY-EIGHT

SCARLETT

HAPPIER THAN I'VE EVER BEEN

"Oh, honey," Jade says, petting my hair. "You two can work through this."

"How?" I wipe my snotty nose on a tissue and fall back onto my bed. I'm wearing his Boston University sweatshirt that he gave me the first night. I never gave it back, and now I don't ever want to if it's all I have left.

Like a good best friend, she came over with donuts and coffee as soon as I called to tell her I ended things with Leo. Paused is the way I'd like to look at it, but who knows when things might blow over. And his reaction. I felt like the lowest of lows. I knew comforting him or trying to ease it would only make things harder. We need a break to let things die down. I hope it isn't forever, but I don't see a way past things right now.

"He was so hurt. You should have seen him. He wouldn't even look at me."

"Well, you did break up with him before the sun rose. That's bound to make anyone a little cranky."

"He went to jail, Jade. Jail." And still, he wasn't going to walk away.

"They probably never even processed him," she says with a wave of her hand, then nods. "But I get your point."

I fling an arm over my face and continue to let the tears fall. Jade sits silently beside me, rubbing my arm.

It's been only a few hours since I walked out on him. I wanted to end things last night, but I couldn't. Instead, I let him make love to me and then clung to him through the night. It was the right thing to do, but it doesn't make my heart hurt any less.

"Scarlett," my mom yells from the top of the stairs, "you have a visitor."

I sit up like a shot.

Jade smiles. "Attaboy, Lohan. I knew he wasn't going down that easily."

She scoots off my bed. "I'm gonna duck out and go search for wedding inspiration. Call me later."

"I will."

Jade goes out through the basement door, and I run a makeup wipe under my raccoon eyes. Then, I take the stairs two at a time. If I were thinking rationally, I wouldn't be so excited to see a man I love and can't be with, but I'm anything but rational right now. Three hours and I already miss him.

Mom's voice is quiet, and I can't make out her words, but I can tell she's chatting with Leo. As I get to the top step, I pause as the deep voice speaks back.

Not Leo.

Rhyse stands from the couch when he sees me and offers a hesitant smile. His handsome and put-together appearance angers me as much as his presence.

"What are you doing here?" My tone is soft and disbelieving even though inside, I feel all the bottled-up anger rising inside of me. Misguided? Probably, but he's the perfect target.

"It was good to see you again," my mom says and shoots me a sideways glance that says, mind your manners, before she leaves us alone.

Rhyse and I stand across the room from one another, taking the other in.

He speaks first. "I'm sorry to just show up here, but you weren't answering my calls or texts."

I open my mouth to tell him the reason I haven't is because I have absolutely nothing to say to him or because he showed up here, blew up my life, and then had his team wipe away his presence in all of it, but one side of his mouth lifts in a hesitant smile, and he steps forward.

"I can still read you as well as ever. I know what you're thinking, and you're right. I'm so sorry. That's why I've been trying to call. I'm going to make a statement explaining why I was in Minnesota."

Well, that isn't what I expected.

"Explain it how?" I take a seat on the couch.

"That's up to you. I could be an old friend, an ex-boyfriend, someone you just started dating again." He moves to sit beside me. "Give me another shot? No more hiding."

"Your team is okay with this?"

"I didn't give them an option." His blue eyes search my face.

"Wow," I say. I'm glad he's standing up for himself, but it's too little too late for us. He's no longer the man I'm in love with.

"I'm too late," he says.

Damn. He's good. I've never been good at hiding my emotions. I wonder what Leo saw this morning.

"You're truly happy with the hockey guy then?"

I nod and smash my lips together to keep them from quivering with the weight of the white lie. I was happy with Leo. Happier than I've ever been. I love him so much. The kind of love I dreamed of my whole life. I thought I was in love with Rhyse, but it feels small in comparison. Or maybe it's just that too much time has passed.

Traveling the world with him was exciting. I got to see so much, and I felt so special that he chose me. I owe a lot of good memories to him. They outweigh the bad by a lot. I hope for his sake he really is ready to stand up to his team and live his life, but it won't have me in it.

I wanted Rhyse to blow up his life to make room for me, and he didn't. Now Leo is doing just that and I broke up with him to stop him. Rhyse wasn't wrong. Maybe I just didn't love him enough to realize what I was asking of him.

"I'm sorry," I say.

"You're sorry?" Full lips exhale with a long breath. "I'm the idiot that let you walk away."

"I understand better now why you made the choices you did. I hope you let yourself have everything you want."

"Yeah. Me too." He runs a hand along his jaw.

"Can I ask you a question?"

"Anything."

"Why now? You've spent years letting other people dictate your life. What's changed?"

He's quiet for a beat. The leather of his jacket creaks as he rubs at the back of his neck. "I don't know. I probably should have done it years ago, but I was winning." He chuckles quietly. "Am winning. I'm having the best season of my life. I'm on track to beat my dad's record."

"I heard, or I read. Congratulations."

"Yeah, thanks."

Beating his dad's record and proving himself consumed Rhyse while we were together. I doubt that's changed. I think he has a long way to go before he has complete control of his life, and that makes me sad for him.

"It won't be enough," he says. "I know that now. It won't bring him back. Won't change anything." He stands abruptly and pulls an envelope from his back pocket. "Take care of yourself, Scarlett."

The folded manilla envelope is heavy in my hands. "You too."

I walk him to the door, and we hug awkwardly. He steps out onto the porch and then faces me one last time, lifts a hand in a small wave, and jogs to the waiting car.

I spend the rest of the day eating my feelings and watching sappy movies. And avoiding opening the envelope from Rhyse.

At dinner, Dad tugs on the end of one braid, but he doesn't say a word about Leo. The team is leaving tomorrow for an away game, and I'm hoping the distance makes my heart hurt less. There's something about being so close and not talking to him that makes it that much more brutal.

Later, I lie in bed and scroll through all the photos I've taken since I've been back. Friends, pets, businesses, landscapes. I've taken so many. Lots of them really good. But the one I fall asleep staring at is of Leo on the beach. The lighting isn't perfect, and I didn't center him in the frame. It isn't even close to being the best photo I've taken, but the man inside of the imperfect picture smiles at the camera, at me, exactly like I always wanted someone to see me.

Jade wanted him to fuck me back on my feet. He did so much more than that.

CHAPTER THIRTY-NINE

LEO

B.S.

I arrive at the plane anxious to get out of town and play some hockey.

Jack falls in next to me as we walk out to the plane. We're heading to New York for a game tonight. My captain's face asks all the questions before he opens his mouth.

"My head is on straight," I tell him.

"Everything worked out then?"

I consider lying, but the sardonic laugh that escapes my mouth wouldn't make it very believable anyway. "No, everything didn't work out."

"You and Scarlett..." He treads carefully.

"She ended things." My voice sounds scarily calm for the rage warring inside of me.

"I'm sorry to hear that."

"Yeah, okay." I give him a look that tells him I know differently. He never thought it was a good idea, and I guess I get his point, but it isn't like I chose to fall for her. It just happened. Nothing could have stopped me after that one night together.

"What the fuck do I know?" He shrugs. "This team is my whole life."

Jack doesn't date, at least not seriously. I never bothered to ask why. It always made sense to me before. The schedule, the travel, and everything else that comes with the job make it an easy excuse. But now I know that he just hasn't met the right person. Or fuck, maybe he did and screwed it up like me. Our job might make dating tricky, but we're playmakers. We know how to make things work if we really want to.

I stew with that thought the entire flight. It isn't like I haven't thought about calling Scarlett before now. Last night I eventually had to turn off my phone to stop myself from texting her. But this is a different impulse. I'm going to make this work. I know she wants to be with me. Or she did before I started acting like an asshole. Step one, stop doing that. After that? I'm not sure, but I'm a playmaker, and there's something I really want: Scarlett.

I'm on the pre-game interview list, and it's brutal. No one outright asks about Scarlett, but I have to say "no comment" and remind them I'm only answering questions about the game more than once.

True to my words, I have my head on for the game. I push everything else out. It's cathartic in a way, not allowing anything else in for a few hours. Avoidance? Probably. But it works.

At least until we hit the locker room and the guys start celebrating the win, then everything else creeps back in. I check my phone for the usual texts from family congratulating me on the game. My parents might not come to the games, but they follow along. The only person missing is Scarlett. And fuck if taking one person out of the equation doesn't screw with me.

On Tuesday, Ash and I workout in his garage after our run. I call uncle first, wiping the sweat from my forehead and lying on the rubber floor.

"Thank fuck." He collapses onto a box and squirts water into his mouth.

We have a three-day break in between games, and we're spending most of our time working out at the arena and on our own. Talia is out of town, Scarlett's gone, and it's almost like the old days. B.S. Before Scarlett. Fitting, because it's absolute bullshit.

"Shower and go out for dinner?" he asks.

"I don't feel like going out." I glance at my phone next to me as it lights up with a text. I don't even bother reading it after I see it isn't from Dream Girl.

We stay in, eating dinner in Ash's living room and playing video games. I can't focus on anything. Ash doesn't even trash talk me when he beats me.

I toss the controller on the couch beside me. "I should probably go home."

"It's early. Stay, we can catch up on Ted Lasso."

"You haven't watched it?"

"Nah. It's our thing," he says and navigates to where we left off a month ago.

I was so busy with Scarlett I didn't realize I neglected my buddy. Ash always has my back.

"Do you have any beer?"

His brows lift.

"I'm not going to blaze through a case," I say. "Beer and Lasso, they go together like...peanut butter and jelly."

He chuckles. "All right. Whatever you want, man."

He comes back with two beers and hands me one. He holds it up, and I clink the neck of his with mine.

"I can't believe you held off on watching the rest of the season," I say as the show starts.

"Not the same without you."

"You could have said something. I would have made time."

He smiles. "Then what would we watch to cheer up your mopey ass?"

The next night I come back over, hoping for more of the same, but we only make it through a single episode before he gets a call, and we have to pause the show.

I'm staring down at my phone when he gets done. He must read the disappointment on my face. Another text, but still not from Scarlett.

"Nothing from her all week?" he asks.

"Nope. Radio silence. She probably blocked me again."

"Highly doubtful. She said that she needed space not to fuck off and die." He kicks up his feet on the coffee table. "Have you reached out?"

"I haven't figured out what to say. Nothing has changed. I'm still me. How do I ask her to be with me, knowing what that means for her?"

"I don't know." He finishes off his beer and stands. "God, we're pathetic. Come on."

"Another run?" I ask hopefully. Three to five miles ought to clear my head again.

"Fuck no. We're going out."

Before I can protest, he adds, "You're going."

We meet up with Declan, Maverick, and Tyler at Wild's.

"He's alive," Declan says when he sees us. "How are you?"

"Breathing." I slump into the seat across from him.

"He hasn't heard from Scarlett all week," Ash says. "He's shit. Hence the need for forced fun."

My buddy pours himself and then me a beer.

"You need a plan," Maverick says. "Do you have a plan?"

"If he did, he wouldn't be here." Tyler lifts a brow, begging me to argue.

"What's the problem?" Declan asks. "The news has died down. You stayed out of jail. Though I'm a little disappointed you didn't have mug shots taken. Can you imagine how awful those would have been? A normal person can't take a good one of those."

I flip him off but can't help but smile. It eases a little of the hurt in my chest. These guys are like my own little dysfunctional family, and I wouldn't have it any other way.

"She deserves more than being called a slut every time she's seen out with me or watching me get carted off to jail and leaving her alone on our date."

"Fuck that noise," Declan says, tone hard as he sits forward.

We all stare at him. He's so chill and quiet most of the time that when he gets riled up about something, he has our undivided attention.

"You did the same thing any one of us would have. You protected your girl."

The guys all nod.

"And she still left." To protect me. I can't even wrap my brain around the endless loop of that fuckery.

"Then go after her. Swallow your damn pride." This comes from Tyler.

"What is it with you two?" I ask of the quietest two members of our team. All of a sudden they're fired up on my behalf?

Tyler shakes his head. "She's your dream girl?"

"Yeah." I let out a breath.

"I had one of those, and I let her go for the same sort of bullshit reason. I regret it every single day."

I can hear the genuine regret in his voice, and I nod. "Sorry, man."

"It's too late for me, but not you."

"You know what that means then?" Maverick asks as he rubs his hands together.

"What?" Ash asks for all of us.

Maverick dances in his seat. "It's time to come up with a plan."

I appreciate their interest and enthusiasm. Though I leave the bar without a solid plan, I'm more determined to find a way through this. I don't want to live with regret.

At home, I fall into bed. Exhaustion falls over me from a long day of pushing my body and staying occupied. She took all of her stuff, but I still feel her and my bed smells like her shampoo.

I pull out my phone to text her, but I have no idea what to say. I'm sorry. I fucked up. Both things are true, but I know it isn't enough.

THE NEXT DAY Coach asks me to hang back after the morning skate. Ash sends me a pitying glance as he skates off with the rest of the guys.

I've talked to him since the breakup. In fact, the very next morning, I sought him out as soon as I got to the arena, so I could tell him about the altercation at the brewery. I left out the awful things that fuckface said about his daughter, but I didn't want him to hear that I hit a guy and went to jail from someone else. If Scarlett had already told him, he didn't let on.

He nodded and asked if I needed a day or two off after our New York game, which I adamantly refused, and since then, it's been business as usual.

I'm definitely hoping to earn back his trust and respect and wear the A again, but I don't blame him for taking it from me.

So far, there hasn't been any blowback from the almost arrest. A local gossip rag ran a small article about a fight involving one or more of the Wildcat Hockey players, but they must not have been able to get anyone to comment because the details were vague.

"Tomorrow night after the game, we're doing some extended interviews. More reporters, longer sessions." He rests his hands on his hips. "I've added you to the list to be available. I can probably work it so that you go last. It'll give you a clean out."

"Not necessary. I can handle it." I wipe the sweat out of my eyes. "Anything else?"

"Just one more thing." He shifts his weight from one leg to the other. "I wanted to thank you."

"For?"

He makes a clicking sound with his tongue before he speaks. "Things may not have worked out between the two of you, but the past couple of months, Scarlett has smiled more than I can remember since she's been back. I think that was your doing."

Like a dagger to the heart. Fuuuck.

I clear the lump in my throat but still don't trust my voice, so I nod.

"You're a good kid, Leo." He claps me on the shoulder. "Keep your head up."

CHAPTER FORTY

SCARLETT

MANIFESTING MY DREAMS

"No regrets?" Jade asks as I read the sports headlines. She forced me out of the house, and I'm going with her to scout out another possible story.

"About Rhyse?" I ask as his face stares back at me on the screen of my phone.

"Yeah. I know how much you cared about him."

I shake my head. "It never would have worked between us."

Also, I'm not so sure his team is going to make it that easy on him now that he's ready to call his own shots. He took the first step, though.

Yesterday's top headline reads, *Women of the world rejoice, playboy Rhyse Fletcher is still single.* The short article explains his recent trip to Minnesota to visit an old friend and former staff photographer and says he's not currently dating, so he can focus on bringing his team another win.

Okay, so it's basically the same verbiage they've been using in every article ever written about him, but I feel more confident than I ever did before that my title, old friend, could have been girlfriend if I'd given him another shot.

And...I finally got credit for all of the images I took of him that his team used. When I finally braved the manila envelope, I found a letter of reference from his social media manager, recommending me and detailing the metrics and reach my photos garnered for Rhyse. I never cared that they used them, but seeing my name under the photo on this news story is pretty damn cool.

And today, for the first time in a week, I don't have a single Google alert, notifying me of a news article written about me and all my whore-ways (major eye roll).

Rhyse inspired me, though. It's time to start living my life the way I want without worrying about the headlines. The impact of those headlines on the people I care about will always matter, but I'm not going to hide.

"I was thinking it's time for me to come out of hiding," I say.

"We're hiding?" She looks around.

"Online."

"Ooooh. Really?"

"Nothing crazy," I say. "I thought I'd start by making my Instagram profile public. It's mostly photos I've taken from traveling or with friends, but it's a little piece of me that I think I'm willing to share.

I don't feel like I owe anyone anything, but I am tired of feeling like I need to hide behind the curtain.

"Well then, we need to have a proper coming out party." She claps her hands. "Photo shoot at my place tonight?"

"Maybe tomorrow night?" I ask. "There's somewhere I need to go tonight, and I need to stay under the radar. Can you come with me for moral support?"

"A secret mission?" My best friend looks way too excited. "Absolutely."

When we get to the arena, Jade laughs. "When you said under the radar, I thought we were going somewhere new and exciting."

"I've been to every home game so far this season, except the one we worked at Wild's." Which basically felt like being there thanks to all the excitement of the nearby bar. "I can't miss this even if Leo and I are…" I trail off. "Whatever."

"Okay, fine. Two games in one season. I might be Coach's favorite daughter at this rate." She links her arm through mine.

I call Lindsey when we're inside. She comes out to the lobby where Jade and I wait.

"It's so good to see you," she says and hugs me. "How are you?"

"Hanging in there," I say, then I introduce her to Jade.

Lindsey tells me how the brewery event was really successful and that the drama only made it so that people talked about it even more. She smiles and chats away in her usual excited, fast-talking voice. I'm glad I didn't screw things up between us.

She stops and lets out a breath. "I should get back in there. I might have a break after the second period. Are you sitting behind the bench?"

"Actually, I was wondering if you could get us into different seats? Something a little farther away."

Jade hitches her thumb toward me. "This one is trying to go unseen."

I don't want to be a distraction. And I'm also afraid Leo might take one look at me, snarl, and then avoid looking in my direction the rest of the game, further smashing my heart. I know, I know, it's what I said I wanted.

I'm still worried that I'm not good for him in the same way he is for me, but I can't deny how much I miss him.

"Gotcha." Lindsey nods. "I think I have just the spot."

She leads us up to one of the suites. A group of women turns to watch us walk in. I spot Maverick's wife, Dakota, among them, and she smiles, easing some of my trepidation.

"Hey, girls," Lindsey says. She hugs several of them, including Dakota, then waves Jade and me over.

"This is Coach Miller's daughter, Scarlett, and her friend, Jade. Is it cool if they sit up here tonight?"

"Leo Lohan's girlfriend," one of the women says as she nods and looks me over.

I don't have time to correct her before Lindsey says, "This is Quinn. Honorary member of the group."

"The group?"

"Wives and girlfriends," Dakota says. "Quinn is dating one of the equipment managers."

"You brought me to the WAG box?" I screech at Lindsey.

"He'll never think to look up here." She winks. "Now everyone get together so I can snap a few pictures before I go back down to the ice."

"Evil genius." Jade laughs.

We hang off to the side while Lindsey takes pictures of the Wildcat's girlfriends and wives. It isn't a big group, but within a few minutes, I feel at ease here. No one asks me about Leo, at least not until the game starts.

I pull out my Lohan jersey from my purse. I've worn it every game. It feels like bad luck if I don't. Also, I still want to pretend I'm his girl.

Dakota takes the seat beside me. "Johnny doesn't know I'm here either. I came up this weekend to surprise him."

Dakota's still in college in Arizona. I don't know how they do it, only seeing each other a couple of times a month, but as we watch the game, she tells me she's planning on moving here as soon as she's done with school. The huge rock on her left ring finger sparkles as she claps for him.

"Now, I've waited as long as I can stand. Tell me what happened with you and Leo. Maverick is a terrible gossip and said Leo's been a total grump all week."

"It's complicated," I say.

Jade leans over me. "Some asshole called Scarlett a hooker at an event, Leo hit him, may or may not have been arrested."

"Go, Leo," Dakota says.

Jade shakes her head. "Then this one ended things."

"That isn't the entire story, but yes, our relationship was turning into one big distraction," I say. "Hockey is everything to him."

"I get that." Dakota gives me a reassuring smile. "There's a lot of pressure on them."

The view of the game from here is nice, but I miss my seat behind the bench, where I can see every expression on Leo's face as he comes on and off the ice. Though maybe it's for the best because even being in the same space as him, nervous energy bounces through me. I twist my hands in my lap and worry my bottom lip.

The game is fast-paced, and at the end of the first, neither team has scored.

"Doing okay?" Jade asks as she sits back down with fresh drinks.

"This is torture," I admit.

She rests her head on my shoulder. "Maybe you should talk to him."

"And say what?"

"I don't know, I miss you, and I want to be with you."

I tilt my head and purse my lips.

"What? It's the truth, isn't it?"

"Of course it is, but—"

"No buts. If it had been me there that night, I would have gladly gone to jail to hit that dude. And I bet any other guy would have done the same thing if it was their girlfriend."

Dakota's listening in and nods emphatically. "She's right. I mean, I barely know you, and I'd like to take a swing at that asshole."

"You can't live your life hoping bad shit won't happen," Jade says. "Manifest your dreams."

I laugh softly.

"Which is why I decided to get engaged."

My head snaps around, and I stare wide-eyed at my best friend. "What?! Sam proposed?"

"Not exactly."

"This sounds like a story that needs drinks." Dakota stands and goes to the bar at the back of our suite. She comes back with three vodka tonics, and Jade starts in.

"You know how all of my story ideas were getting shot down by my editor?"

I nod along.

"Well, I finally came up with a killer angle. I'm going to write a weekly column chronicling my experience from engagement to honeymoon. Finding a photographer, picking venues, the perfect wedding planner, invitations…" She trails off waiting for me to comment.

"I don't understand. Sam didn't propose?"

She rolls her eyes. "God, no."

The game is lost to us as Jade tells Dakota and me how she was scoping out a jewelry store to do a write-up on wedding rings when she found herself trying them on and imagining herself as the bride.

"So you're not really engaged?" I ask at the end of her story.

"Sam has agreed to go along with it."

Dakota leans in. "Okay, stupid question, but how are you going to pull off a wedding at the end of this when you're not really engaged?"

Jade waves it off. "I have months, maybe a year's worth of content to drag this out."

I laugh. "Well, it's bold."

"Manifesting my dreams," she says happily. "Now, what is it that you want?"

"Leo," I say without a second thought.

The final buzzer sounds with the Wildcats winning by one. I see him skate off the ice with the rest of the team. I could swear he looks right at the empty seat next to my mom.

Jade squeezes my leg. "Then you need to talk to him. Now."

"I'll text him," I say, nerves making my fingers shake as I pull out my phone. After the way I walked out, I'm not so sure he's going to be as eager to see me.

"I have a better idea," Dakota says. "Come with me."

CHAPTER FORTY-ONE

LEO

WHERE SHE BELONGS

She didn't come. Yeah, she walked out of my house six days ago, and we haven't talked since, but her not showing up here tonight feels a hell of a lot more final. I don't think it's a coincidence that the first time she doesn't come in a month is after things with us went south.

"The guys are heading to Wild's," Ash says.

"I don't think I'm feeling it tonight." I run a towel through my hair and get dressed.

"All right. Lord of the Rings binge? Strip club?"

I laugh a little. "Go on without me. I have to hit the media room anyway."

"Hey," he says and grabs my shoulder. "No comment."

He says the two words slowly and then smiles big.

Fucker.

"Lohan!" Maverick calls my name from across the locker room and beckons me. I don't feel like talking to anyone else, so I make a motion that I'm heading in the other direction and start toward the interview room. Jack is already there, answering questions from the podium.

Blythe walks over to me and offers a smile. "Nice game."

"Thanks."

She lingers.

"I know the drill. Say 'no comment' and smile. I won't let you down."

She quietly laughs and shoots me a sideways glance. "They've already been prompted to keep all questions on the game. If they go rogue, I'm here to deal with them."

"Thank you." The last thing I need is to cap off the night with another jog down memory lane of my actions the past few weeks and how I lost my position and the girl.

Jack takes his last question, and I push off the wall.

"Hey, Leo." Blythe stops me before I go upfront. "You have this. If you don't know how to answer a question, you can always fall back with a good shrug or shake of the head, say how much you enjoy being a part of this team."

The room buzzes with noise as Jack thanks the reporters and waves. A few shout out final questions, hoping he'll answer, lots of flashes go off. They're still focusing on him when I take his spot and adjust the hat on my head to show more of my face.

Nervous energy makes me shift on my feet. I fiddle with the zipper on my team jacket and nod to the first reporter. He lobs me an easy question about L.A.'s defense.

I answer with confidence, but as soon as I finish and the next reporter starts to speak, I hold my breath. Whatever Blythe said before the interviews seems to have worked, and I settle in, feeling more like my old self with each one.

On the surface, I'm cool, calm, and collected. But as I blather on about hockey and tonight's game, I realize on the inside I'm not any of those things. Even if I play every game perfectly and ace every interview, I'm never going to be the same.

Scarlett isn't here, and she won't be here unless I do something about it.

"Final question," Blythe says from the side of the room.

I wave to a reporter in the front row. I realize my mistake too late. I've never seen her before, and she has that eager and wide-eyed look of a newbie. New reporters are a pain. They think their big break question is just around the corner, and they don't hold back any punches. She smiles nervously and glances at Blythe, like she knows she's going to get shot down as soon as the question leaves her mouth.

I recite no comment in my head over and over again, while I wait for her to deliver whatever hardball question she has up her sleeve.

"Your personal life has gotten a lot of attention this season." She pauses, and Blythe steps forward. She continues on, speaking faster, "It isn't the first time that you've had bad press. There was the incident in Boston your rookie season."

"That will be all for tonight," Blythe says, giving me an out.

"No, it's fine." I hold up my hand to stop Blythe from intervening. So far, she hasn't said anything that isn't straight facts.

The reporter blushes. "I only wonder how you drown out the noise after something like that and come in and play a game like tonight where you're so sharp and focused?"

I rest my hands on either side of the podium. "We have a great group of guys with a lot of talent. Coming to work every day is fun."

She nods. I can read the disappointment on her face from my bullshit answer. Blythe smiles proudly. She should. She crafted it herself.

I think of Scarlett. What's she doing? Where is she? Does she feel empty on the inside like me?

I'd do anything to get her back. An idea hits, and I run through it at lightning speed, like I'm skating down the ice trying to read the play. *Ah, fuck.*

A few reporters stand to leave, but as soon as I start speaking again, they all freeze and retake their seats.

"You want to know how we drown out the noise? The truth is we don't. Not really. Even the most dedicated and focused guy has his moments. How can we not? The very reason most of us play the game is personal. The people in our lives are a part of that, and yeah, when our relationships are rocky, then it sometimes shows out there." I hang my head. "These guys on the team are like family. On the ice, we protect one another. Above all else, we're a single unit with a single goal."

I look to Blythe, and she nods, encouraging me. That's because she has no idea where this little speech is going. I'll apologize later.

"I fell in love with my coach's daughter, and when people attacked her and our relationship, my instinct was to protect her, just like it would be out there with my guys. Then a lot of people told me the best thing for everyone was if I stayed silent. And that probably is what's best for the team, maybe even for me, but it isn't fair to her. I love this team. I'm proud to be a part of it, and I give a lot to it because I want us to win. You can play the best defense and still lose. I lost the girl because I was so busy protecting everyone that I forgot to ask myself what really mattered. That stops right now. Make no mistake about it, I'm still here to win, and when I step out on the ice, I will do everything in my control to be a good teammate and player, but right now… I need to play a little offense."

I take off with reporters calling after me. I blaze past all of them and head straight for the door. Some follow, but I don't have time to care. I'm on a mission.

Johnny Maverick is in the hallway and steps beside me like he's going to say something.

"Not now, Maverick. I need to find Scarlett."

"That's what I was trying to tell you." He jogs beside me to keep up. "She's here."

I stop. "Here?"

He points to the far end of the hallway, where family and friends wait for players.

She's here. All the air is knocked from my lungs. My legs can't take me to her fast enough.

Her expression is impossible to read, but the Leo Lohan jersey she's wearing isn't. She's mine. We belong together. She's my most important teammate.

I circle her waist with an arm and kiss her. She lets out a shocked squeak but then lifts up on her toes and places her arms around my neck.

Everything else feels insignificant without this. Without her.

Flashes bring me back to reality. When I finally look up, it's to see a crowd of people, including the reporters I just left.

Scarlett tries to hide behind me, but I take her hand and pull her to my side. Right where she belongs.

CHAPTER FORTY-TWO

SCARLETT

DICK OVER DONUTS

"**W**hy is everyone staring at us?" I whisper as Leo tightens his grip on my hand to keep me next to him.

"Probably because I just told them all I was in love with you and going to win you back."

"What?" My voice is shaky as I look up at him. He grins, waves at the reporters, and pulls me farther down the hallway to a quiet area that's off-limits to the media.

The smell of his soap is like a hit to the memory bank, unlocking all the feelings I've tried to repress since I last saw him.

"You came," he says, and his gaze drops to take in my jersey.

"Of course I did."

"None of this matters without you." He fists the material at my hip. "I'm sorry that I didn't do a better job of protecting you. And I'm sorry if I scared you or embarrassed you by hitting that guy. I've spent the last few days going over it and over it."

"And?"

"I still want to hit him." One side of his mouth lifts in a rueful smile.

"I love that you stood up for me, but I hate that you needed to. I don't want to be the person that causes the drama and distractions in your life."

"Too late," he says and leans in close. "I'm officially distracted. Besides, everyone deserves to have someone risk going to jail for them. I love you, dream girl. I have a lot of bail money."

"I love you too." So much. "I want to be good for you."

"You are."

We have things to figure out, but I know I want to find a way to do this.

"Say it again."

"I love you, Leo Lohan."

His grin is slow, and he's quiet for several seconds like he's soaking in my words.

Blythe steps up to us out of breath. "You two might want to take security when you leave. They're camped out waiting for another glimpse of you."

"I'm sorry," Leo says to her. "No comment would have made things easier, huh?"

She laughs. "What fun would my job be if you always did what I said?"

I'd been standing with Dakota and Jade when I was waiting for Leo, and they find us, bringing along Maverick, Ash, and a few other guys from the team.

"Dude. That was amazing." Maverick slings an arm around Leo's shoulders. "We have to celebrate."

"Wild's?" Ash asks.

"Nah." Leo looks at me. "Party at my place."

Ash chuckles. "For real? Hot tub?"

"Yep." He pops the p. "You'll let the boys know? I need an hour's head start."

Jade hugs me and makes her excuses to find Sam, so they can talk about her, or I guess, their engagement.

I ride with Leo to his place. The team won't be far behind, even with the hour warning, but neither of us cares. He drags me upstairs to his room, and his mouth slants over mine. Oh, how I missed this.

"I'd go to jail for you too," I say, and we both burst into laughter. "I meant it to sound sweet."

We start laughing again so hard that tears form in my eyes.

"Let's try to stay out of the clink." His hands cup my ass through my jeans. "I like sharing the same air as you."

"And the same bed." We both eye the king-size mattress. There are things to discuss, but I've missed him so much.

I thread my fingers into his thick hair at the nape of his neck and lift onto my toes to kiss him. Our mouths linger there, the smallest contact, reveling in the feeling. We're so good like this. We're good, period.

"I want this to work," I breathe him in.

"It will." He lifts me into his arms and places me on the bed.

Slow isn't working for either of us anymore, and I scramble to undo his pants as he kicks off his shoes and basically rips off my shirt.

His big hands go straight for my boobs, and he squeezes them together like he's refamiliarizing himself with my chest. His trance continues until I wrap my fingers around his shaft. His lids close, and he lets out a low groan.

"Need you," he mutters.

We hurry out of the rest of our clothes, and he quickly pushes inside, like waiting another second might physically harm him.

"Oh goddamn." Leo rests his forehead against mine.

There is no other feeling like this with him. We fit together so perfectly.

I'm certain if I could bottle up this feeling, this connection with another soul, I could solve all of the world's problems.

"Love you, dream girl," he whispers.

THE NEXT MORNING, we're downstairs, and I'm in my favorite spot on the couch next to Leo.

Dakota and Maverick ended up crashing here, so did Tyler.

Ash comes through the front door in sweats and a t-shirt, bags looped over each arm and a tray of coffees in one hand.

"Wow," I say. "Where was this service all the other times I stayed over?"

He hands me a coffee first. "Dick over donuts."

"Oh my god," Dakota mutters. "What does that even mean?"

"Since it seems you're sticking around, I thought I'd get on your good side," Ash says. "We need to talk about scheduling, Miller."

"Scheduling?" I quirk one brow as I take a sip of the coffee. It's too early for Ash.

Leo's chest rises and falls with silent laughter.

"Yeah. My boy disappeared for the past month. It got lonely over there."

"I see." I really try to keep a straight face, but damn, is it hard. "You can have Tuesdays and Thursdays."

"And Sundays during football season," Ash counters.

I bite my lip. "Sure."

Ash nods, obviously pleased with our arrangement.

"You gave up half the week just like that?" Leo asks. "Man, I see how it is."

I lean forward and place my lips over his. "I'll sneak back over when you're done having bro time."

We enjoy a lazy morning. Eventually, everyone leaves, and it's just the two of us. Neither of us got a lot of sleep last night, so we nap, and I wake up to Leo hovering over me with a camera.

"What are you doing?" I ask, hiding my face.

"You're ruining my shot," he whines.

I peek out between my fingers, and he takes another.

"I didn't know you had a camera."

"I don't." He places it on the bed beside me. "It's for you."

I sit up and take it in my hands. It's a small, simple black Canon with only a few buttons and settings. "It looks like my very first camera. I loved that thing."

He smirks, and it hits me.

"You already knew that. How did you already know that?"

"Your dad told me the story once, and I had a little help finding one that was similar." He shrugs. "I know it isn't as fancy as your other one, but I thought you could leave this one here. We can start our own photo book of memories."

"I love that." I hold the camera out in front of us and then kiss him as I take the picture.

"And, uh, maybe you want to leave a few more things here too?"

"I will bring my toothbrush back, so I don't have to use yours again," I say. The man is super protective over his toothbrush. "Are my drawers still available?"

He nods slowly. "And half the closet, or an entire closet in one of the spare rooms if you want."

"I don't think I'm going to need that much—" I stop.

He grins. "Move in with me?"

My heart races. "Really?"

"Yeah, I mean, it'll make it easier for you to sneak into my room on Tuesday, Thursdays, and Sundays."

CHAPTER FORTY-THREE

LEO

LEO LOHAN, LUCKIEST MAN ALIVE

The days and weeks start to blur together. Hockey takes up most of my time, and I spend every other spare minute with Scarlett.

Or almost every other minute. It's Sunday, and officially, it's Ash's day. I shake my head at the thought of my girl and my best friend splitting custody of me like I'm a child, but in all honesty, I feel pretty fortunate to have both of them.

Me, Jack, Declan, Maverick, and Tyler are at Ash's house to watch the Vikings play. It's halftime, and we're outside, braving the December cold for a game of washers and a couple of beers. Tyler's been on the phone basically since he walked in.

"Wonder what's up with him," Ash says.

I shake my head. "No clue."

When we head back in for the second half, Tyler finally rejoins us. He plops onto the couch, jaw set and brows furrowed.

"Everything okay?" I ask.

"Yeah." He roughs a hand through his hair. "No. Not really. My sister got suspended from school. Again."

"Sorry, man," Ash says.

"You have a sister?" Maverick asks.

Tyler nods. "She's in high school. Or was. She's one more fuck up from being expelled. She wants to come live with me."

We're all quiet. His phone pings with a text. He sighs and stands. "And she just got on a bus headed this way. I have to go deal with this. Sorry, guys."

I stand to bump his fist and wish him luck.

"Let us know if you need anything," Jack says.

"Unless you know how to speak seventeen-year-old girl, I'm probably on my own. Hopefully, I can talk her into turning around and going back home." Ty shakes his head and heads out.

After the game, I jog across the street. Scarlett is just pulling in. She hasn't moved in yet. She wanted to take some time and make sure things were solid with us first, but she spends almost every night here. I have to bite my tongue to keep from bringing it up daily, but the offer is out there, and when she's ready, I'm excited to live with her.

She rolls the window down and lets the music filter out. She sings along to a Backstreet Boys song, not missing a single lyric.

"You sang this song the first night we met," I say as I open her car door.

"I know. It's my secret weapon." She gives me a sexy and playful look. "It got me one night with Leo Lohan."

"Got you a lot more than that." I smack her ass. "What are you using it to get this time?"

"I know you have practice early tomorrow, but any chance you want to attend a fake engagement party?"

I chuckle. "A fake one?"

"Jade and Sam. They rented out Mike's bar for the night."

When I don't immediately agree, she adds, "I bought a new dress to wear."

I'm a sucker for her sexy little dresses and skirts.

"Yeah, it sounds fun. As long as we can duck out early enough I can still get under your new dress when we get home."

"Deal."

I haven't been back to Mike's in a while, but the small dive bar has been transformed tonight. The tables are all covered in white cloths. Flowers and candles are set on each one. The neon signs are off tonight, and someone strung twinkling lights from the ceiling.

"Wow," Scarlett mutters as she hugs her best friend. "How did you pull this off?"

"Vivian." She nods toward a woman in all black bossing Mike and another bartender. "And the magazine is paying for a lot of it since I'm using it for the article."

Her fiancé looks less than thrilled. We offer our congratulations to Sam, which feels a little weird since they aren't really engaged. Or they are. I don't understand it.

But my girl is smiling, and she looks fine as hell.

"Leo Lohan," Mike booms my name when he finally sees me. "I had no idea it was you."

"I get that a lot." I squeeze Scarlett's leg, eliciting a giggle out of her.

"I'd love to have you sign something to hang in the bar," the likable bar owner says.

"Yeah, of course. I'll bring a few things the next time I'm in."

He starts to question me about our upcoming games, but Vivian interrupts and shoos him back to work.

"Does she know it's his bar?" I ask Jade. She's hiding out and chugging champagne like it's her job.

"Vivian's amazing, right? I think she's my hero." Jade finishes her glass of champagne and then stares at the empty flute, and blows out a breath. "Okay, going back out there."

"Good luck," Scarlett calls. She leans into me. "I forgot how much I enjoyed a night out with you. You look sharp, boyfriend. We should do this more often."

We've been laying low in the weeks since we got back together. The media storm has died down, but neither of us wanted to burst our happy little bubble.

"Yeah?" I ask.

"Don't get me wrong, I love staying in with you, but I don't want to hide. Maybe we can pencil in a few Daria-approved events."

"I'll send you the list, and you can pick whatever you want." I lean in, kissing her shoulder and whispering, "Are you sure you want to be photographed with the least photogenic guy in history?"

She smiles. "It'll make it seem like you're the one dating up instead of the other way around."

"Oh, I am," I tell her and slide my hands up her bare legs. No doubt about it.

The following day I slip out of bed, careful not to wake Scarlett as I get ready for my run with Ash.

"Did you do it?" he asks as soon as we start jogging away from our houses.

"No." I chuckle, my breath appearing in front of me. "Guess where she took me last night?"

"Where?"

"Her best friend's engagement party."

Ash throws his head back and laughs loudly into the silent

morning. I bought a ring two weeks ago, but every time I make plans to give it to her, something happens, and it doesn't feel like the right moment.

I'm one hundred percent certain, but I'm not sure Scarlett is. She hasn't even agreed to move in yet, and I'm about to ask her to do a lot more than that. I think I knew from that one night that she was it for me. I don't want to rush her. We can be engaged for a long time if she wants. The point is, I'm in this for as long as she'll have me.

"You need a solid, fool-proof plan."

"You might be right." I'd been avoiding planning a night out, unsure how Scarlett would feel about making any more of our moments public, but winging it isn't working, and it sounds like she's ready to be seen with me again.

Friday, I swing by her house to pick her up for our night out. Coach answers the door, holding a golf club in one hand. "Come in. She's still getting ready."

The clubface on that driver could kill a man. I wonder if this is his equivalent of cleaning his gun to let me know he has no problem disposing of my body if I hurt his little girl again.

"Hi, Leo." Scarlett's mom waves from the kitchen.

"Hi, Mrs. Miller. Good to see you."

"How many times do I have to tell you to call me Emilia?"

"Emilia," I say to appease her.

Scarlett comes up the stairs, placing her phone into her purse as she gets to the landing. "Sorry, I couldn't decide which shoes to wear."

I haven't even made it to her feet. My gaze is glued to her ass, and I'm struggling to pry it away. Her dark red dress is molded to her, pushing those perfect tits up and hugging her ass. Fuck me.

Coach clears his throat, breaking me from my trance.

"You look beautiful," I say as I place a kiss on her cheek. I step back, afraid I might maul her in front of her parents. "Ready?"

"Staying at Leo's tonight," she says as we leave.

"Have fun," Emilia calls after us.

Coach walks us to the door. Before I can step outside, he stops me with the end of his club.

Scarlett pauses to see why I'm not following.

"Be right there," I tell her.

She lifts her brows at the man stopping me. "Daaad."

"One minute. I just want to have a quick chat. Hockey stuff." He waves her off.

She doesn't look like she believes him, but I hit the automatic start on my car, and she gets in.

"You'll keep an eye on her?" he asks, shifting his weight and leaning on the club.

"Of course."

"We have tomorrow off."

I nod. This isn't news. It's a scheduled rest day.

"But if my baby girl comes home crying, just go ahead and meet me there at eight sharp."

I choke back a laugh. "Yes, sir."

We shake hands, and I jog toward my car.

"And Leo," he calls before I open the door.

I look up as his lips pull into a wide grin.

"If someone does try something, do me a favor. Don't hit anyone."

Tonight's event is a formal, black-tie charity shindig for local at-risk youth. We valet and hit the red carpet. I'm holding tight to Scarlett's hand. I don't expect any altercations here, but I don't want to give the media anything to use for tomorrow's headline unless it's *Leo*

Lohan, Luckiest Man Alive.

We pose for a few photos then head inside where we find our place cards for dinner and roam around the room drinking and talking. Jack is here with a date, and Ash came solo since Talia is out of town.

My arm is draped around her waist, and Scarlett leans into me. I like being out with her like this, and that's saying something because I used to avoid these things at all costs. Hence Daria's demands to do more of them.

I've got the ring box in my pocket, and the plan is to do it right before dinner, somewhere semi-private, and then we can spend the rest of the night celebrating.

We're about to take our seats for dinner, and I'm eyeing the perimeter to find a secluded spot to spill my guts when Tiffany Ryan approaches, holding onto the arm of Ryan Moore.

"Leo," Tiffany says by way of greeting. She smiles at Scarlett.

I hold tight to my girl's hand as Ryan gets a slimy grin on his stupid face. "What are you doing here, Moore?"

"Came in a few days early." He shrugs one big shoulder.

We play Seattle again on Tuesday, and I've been waiting for another chance to face this asshole on the ice.

"Still having your coach pick out your dates, I see." He gives her a once-over that makes me want to knock him out. "If my coach had a daughter like this, I wouldn't mind so much either. What do you say, Seattle wins on Tuesday, and I get a turn?"

I squeeze Scarlett's hand tighter. I swear to god I cannot make a scene here.

I'm about to walk away when Scarlett steps forward, rests her free hand on his shoulder, and knees him hard in the balls. "You wish."

She's so sly about it that few people even look our way. Plus, with the commotion of everyone going to their seats, most are too preoccupied to notice Ryan crumble all the way to the ground.

A chuckle breaks free. "I've been waiting to see you stare up at me from the ground, but damn if it isn't twice as satisfying seeing her do it." I lift Scarlett's hand and kiss it. "See you Tuesday, Moore."

EPILOGUE

SCARLETT

TO LOHAN AND HIS DREAM GIRL

After the newspaper story about Rhyse gave me credit for his racing photos, my phone blew up with job offers. I went from no experience and being unemployable to magazines and teams begging me to come on board. Life is weird.

I took some time to think about what I wanted and finally accepted a position at the same bridal magazine Jade works at. What's better than working with your best friend? Nothing, that's what.

While I don't always get assigned to work on her articles, we spend almost every day together, either at the office or working at the coffee shop.

Tonight, I'm at a bridal expo taking pictures of couples in front of a white floral backdrop that makes whoever stands in front of it look like they're on the cover of the magazine.

Jade and our boss, Melody, are working in the booth next to it.

My phone buzzes in my bra, and I retrieve it during a break in the line, smiling when I see Leo's name. *Just landed in Minnesota. What time are you done?*

I let him know I still have another hour and that I'll come over after. I love taking pictures, capturing smiles and memories. It feels like such a privilege. They won't remember me, and I probably won't remember them, but in twenty or thirty years, they'll still have something that I helped make.

"Thanks for your help tonight, Scarlett," Melody says when the event ends.

"I took a few of the booth before and during. I'll get them edited and sent to you this week."

"Looking forward to it." She looks at Jade. "What's next on Jade's Bridal Blog?"

"I'm meeting with venues this week," Jade answers. She might be faking an engagement, but her dedication to this job is real.

Melody's face lights up. "Can't wait. See you two on Monday."

My feet are killing me by the time Jade and I tear down the booth and load up our cars.

"I hate lying to that woman," Jade says.

"Little late now."

"No kidding." She hugs me. "I'll call you in the morning."

In my car, I start the engine and turn on the heat, rubbing my hands in front of the vent to warm up. It's the middle of December and winter is officially here. Another text comes through, an image of Leo's bed. His hand is stretched out on the empty side—mine.

I tap out a quick response, *On my way.*

I get halfway to Leo's before I cut the wheel and make a U-turn, heading to my parents' house instead. I rummage through my room downstairs and pack two bags worth of clothes and all my toiletries. When I go back upstairs, Dad is in the kitchen eating cereal.

"Hey." I drop my bag and join him. I still haven't changed out of the black dress I wore to the expo, and he smiles as he sees my outfit.

"You look beautiful." He motions toward the bags. "Going on a trip?"

"Sort of." I take a seat beside him. "I'm moving in with Leo."

My heart hammers in my chest. Dad's mouth pulls into a somber smile, and he nods. "I'm going to miss you around here."

We're barely home at the same time anymore, but I'll miss him too, and I tell him as much.

"I promise to come by for Sunday dinners."

"Good. I don't know if I ever told you how much I missed you when you were in London, but I hope not to ever go that long again without seeing you."

"Same." I smile and hug him around the neck.

"Need any help?" he asks, pointing to my stuff.

"No, I think I got it. I'll come by tomorrow to get the rest and tell Mom."

I load up, one bag on each shoulder, but before I can get out the door, Dad halts me. He goes to the pantry and pulls out an unopened box of Fruity Pebbles, then walks it to me. "For your midnight snacks."

"Won't be the same without you." My throat tightens and I give him another hug. "Love you, Daddy."

When I get to Leo's, he's clearly worried about the length of time it's taken me. He stands at the front door in only a pair of sweatpants, brows furrowed. "Everything okay? I was getting nervous."

"Everything is great." I get the bags and lug them once more into his house. He takes one from me and quirks a brow. "Is this all photography equipment?"

Suddenly, I'm nervous. He hasn't asked me to move in with him again since we first got back together. I assumed he was giving me space and letting me get there on my own, but now I'm a little worried he won't be as excited about my sudden desire to shack up.

I needed to feel more settled, like I had some clue what I was doing with my life. Some days I still feel like I'm about ten steps behind my peers, but I wouldn't be me if I didn't need to take a detour or ten to find my way.

And I'm sure that my way includes Leo.

"I decided that I didn't want to stay at my parents' house tonight."

His face scrunches up. "Yeah, no kidding."

"Or tomorrow night. And not the night after that either."

I watch realization dawn on him, and his mouth pulls into a wide smile. That dimple on the left side of his face appears. He sweeps me off my feet and clutches me to his chest. "Really?"

"Really."

He kisses me quickly and then takes both bags and hustles up the stairs with them. He tosses them in his walk-in closet, moves everything from one side, and tosses it in the other direction, making room for me.

"I think we can do that tomorrow." I'm laughing as I watch him so eager to get me unpacked.

I take off my coat and toss it at his head. The black dress finally gets his attention. It's modest, but the way Leo looks at me always sets me on fire.

"I'm never letting you leave now."

"I can live with that."

He kneels in front of me. Those hands I love so much slide up my calves and under the skirt of my dress as he places open-mouth kisses along my leg—the right and then the left.

The first time is almost never slow between us. I wonder if it'll always be this way, physically impossible to get enough and rushing to get naked.

He slides my panties down my legs, and I step out of them. When he disappears under my dress, and his talented mouth finds my pussy, I sway and steady myself on the now-empty clothing rack.

He squeezes my ass with both palms as he licks and sucks.

What a way to christen a closet. Holy crap. I'd say as much if I were capable of forming words. Instead, I moan and lift one leg onto his shoulder to give him better access.

I come with his name on my lips, and before I've recovered, he has me in his arms and is pushing inside of me, filling me so completely in the way only he does—body and soul.

At some point, we end up on the floor. Closet sex, that's something I didn't know I needed in my life. Half of his side is orderly and neat, and the rest looks like a bomb went off where he tried to make some grand gesture in clearing room for me.

"This closet has a real vibe."

"It sure does." He rolls on top of me, kisses me, and smiles. "The whole house has a better vibe with you in it. My whole life, really."

"Mine too."

"Welcome home, baby."

I SLEEP FABULOUSLY that first week in my new place. On Thursday, I wake and Leo's already gone to the arena, but he left me a note to meet him at Mike's bar for drinks to celebrate. As if that isn't what we've been doing the past four days. We have had sex in every square inch of this house—inside and out.

An hour later, two delivery guys show up with a new desk and office chair, which they place in one of the spare rooms. I find a card with my name on it taped to the door. It tells me it's all mine or if I don't like this room, pick any other for my office.

I bring in my photography stuff and my laptop, but I'm too excited to be very productive. Instead, I plan the perfect outfit for drinks and call Jade to come over.

"This place is amazing," she says when I open the door for her.

"I can't believe I live here."

She walks to the back windows and looks out at the pool. "Hope Lohan's okay with a third roommate come summer."

"Non-negotiable best friend clause," I say. "You are always welcome."

Jade helps me pick a dress and do my hair. It's nice to spend a day just talking and playing dress up. I'm way too overdressed for Mike's, but I don't care. There is so much to celebrate.

"We better go, or we'll be late," Jade says as I add another layer of lip gloss.

"We'll?"

"Oh, did I not mention that." She waves me off. "I'm covering a shift at the bar."

"Still? I thought you stopped doing that weeks ago."

"It's a one-time thing. You know how crazy trivia night can get."

"Oh right." I smile thinking back to the night I first met Leo. "I'll ride with you then, that way I can come back with Leo."

"Great." She claps in front of her and we head to the bar.

Leo's already there, along with Ash and a few other guys from the team. A small wave of disappointment washes over me that it won't be just the two of us, but when he stands to hug me, he says,

"Sorry, the guys still haven't forgiven me for going to trivia on my own and finding my dream girl. They're convinced it'll be just as lucky for them."

Ash raises his beer. "Here's hoping."

The bar isn't as busy tonight and Jade spends as much time hanging out at our table as she does the bar. When trivia finally starts, Leo finds my leg under the table and his fingers spread out, covering my bare thigh.

Just like last time, he's ridiculously good at trivia. The rest of the guys, too, but Leo and me take the first game. Okay, fine, it's mostly him. But I'm clutch on actors and movies.

"Yo, college," Ash says narrowing his gaze. "You're going down."

"No way." I sit forward. "We're unbeatable."

Jade drops off fresh drinks as Mike and another bartender get set for another round of trivia.

I've never seen Mike smile so much. He's loving having so many of the Wildcats in his bar. They're good sports and sign everything he pushes in front of them. Leo even brought him a signed jersey, just like he promised. My boyfriend is a pretty great guy. His friends too.

I snuggle into his side, and he wraps an arm around my shoulders. Jade takes over the trivia for Mike. She perches on a stool at the bar and swivels to face all the tables.

She laughs as she reads the first question, which so happens to be Wildcat history. Jack shouts out the answer before she's even finished.

"Correct."

I look to Leo. "Where were you?"

"Where were you?" he taunts back. "You've lived in Minnesota way longer than me."

Yeah, fair point. "Okay, this one we've got."

"Since when did you get so competitive?"

"I think your teammates are rubbing off on me."

"Not too much, I hope." He brushes his lips over mine.

Jade raises her voice to call out the next question. "What is the most popular diamond shape for engagement rings?"

"Round cut," I yell quickly. Jade wrote an article on this a few weeks ago, so I'm confident in my answer.

"Nice job," she says. "Point to Leo and Scarlett."

Leo moves his arm from around me and holds it up for a high-five. I slap my hand against his and toss out some trash talk to Ash and Tyler.

They give it back two-fold. The quieter of the two, Tyler, grins but mumbles about the questions being rigged.

It must be our night because the next one Jade reads from her trivia note cards is a complete these lyrics question, and while the other guys are still thinking, Leo finishes it off singing the end of the Backstreet Boys tune.

After another handful of questions, Leo and I are tied with Ash and Tyler. Jack and Declan are so far behind that Jack has given up completely and goes to the bar to order a round of drinks.

"Final question," Jade says, and we all go quiet. "What is the most difficult question for a man to ask?"

My brain freezes. What the hell kind of question is that? Adrenaline shoots through me as I wrack my brain for an answer before someone else gets it.

Ash throws his hands up. "Oh, oh. I know. Asking for directions."

Jade shakes her head. "Sorry, wrong answer."

"Oh, we still have a chance." I look over to Leo, except he's no longer sitting next to me. Everyone goes quiet, and it takes me an embarrassingly long time to figure out why he's down on one knee.

I'm not sure I've ever seen my boyfriend look so nervous. His confidence in himself and me has always been something I loved about him, but seeing him like this and knowing what it means makes tears sting my eyes.

"Scarlett Miller, will you marry me?" His voice quivers, and he opens the black box in his hands.

I nod and get to my feet. My vision is too blurry from crying to even see the ring, but I already know it's perfect. I blink away the tears, and he raises up and places the round-cut diamond on my left ring finger.

And then he kisses me. The guys cheer and Jack brings the round of drinks he ordered to the table. Champagne, of course.

"Cheers," the team captain says as he lifts a glass. "To Lohan and his dream girl."

PLAYLIST

Happier Than Ever by Billie Eilish

Miss You a Little by Bryce Vine feat. Lovelytheband

Rumors by Lizzo feat. Cardi B

Sheesh! by Surfaces feat. Tai Verdes

Heat Waves by Glass Animals

Pink Ferrari by Zach Hood

Need to Know by Doja Cat

Stay by The Kid Laroi feat. Justin Bieber

Fuck Being Sober by Annika Wells

Fine Apple by Nic D

18 by Jeremy Zucker

FMRN by Lilyisthatyou

Bad Day by Justus Bennetts

Numb by Chri$tian Gate$

@ **My Worst** by Blackbear

I Don't Want To Watch The World End With Someone Else
by Clinton Kane

Real Life Sux by Justus Bennetts

I Like That by Bazzi

Icee Pop by Nic D

Suga Suga by Dorian Lackey & The Song House

ALSO BY REBECCA JENSHAK

Wildcat Hockey Series
Wildcat
Wild About You

Campus Nights Series
Secret Puck
Bad Crush
Broken Hearts
Wild Love

Smart Jocks Series
The Assist
The Fadeaway
The Tip-Off
The Fake
The Pass

Standalone Novels
Sweet Spot
Electric Blue Love

ABOUT THE AUTHOR

Rebecca Jenshak is a USA Today bestselling author of new adult and sports romance. She lives in Arizona with her family. When she isn't writing, you can find her attending local sporting events, hanging out with family and friends, or with her nose buried in a book.